"We stand poised on the brink of godhood. The knowledge and wisdom that modern scientific research offers can help us to take the next evolutionary step, and transform ourselves into a race of intelligent beings who truly understand themselves and the universe around them. . . ."

**—BEN BOVA—**

Five-time Hugo Award-winning editor of *Analog* magazine, now editor of the brilliant OMNI, Bova presents a collection of his own personal demons and heroes.

Here is science fact and science fiction, humor and adventure, as you enter the unpredictable world of

# MAXWELL'S DEMONS

## ANALOG BOOKS

— Series Editor: Ben Bova —

CAPITOL by Orson Scott Card
PROJECTIONS by Stephen Robinett
CAPTAIN EMPIRICAL by Sam Nicholson
MAXWELL'S DEMONS by Ben Bova
THE BEST OF ASTOUNDING Tony Lewis, Ed.
THE ANALOG YEARBOOK Ben Bova, Ed.

*look for these and other* Analog *books from*

*ACE SCIENCE FICTION*

**SF**

# MAXWELL'S DEMONS

## BEN BOVA

SF
**ace books**
A Division of Charter Communications Inc.
A GROSSET & DUNLAP COMPANY
360 Park Avenue South
New York, New York 10010

An ACE Book by arrangement with BARONET Publishing Company

*Cover art by Ken Barr*

First printing: September 1978
First Ace printing: January 1979

Printed in U.S.A.

# Acknowledgements

**What Chariots of Which Gods?** copyright © 1974 by AstroMedia Corp., originally published in the August 1974 issue of *Astronomy* magazine.

**The Great Supersonic Zeppelin Race,** copyright © 1974 by Roger Elwood, originally published in THE FAR SIDE OF TIME, edited by Elwood, published by Dodd, Mead & Co.

**Foeman, Where Do You Flee?** copyright © 1968 by Galaxy Publishing Corp., originally published in the January 1968 issue of *Galaxy* magazine.

**The Sightseers,** copyright © 1973 by Roger Elwood, originally published in FUTURE CITY, edited by Elwood and published by Trident Press.

**The Secret Life of Henry K.,** copyright © 1973 by Gallery Enterprise Corp., originally published in the May 1973 issue of *Gallery* magazine.

**The Man Who Saw "Gunga Din" Thirty Times,** copyright © 1973 by Roger Elwood, originally published in SHOWCASE, edited by Elwood, published by Harper & Row.

**Priorities,** copyright © 1971 by The Condé Nast Publications, Inc., originally published in the December 1971 issue of *Analog* magazine.

**Build Me a Mountain,** copyright © 1974 by Ben Bova, originally published in *2020 Visions*, edited by Jerry Pournelle, published by Avon Books.

**The System,** copyright © 1967 by The Condé Nast Publications, Inc., originally published in the January 1968 issue of *Analog* magazine.

# About the Author

Ben Bova is a novelist, lecturer, and editor of *Analog Science Fiction-Science Fact* magazine, the most widely read and influential science fiction magazine in the world. He has received the Science Fiction Achievement Award (Hugo) for Best Professional Editor for five consecutive years, 1973 through 1977.

The author of more than forty books of both fiction and nonfiction, Bova has also been a working newspaperman, an aerospace-industry executive, a motion-picture writer, and a television science consultant.

As manager of marketing for Avco Everett Research Laboratory in Massachusetts, he has worked with leading scientists in advanced research fields, such as high-power lasers, magnetohydrodynamics (MHD), plasma physics and artificial hearts. Prior to joining Avco, he wrote scripts for teaching films for the Physical Sciences Study Committee, working with the MIT Physics Department and Nobel Laureates from many universities. Earlier he was technical editor on Project *Vanguard*. He also worked on newspapers and magazines in the Philadelphia area, where he was born and where he received a degree in journalism from Temple University.

Bova has lectured before audiences ranging from the U.S. Department of State to the Institute of Man and Science, from college campuses to international meetings of businessmen and scientists. He has also appeared on numerous radio and TV talk shows. His lecture topics include "How to Predict the Future", "How We Lost the Energy Battle (But May Still Win the War)", and "The Future of Our Cities." He has directed film courses and taught science fiction at the Hayden Planetarium in New York City.

His short stories and articles have appeared in all the major science-fiction magazines, as well as in *Harper's, Smithsonian, American Film, Vogue, The Writer*, and many other periodicals. His book, *The Fourth State of Matter*, was honored as one of the best science books of 1971 by the American Librarians' Association. He is a charter member of the National Space Institute and the Science Fiction Writers of America. He was the 1974 recipient of the New England Science Fiction Association's E. E. Smith Memorial Award for Imaginative Fiction.

Further biographical details may be found in *Who's Who in the East, The International Author's Who's Who, Contemporary Authors*, and *Who's Who in Science Fiction*.

# Contents

# Introduction:
# The Hero as Sociopath

Maxwell's Demon is a strange little fellow. He was invented by James Clerk Maxwell, the nineteenth-century British physicist and one of the greatest scientists of all time.

Maxwell imagined two flasks of gas—air, for example—connected by a tube. The tube has a gate in it. The gas in each flask starts out at the same temperature. And the Demon works the gate. Every time he sees a fast-moving (hot) molecule approaching the gate from one direction, he opens the gate and lets that molecule through into the opposite flask. And when he sees a slow-moving (cold) molecule heading for the gate from the other direction, he lets it go through into the first flask.

In time, one flask gets colder and colder, while the other flask gets hotter and hotter.

Now, you need a Maxwell's Demon to accomplish this trick, because in the real world, if you start out with two flasks of gas at the same temperature, you will end up with two flasks of gas at the same temperature, no matter how long you wait. There are no Maxwell's Demons in the real world.

But there are in fiction.

Consider another term, one that's used often by social scientists. The term is *sociopath*.

Webster's New World Dictionary (Second College Edition, 1972) defines sociopath as: "a psychopathic personality whose behavior is aggressively antisocial."

If you leave out the perjorative word "psychopathic," then another definition of sociopath could be: *hero*.

Especially in science fiction stories, the hero actively tries to change the society in which he finds himself. He is aggressively antisocial in the eyes of those around him. Like Maxwell's Demon, the science fiction hero tries to do things that would not happen naturally. He labors to make things different, to engender *change*.

The Baker's Dozen of stories in this collection all revolve around protagonists who are, to some degree, sociopaths. Heroes. Maxwell's Demons. They strive to change their worlds. In some cases their struggles are funny. Maxwell's Demons aren't all dour and serious. Some of them are definitely pixieish.

The short stories and novelettes are framed, front and back, by a pair of nonfiction pieces. The first takes a hard look at the psuedo-scientific frippery that purports to "prove" that we have been visited in the distant past by extraterrestrials who built strange monuments. The second is a personal view of where science is leading us.

Because today's scientists—those descendants of Galileo, Newton, Maxwell and Einstein—well, if we have any Maxwell's Demons in the real world, the best of our scientists are it. Why do you think so many unthinking people fear and oppose scientific research? Why do you think scientists have been called antisocial, even sociopathic?

# What Chariots of Which Gods?

When I started bouncing the ideas contained in this essay off Erich von Daniken, during a TV talk show we did together in Toronto, he sputtered that we couldn't possibly discuss such a complex subject in just one hour. I agreed, and suggested that his publisher and mine would gladly arrange a three-hour radio or television debate in New York City. Once I returned to New York, I quickly found that both publishers were eager to stage the debate. It would make great publicity for all concerned. Alas, Mr. Von Daniken disappeared on us, and has never come back to do the show.

So here are my own highly prejudiced views on the Chariots of the Gods syndrome.

An astonishing amount of the public's attention has been focused lately on the idea that our planet was visited in prehistoric times by astronauts from other worlds. Presumably, the visitors were wise, benign, and maniacs about large construction projects such as the pyramids and the Easter Island statues.

Maybe there are older, wiser races "out there" among the stars. Maybe they have visited here. Perhaps they are watching us now with gentle amusement as we sweat over our Skylab and Mariner and Pioneer space probes.

But what *evidence* do we actually have? With our optical and radio telescopes, our Orbiting Astronomical Observatories, our penetrating studies of cosmology; what evidence can we put together that shows: (1) that there are indeed other intelligent races in space, and (2) that they have visited Earth?

We could argue for a lifetime over the kinds of evidence offered by the *Chariots of the Gods?* (by Erich von Daniken) believers: quaint paintings found in ancient caves or markings carved into hillsides and remote plateaus. We could spend equally fruitless time debating whether it was humans or alien astronauts who actually built the pyramids, Stonehenge, etc. That evidence is highly equivocal.

Instead let us turn to the unequivocal laws of physics and chemistry, and the solid observations of astronomy, to see if we can find definite answers.

Are there other intelligent races in space, and have they visited Earth?

It seems almost certain that there is no other intelligent species among the planets of our solar system. Mars and Venus have been exposed by spacecraft probes and radar studies. Mercury, Pluto and our own moon were never expected to be habitats for intelligent races. The Jovian planets are too alien for our purposes—more on that later.

If we seek another intelligent race, it must be out among the stars. Assuming for the moment that brainy aliens are out there, what are the chances that we could find them *now*, today, and have meaningful, fruitful contact with them? Not just radio chats, but long term meaningful interaction in the way the United States interacts with the other nations of Earth—trade, cultural interpenetration, tourism, politics, and even war.

That all depends, of course, on attaining some means of traveling interstellar distances. More than that, it must be fast, cheap interstellar transportation. Otherwise there can be no large-scale interactions, no politics, and no trade between us and them. Look at a parallel from Earth's history.

Since at least Roman times, western Europeans knew that China and the Orient existed. In the Middle Ages, Marco Polo got there and back, spreading wondrous tales that grew each year. But Europe did not interact with China in any significant way. True, Europe engaged in trade with the Arab Middle East and obtained goods from the Orient through Arab middlemen. The Middle East was close enough for Europeans to reach on foot, if they had no other way to get there. Europe traded with the Middle East, exchanged scholarly works (which is why most of the stars in the sky have Arabic names) and engaged in the pious slaughters called the Crusades.

But there was no direct trade and no conflict with China. Once deep-ocean sailing vessels were perfected, however, Europe did indeed contact China directly and treated the Orient to Western technology, trade, disease and war. Today, of course, with intercontinental rockets and instant communications, everybody on the globe can interact politically with everybody else.

The same rule will apply to interstellar politics. There may be glorious civilizations in the Orion complex, or even as close as Alpha Centauri. But we know less about them than Hannibal knew about China.

Yet even today it is possible for our scientists and engineers to visualize starships based on technology that might be available in less than a century. If and when we can make trips to the nearest stars within a human lifetime, we'll have reached the Marco Polo stage of interstellar contact—adventure, strange tales, and stranger artifacts. But no lasting political relations, for better or worse. This is the stage that *Chariots of the Gods?* advocates are talking about: rare visits, spaced thousands of years apart, by Marco Polo-type explorers from other civilizations.

There can be little tourism—except of a scientific variety—when a person can visit another star system only once in a lifetime, and the trip would consume a fair portion of his lifespan. It is also difficult to picture commerce and trade relations based on one ship per human generation. That's more like a cultural exchange. And even the sternest, most fearless and ruthless general might feel a bit foolish about mounting an attack when he knew he could never see the outcome in his own lifetime.

But the real importance of Marco Polo's adventure was the spur it gave to Prince Henry the Navigator and others, including Columbus. We might wonder, then, why the alleged visits of alien astronauts in ancient times have not been followed up more recently. Have the chariots of the gods metamorphosed into flying saucers?

Now, if you corner a theoretical physicist and feed him enough drinks, chances are that you can get him mumbling about tachyons and things that go faster than

light. Einstein's light barrier is starting to look—well—
not leaky, perhaps, but at least a little translucent.
Perhaps one day spaceships will be able to travel among
the stars at speeds far greater than light. Perhaps they
do now—alien spacecraft, that is—although we have
not seen any evidence of this in our astronomical studies
of the heavens.

If we had ships that could go faster than light, so that
we could easily explore interstellar space, we might get
as close and friendly with our stellar neighbors as we
are today with the Chinese. But we must realize that
there will be many races out among the stars that we
simply *cannot* interact with in any useful way, even
though we may be able to reach them physically.

For example, we may find races much younger than
ours with a correspondingly simple technology and social development. To them, we would appear to be
gods, and there would be little we could do for them—or
that they could do for us. Would we parade around
their world building pyramids and doling out tidbits of
our technology?

Certainly we would want to study them to learn more
about how intelligence and societies evolve. That would
best be done from orbit, where we could remain "invisible" and not disturb them in any way. What could
they offer us, except their own artifacts or their own
bodies? The artifacts might be interesting as examples of
alien art. No matter how lopsided or gruesome they appear, there will be at least one art critic who will
discover hidden esthetic values that everyone else has
missed and sell the stuff at a huge markup.

And their bodies?

We wouldn't use them for meat, for biochemical reasons if no other. If their bodies contained some precious chemical substances that could not be found elsewhere—the key to immortality or something equally exotic—we would be in a lovely ethical bind. But the chances of that sort of thing are vanishingly small. We certainly would not need muscular slaves in our technological society; electricity is cheaper.

What could we offer such younger neighbors? Only the things that would destroy their culture just as surely as western Europe destroyed the American Indians. Hopefully, by the time we do study such a race, we will have learned not to interfere with them.

If we should try to meddle with a race that is only slightly younger or technologically weaker than we are, their reaction could very well be the same as the Indians—they would resist us as strongly as they could, probably with guerrilla warfare. As Custer learned a century ago and we learned in Vietnam, "unsophisticated" and "simple" people can turn our own technology against us very effectively. But the Indians were either killed or absorbed into our culture, and the Vietnamese are going through the same process. That part of the world will never again be a simple, unspoiled, isolated Asian backwater. The same thing would probably happen to a younger race that fights against us; the very act of resistance would destroy their native culture.

What would happen if we contacted a race much more advanced that we are? The same situation, only in reverse. We would have precious little to offer them, except possible curiosity value. And they would be wise

enough not to tamper with us—we hope. Playing cow-
boys and Indians is no fun when you're on the fore-
doomed side.

A really far advanced race would most likely go its
own way, aloof and serene, even if we tried our hardest
to make friends. The picture that comes to mind is a
puppy chasing a monorail train.

That leaves us with races that are more or less at our
own stage of development—intellectually, morally and
technologically. That's the kind of race we will have
some interactions with. And conversely, if we have been
visited in the past by extraterrestrial astronauts, only
those whose development is relatively close to our
own—give or take a millennium or two—would take
any interest in us.

Whether we visit them or they visit us, we will
interact strongly only with races that have something to
gain from us, and vice versa. Gorillas and angels have
so little in common with us that we won't bother them if
we find any "out there," nor would they bother us. But
other people at our own stage of development, more or
less, will provide the interstellar action—even if they are
purple and have sixteen legs.

Furthermore, any race that interacts with us would
probably come from a planet enough like our own home
to make this Earth attractive to them. And their home
world would similarly be attractive, or at least bear-
able, to us. This is why, even if an intelligent race exists
under Jupiter's clouds—or Saturn's, Uranus' or Nep-
tune's—we probably will interact with them about as
much as we do with the denizens of the Marianas
Trench. There is simply no common meeting ground.

We do not have political relations with dolphins, even if they are as intelligent as we are. We have nothing to trade or fight over.

It boils down to this: Although there may be millions of strange and marvelous races among the stars, if they are physically or intellectually far removed from us we will have little but the most cursory contacts with them—except for possible scientific expeditions. This, of course, does not deny the *Chariots of the Gods?* thesis—a strange race visited our planet thousands of years ago and departed after a rather brief stay. But let's go from the general to the specific, to see if this thesis really stands up in the light of modern knowledge.

There are thirty-seven stars within sixteen light-years of our sun; these are our nearby neighbors, and we know quite a bit about them. Of these thirty-seven stars, twenty-seven are single, eight are binary stars, and two are triples. Four of these stars are believed to have "dark companions," bodies of planetary mass that are too small and too faint to be seen. In fact, two of the nearest five stars seem to have planets. Since planets are extremely difficult to detect over interstellar distances, we might suspect that there are plenty of them orbiting the farther distant stars. But we just cannot perceive them from here.

The Milky Way galaxy as a whole contains about 100 billion stars. Our galaxy is roughly 100,000 light-years in diameter, and our solar system is some 30,000 light-years from the center.

We have no way of knowing how rare intelligence is, nor indeed whether life itself is a common phenomenon throughout the Milky Way. Radio astronomers have found that the basic chemical ingredients of life, such as water, ammonia, and hydrocarbon molecules, exist in interstellar space. In fact, they are found in exactly those locations among the stars where swirling clouds of interstellar gas and dust are building new solar systems. Biological building blocks, such as amino acids, have been found in meteorites reaching our planet, and organic chemicals exist in the soil samples and rocks brought back from the moon.

Based on balance, it would seem that life is not restricted to our own planet, nor even to our own solar system. Every cosmological test that has been applied to Earth and the solar system has shown that we are not unique. Quite the opposite. Our sun is a rather average star. It appears that planets form around stars naturally. Planets at our temperature range from their star should turn out to look roughly like Earth, with plenty of liquid water. Life on such planets should be based on carbon, oxygen and water, making use of the most abundant materials and the most energetic chemical reactions available. Given enough time, the natural forces that led to the evolution of life on Earth should lead to similar results on similar planets.

But what about *intelligent* life? The underlying question is: What are the ages of the stars around us? If they are about the same age as the sun, shouldn't we expect that they would have had time to develop not only life, but intelligent life—just as we have?

Is it really that simple?

The sun's age has been pegged at roughly five billion years. This is based chiefly on estimates of the amount of the sun's original hydrogen that has been converted to helium through the thermonuclear fusion process that makes the sun shine. Although no one knows how much helium, if any, the sun contained when it first began to shine, five billion years is probably a reasonable estimate of the sun's age since it tallies well with the ages of the oldest rocks found on Earth, the moon, and in meteorites.

Many of the stars around the sun are clearly much younger. The table shows classes of typical stars according to their spectral types, together with estimates of their stable lifespans. By stable lifespan, we mean the length of time that the star remains on the main sequence.

To explain: Stars go through an evolutionary path, a lifespan, much as do living creatures. In the vast spiral arms of the Milky Way, stars are constantly being born and dying. The evolutionary path for an ordinary star, such as our sun, goes like this:

1. A protostar condenses out of interstellar gas and dust. The protostar, a dark clump fo mostly hydrogen, is about a light-year wide. It contracts rapidly, falling inward on itself under the gravitational force of its own mass. As it contracts, it naturally gets denser and hotter; its interior temperature rises sharply.

2. When the density and temperature at the core of the protostar reach a critical value, hydrogen fusion reactions are triggered. The gravitational collapse stops, because now heat and light produced by the thermonuclear fusion reactions are making outward-pushing pressures that balance the inward-pulling gravity. The star shines with fusion energy, and it becomes a stable member of the great family of stars that astronomers

call the main sequence. Its size and surface temperature will remain stable as long as hydrogen fusion provides the star's energy. The sun is about half way through this stage.

3. The bigger and more massive the star was to start with, the hotter it "cooks," and the faster it runs through its hydrogen fuel supply. When the hydrogen runs low, the star begins burning the helium "ash" that is left in its core. Helium fusion, producing oxygen, neon and carbon, runs hotter than hydrogen fusion. The star's central temperature soars, and the outer layers of the star are forced to expand. The star is no longer a main sequence member—astronomers call it a red giant. Soon, in astronomical time scales the helium runs low, and the star begins burning the heavier elements in its core. The star continues to create, and then burn, increasingly heavier elements. All the while, the core is getting hotter, and the star's outer envelope is swelling enormously. When the star goes into its red giant phase, it may become so large that it swallows its closest planet. The sun, someday a few billion years from now, may engulf Earth.

4. The eventual fate of the star depends on its original mass. A star of the sun's mass will probably end as a white dwarf, about the size of an Earth-type planet. More massive stars could become 10-mile-wide neutron stars, or even disappear from our universe altogether by becoming black holes.

The important point for us right now is that the star remains stable for only a certain finite period of time, depending on its original mass and temperature. After that, things get pretty desperate for any planet-dwelling life near by.

Hot blue giants, such as Rigel and Spica, cannot stay stable for more than a few hundred million years. While this is long in terms of human lifespans, it is an eyeblink in terms of evolution. This means that such stars cannot be more than a few hundred million years old, at most. The dinosaurs never saw Rigel!

We know that it took about five billion years for intelligence to emerge on Earth. As a rule of thumb, lacking any better evidence, we can say that we should not expect to find intelligent life on planets circling stars that are less than a few billion years old. So Rigel and the other young blue giants can be ruled out as possible abodes for intelligent life.

The stars that are smaller and cooler than the sun, such as the K and M dwarfs, have much longer life expectancies. But are they older than the sun? There is no easy way to tell. Moreover, since they are dimmer and cooler than the sun, the chances of their having an Earth type planet orbiting about them, at temperatures where water is liquid most of the time, are consequently smaller. This does not rule them out as possible habitats for intelligent life, but it makes the chances that much smaller.

There is another way to look at the problem of finding intelligent life in the Milky Way galaxy. Consider the geography of our galaxy.

The Milky Way is, of course, a spiral galaxy very much like the beautiful spiral in Andromeda. The core of our galaxy is thick with stars, but we can never see the core because it is hidden behind dense clouds of interstellar dust. Radio and infrared observations have been able to penetrate the clouds to some extent, but observations of the central regions of other galaxies show that they are so rich with stars that these stars are probably no more than a single light-year from each other, at most.

Stars in the core of a galaxy are also much older than the sun. Red giant stars are common there and, as we mentioned, stars become red giants only after they have ended their stable main-sequence phases. Also, in the cores of galaxies there are no young, hot blue giants such as Rigel and Spica. These are found only in the spiral arms of galaxies.

Because the core regions of spiral galaxies seem to contain different types of stars than do the spiral arms, astronomers refer to the two different stellar constituencies as Population I and Population II. This sometimes causes confusion among nonastronomers.

Population I stars are the kind our sun lives among. These are the youngish stars of the spiral arms. Their brightest members are the blue giants. Population I stars contain a relatively high proportion of elements heavier than hydrogen and helium. Although the proportion of heavy elements hardly ever amounts to more than one percent, the Population I stars are said to be metal-rich.

Population II stars are found in the core regions of a galaxy. They are old; their brightest members are red giants, and they are mostly metal-poor.

The heavy-element content of a star is an important clue to its history. Why are the stars in a galaxy's core metal-poor and the stars in the spiral arms metal-rich? Because the elements heavier than hydrogen have been created inside the stars. It works this way:

Consider the Milky Way before there were any stars. Cosmologists have estimated that the Milky Way is between 10 and 20 billion years old; that is, some two to four times older than the sun. Presumably, the whole universe is the same age as the Milky Way. But when you are dealing with tens of billions of years, the numbers tend to become imprecise and hazy.

Regardless of the exact age of our galaxy, it began as an immense dark cloud of gas at least 100,000 light-years across. The gas might have been entirely hydrogen, or it might have been hydrogen-helium mixture. Where the gas originally came from is a mystery that cosmologists argue about, but no one has been able to prove which side of the argument is correct—if either.

The first stars to form had no elements heavier than helium in them—perhaps nothing more than hydrogen. All the heavier elements, from lithium to iron, were "cooked" inside these stars as they went form hydrogen burning to helium burning to heavier-element burning.

Some of these stars exploded, in the last stages of their lives, with the titanic fury of the supernova. In those star-shattering explosions, still heavier elements were created, beyond iron, all the way up to uranium and even beyond that. (There is evidence that the so-called man made element Californium 254, was present in the supernova of 1054 A.D.—which we know today as the Crab nebula.)

So the earliest generation of stars in the Milky Way began with only hydrogen—perhaps laced with a smattering of helium—and eventually produced all the heavier elements. And these stars threw the heavier elements back into space, where they served as the building materials for the next generation of stars. The explosions that marked the death throes of the first generation stars enriched the interstellar gas cloud with heavy elements. It was from these clouds that later generation stars were born.

Judging by the heavy-element content in the stars, most astrophysicists estimate that the sun must be a third generation star, grandson of the original stars of the Milky Way. The elements inside the sun today were once inside other stars. The atoms that make up the solar system were created in other stars. The atoms of your own body were made in stars. We are truly star children.

Beware of a clash of jargon when we speak about generations of stars and Population I or II. Population I stars are younger, late generation stars. Population II stars are the older, early generation stars. Two came before I, historically.

What has all this to do with receiving visitors from the stars?

Just this: Those first generation stars *could not produce life*. There was no carbon, no oxygen, no nitrogen—nothing but hydrogen and perhaps some helium. If those first stars had planets, they would all have been frozen ice balls of hydrogen—somewhat like Jupiter but not so colorful, because there would have been no ammonia or methane or any other chemical compounds to cause the gaudy streaks of colored clouds such as we see on Jupiter and Saturn. There wouldn't even have been any water. Not then.

Second generation stars? It's possible that they would

have most of the heavier elements, including the carbon, oxygen, nitrogen, potassium, iron and such that we need to develop life. Planets of such stars might be able to support life, even our kind of life, if these heavier elements were present in sufficient quantities. If life has appeared on such planets, there's no reason to suppose it wouldn't eventually achieve intelligence. Certainly the long-lived red dwarf stars provide plenty of time for intelligence to develop—much more than five billion years.

Let us assume that an intelligent race could arise on the planets of a second generation star. Could such a race develop a high civilization and technology—high enough to build star-roving "chariots"? It all depends on the abundance of natural resources on the home planets. Fossil fuels, such as coal and oil, should be plentiful enough, since they are the result of the biodegrading of plant and animal remains. But what about metals? Our technology here on Earth is built around metals. Even our history rings with the sound of the Bronze Age, the Iron Age, the Steel Age, the Uranium Age.

Astronomical evidence is indistinct here. Theory shows that second generation stars should have a lesser abundance of metals than we third generation types. But certainly there should be *some* metals on second generation planets.

How much metal is enough? There is no way to tell. Our own Jupiter probably has much more iron than Earth does. But it's mixed with 317 Earth masses of hydrogen, helium, methane, ammonia, and whatnot. The Jovians, if they exist, must find it much harder to locate and *get at* their iron than we do.

We should also realize that intelligence does not depend on heavy metals—but *life itself does!* There is an atom of iron at the core of every hemoglobin molecule in your body. Atoms of phosphorus are crucial to the energy-releasing chemistry in cells of living organisms. Chlorophyl is built around magnesium atoms. Without certain metals, life could not exist on Earth—or elsewhere.

Humankind rose to intelligence before our ancestors discovered heavy metals. They used wood, clay, rock and animal bones for their earliest technology. In a way, the human race went through a Ceramics Age before the discovery of metals. It was wood and ceramics that allowed primitive humans to handle and use fire. Only after fire was tamed could men begin to use metals on a large scale.

Human history shows that once metals were put to use, we took a giant leap forward. Metals allowed men to build effective plows. And swords. And chariots. Even today, our skyscrapers, computers, engines, spacecraft, weapons and household appliances are made mainly from metals. Metals are strong, tough and cheap. They are rather easily found and easily worked, even with low-grade fire.

Could an intelligent race build cities and spacecraft without metals? Today there are many space age materials, such as plastics and boronfiber composites, that are replacing some metals. But the machinery that produces them is made of stainless steel, copper, brass, etc. Modern technology is showing that there are non-metallic materials that can outperform metals in strength, weight and many other parameters. Cavemen, or even the ancient Greeks, could not have produced boron-fiber composites or modern plastics. They did not have the metals to produce them!

Would a metal-poor second generation, intelligent race be stymied in its attempts at technology? Who can say? All we know for sure is that our technology certainly depends on metals, and until metals were available, our ancestors had no culture or technology higher than the Neolithic.

Another vital point: While we have nothing but the history of our own race to go on, it looks very much as if the whole world of electromagnetic forces would never have been discovered without metals such as iron and copper. The discovery of magnetism depended on the abundance of iron on this planet. And from the very beginnings of our experiments with electricity, we used lead, zinc, copper, brass, etc. It is difficult to see how the entire chain of the study and use of electromagnetic forces—from Volta and Faraday and Hertz through to radio telescopes and television and superconducting magnets—could have happened on a metal-poor planet. And where would technology be without electricity? Back in the early 19th century, at best.

It just might be possible for a metal-poor second generation intelligent race to build a complex technology completely out of nonmetals. But tribes on Earth that never had easy access to heavy metals have never developed a high technology. Coincidence?

So there goes the long-standing science fiction dream of an immense galactic empire, run by the older and wiser races of the Milky Way's ancient core region. Like the "steaming jungles" of Venus and the "desert cities" of Mars, the empire at the center of the galaxy simply does not exist. The first generation stars there produced no life. If there are second generation intelligences around they must be extremely rare and, because of their ages, so far advanced beyond us that empires are meaningless trivialities to them. Or, they are so metal starved that they are no doubt gamboling innocently through some version of Eden. They will never find us; we will have to find them. Hopefully, we will be old enough and wise enough to leave them strictly alone.

It's a shame. It would have been pleasant to talk with them—those incredibly ancient, benign and understanding superbeings from the galaxy's core. It is sort of shattering to realize that, although life is probably common throughout much of the galaxy, highly advanced technological races are probably extremely rare.

One final note: The sun seems to be one of the oldest third generation stars in this part of the galaxy. There might not be any older races like us within thousands of light-years.

Could it be that we are the oldest, wisest, furthest advanced race in this part of the Milky Way? That we built the pyramids ourselves? That the only godlike chariots we will ever see will be the starships we build for our own flights through interstellar space?

# The Great Supersonic Zeppelin Race

*This story actually did begin in a laboratory cafeteria, with a pair of friendly aerodynamicists pulling my leg about the supersonic biplane. The aerodynamics is all perfectly valid, however, and by the time lunch was over they had convinced themselves that a supersonic zeppelin could actually be built. They never carried the idea any further, but if they had . . . well, read on.*

You can make a supersonic aircraft that doesn't produce a sonic boom," said Bob Wisdom.

For an instant the whole cafeteria seemed to go quiet. Bob was sitting at a table by the big picture window that overlooked Everett Aircraft Co.'s parking lot. It was drizzling out there, as it usually did in the spring. Through the haze, Mt. Olympia's snow-topped peak could barely be seen.

Bob smiled quizzically at his lunch pals. He was tall and lanky, round faced in a handsome sort of way, with dark, thinning hair and dark eyes that were never somber, even in the midst of Everett Aircraft's worst layoffs and cutbacks.

"A supersonic aircraft," mumbled Ray wuurtz from inside his beard.

"With no sonic boom," added Tommy Rohr.

Bob Wisdom smiled and nodded.

"What's the catch?" asked Richard Grand in a slightly Anglified accent.

The cafeteria resumed its clattering, chattering noises. The drizzle outside continued to soak the few scraggly trees and pitiful shrubs planted around the half-empty parking lot.

"Catch?" Bob echoed, trying to look hurt. "Why should there be a catch?"

"Because if someone could build a supersonic aircraft that doesn't shatter people's eardrums, obviously someone would be doing it," Grand answered.

"We could do it," Bob agreed pleasantly, "but we're not."

"Why not?" Kurtz asked.

Bob shrugged elaborately.

Rohr waggled a finger at Bob. "There's something going on in that aerodynamicist's head of yours. This is a gag, isn't it?"

"No gag," Bob replied innocently. "I'm surprised that nobody's thought of the idea before."

"What's the go of it?" Grand asked. He had just read a biography of James Clerk Maxwell and was trying to sound English, despite the fact that Maxwell was a Scot.

"Well," Bob said, with a bigger grin than before, "there's a type of wing that the German aerodynamicist Adolph Busemann invented. Instead of making the wings flat, though, you build your supersonic aircraft with a ringwing . . ."

"Ringwing?"

"Sure." Leaning forward and propping one elbow on the cafeteria table, Bob pulled a felt-tip pen from his shirt pocket and sketched on the paper placemat.

"See? Here's the fuselage of a supersonic plane." He drew a narrow cigar shape. "Now we wrap the wing around it, like a sleeve. It's actually two wings, one inside the other, and all the shock waves that cause the sonic boom get trapped inside the wings and get canceled out. No sonic boom."

Grand stared at the sketch, then looked up at Bob, then stared at the sketch some more. Rohr looked expectant, waiting for the punch line. Kurtz frowned, looking like a cross between Abe Lincoln and Karl Marx.

I don't know much about aerodynamics," Rohr said slowly, "but that is a sort of Busemann biplane you're talking about, isn't it?"

Bob nodded.

"Ahah . . . and isn't it true that the wings of a Busemann biplane produce no lift?"

"Right," Bob admitted.

"No lift?" Kurtz snapped. "Then how the hell do you get it off the ground?"

Trying to look completely serious, Bob answered, "You can't get it off the ground if it's an ordinary airplane. It's got to be lighter-than-air. You fill the central body with helium."

"A zeppelin?" Kurtz squeaked.

Rohr started laughing. "You sonofabitch. You had us all going there for a minute."

Grand said, "Interesting."

John Driver sat behind a cloud of blue smoke that he puffed from a reeking pipe. His office always smelled like an opium den gone sour. His secretary, a luscious and sweet-tempered girl of Greek-Italian ancestry, had worn out eight strings of rosary beads in the vain hope that he might give up smoking.

"A supersonic zeppelin?" Driver snapped angrily. "Ridiculous!"

Squinting into the haze in an effort to find his boss, Grand answered, "Don't be too hasty to dismiss the concept. It might have some merit. At the very least, I believe we could talk NASA or the Transportation people into giving us money to investigate the idea."

At the sound of the word "money," Driver took the pipe out of his teeth and waved some of the smoke away. He peered at Grand through reddened eyes. Driver was lean-faced, with hard features and a gaze that he liked to think was piercing. His jaw was slightly overdeveloped from biting through so many pipe stems.

"You have to spend money to make money in this business," Driver said in his most penetrating *Fortune* magazine acumen.

"I realize that," Grand answered stiffly. "But I'm quite willing to put my own time into this. I really believe we may be onto something that can save our jobs."

Driver drummed his slide-rule-calloused fingertips on his desktop. "All right," he said at last. "Do it on your own time. When you've got something worth showing, come to me with it. Not anyone else, you understand. Me."

"Right, Chief." Whenever Grand wanted to flatter Driver, he called him Chief.

After Grand left his office, Driver sat at his desk for a long, silent while. The company's business had been going to hell over the past few years. There was practically no market for high-technology work any more. The military were more interested in sandbags than supersonic planes. NASA was wrapping tourniquets everywhere in an effort to keep from bleeding to death. The newly reorganized Department of Transportation and Urban Renewal hardly understood what a Bunsen burner was.

"A supersonic zeppelin," Driver muttered to himself. It sounded ridiculous. But then, so did air cushion vehicles and Wankel engines. Yet companies were making millions on those ideas.

"A supersonic zeppelin," he repeated. "SSZ."

Then he noticed that his pipe had gone out. He reached into his left-top desk drawer for a huge blue-tipped kitchen match and started puffing the pipe alight again. Great clouds of smoke billowed upward as he said: "SSZ . . . no sonic boom . . . might not even cause air pollution."

Driver climbed out of the cab, clamped his pipe in his teeth, and gazed up at the magnificent glass and stainless steel facade of the new office building that housed the Transportation and Urban Renewal Department.

"So this is TURD headquarters," he muttered.

"This is it," replied Tracy Keene, who had just paid off the cabbie and come up to stand beside Driver. Keene was Everett Aircraft's crackerjack Washington representative, a large, round man who always conveyed the impression that he knew things nobody else knew. Keene's job was to find new customers for Everett, placate old customers when Everett inevitably alienated them, and pay off taxicabs. The job involved

grotesque amounts of wining and dining, and Keene—
who had once been as wiry and agile as a weak-hitting
shortstop—seemed to grow larger and rounder every
time Driver came to Washington. But what he was gain-
ing in girth, he was losing in hair, Driver noticed.

"Let's go," Keene said. "We don't want to be late."
He lumbered up the steps to the magnificent glass doors
of the magnificent new building.

The building was in Virginia, not the District of Columbia. Like all new Government agencies, it was head-
quartered outside the city proper. The fact that one of
this agency's major responsibilities was to find ways to
revitalize the major cities and stop urban sprawl somehow never entered into consideration when the site for
its location was chosen.

Two hours later, Keene was half-dozing in a straight-
backed metal chair, and Driver was taking the last of an
eight-inch-thick pile of viewgraph slides off the projector. The projector fan droned hypnotically in the
darkened room. They were in the office of Roger K.
Memo, Assistant Under Director for Transportation Research of TURD.

Memo and his chief scientific advisor, Dr. Alonzo
Pencilbeam, were sitting on one side of the small table.
Keene was resting peacefully on the other side. Driver
stood up at the head of the table, frowning beside the
viewgraph projector. The only light in the room came
from the projector, which now threw a blank glare onto
the wan, yellow wall that served in place of a screen.
Smoke from Driver's pipe sifted through the cone of
light.

Driver snapped the projector off. The light and the

fan's whirring noise abruptly stopped. Keene jerked fully awake and, without a word, reached up and flicked the wall switch that turned on the overhead lights.

Although the magnificent building was sparkling new, Memo's office somehow looked, instant-seedy. There wasn't enough furniture in it for its size: only an ordinary steel desk and swivel chair, a half-empty bookcase, and this little conference table with four chairs that didn't match. The walls and floor were bare, and there was a distinct echo when anyone spoke or even walked across the room. The only window had vertical slats instead of a curtain, and it looked out on an automobile graveyard. The only decoration on the walls was a diploma. Memo's doctorate degree, bought from an obscure Mohawk Valley college for $200 without the need to attend classes.

Driver stood by the projector, frowning through his own smoke.

"Well what do you think?" he asked subtly.

Memo pursed his lips. He was jowly fat, completely bald, wore glasses and rumpled gray suits.

"I don't know," he said firmly. "It sounds . . . unusual . . ."

Dr. Pencilbeam was sitting back in his chair and smiling beautifully. His Ph.D. had been earned during the 1930's, when he had to work nights and weekends to stay alive and in school. He was still very thin, fragile looking, with the long skinny limbs of a praying mantis.

Pencilbeam dug in his jacket pockets and pulled out a pouch of tobacco and cigarette paper. "It certainly looks interesting," he said in a soft voice. "I think it's technically feasible . . . and lots of fun."

Memo snorted. "We're not here to enjoy ourselves."

Keene leaned across the table and fixed Memo with his best here's-something-from-behind-the-scenes look:

"Do you realize how the Administration would react to a sensible program for a supersonic aircraft? With the *Concorde* going broke and the Russian SST grounded . . . you could put this country out in front again."

"H'mm," said Memo. "But . . ."

"Balance of payments," Keene intoned knowingly. "Gold outflow . . . aerospace employment . . . national prestige . . . the President would be awfully impressed.

"H'mm," Memo repeated. "I see . . ."


The cocktail party was in full swing. It was nearly impossible to hear your own voice in the swirling babble of chatter and clinking glassware. In the middle of the sumptuous living room, the Vice President was demonstrating his golf swing. Out in the foyer, three Senators were comparing fact-finding tours they were arranging for the Riviera, Rio de Janeiro, and American Samoa, respectively. The Cabinet wives held sway in the glittering dining room.

Roger K. Memo never drank anything stronger than ginger ale. He stood in the doorway between the living room and foyer, lip reading the Senators' conversation about travel plans. When the trip broke up and Senator Goodyear (R., Ohio) headed back toward the bar, Memo intercepted him.

"Hello, Senator!" Memo shouted heartily. It was the only way to be heard over the party noise.

"Ah . . . hello." Senator Goodyear obviously knew

that he knew Memo, but just as obviously couldn't recall his name, rank, or influence rating.

Goodyear was nearly six feet tall, and towered over Memo's paunchy figure. Together they shouldered their way through the crowd around the bar. Goodyear ordered bourbon on the rocks, and therefore so did Memo. But he merely held onto his glass, while the Senator immediately began to gulp at his drink.

A statuesque blonde in a spectacular gown sauntered past them. The Senator's eyes tracked her like a range finder following a target.

"I hear you're going to Samoa," Memo shouted as they edged away from the bar, following the girl.

"Eh . . . yes," Goodyear answered cautiously, a tone he usually employed with newspaper reporters.

"Beautiful part of the world," Memo yelled.

The blonde slipped an arm around the waist of a young, long-haired man and they disappeared into another room together. Goodyear turned his attention back to his drink.

"I said," Memo repeated, standing on tiptoes, "that Samoa is a beautiful part of the world."

Nodding, Goodyear said, "I'm going to investigate the ecological conditions there . . . my committee is considering legislation on ecology."

"Of course, of course. You've got to see things first-hand if you're going to enact meaningful laws."

Slightly less guardedly, Goodyear said, "Exactly."

"It's such a long way off, though," Memo said. "It must take considerable thought to decide to make such a long trip."

"Well . . . you know we can't think of our own comforts when we're in public service."

"Yes, of course. . . . Will you be taking the SST? I understand QUANTAS flies it out of San Francisco . . ."

Suddenly alert again, Goodyear snapped, "Never! I always fly American planes on American airlines."

"Very patriotic," Memo applauded. "And sensible, too. Those Aussies don't know how to run an airline. And any plane made by the British *and* the French . . . well, I don't know. I understand it's financially in trouble."

Goodyear nodded again. "That's what I hear."

"Still—it's a shame that the United States doesn't have a supersonic aircraft. It would cut your travel time in half. Give you twice as much time to stay in Samoa . . . investigating."

The hearing room in the Capitol was jammed with reporters and cameramen. Senator Goodyear sat in the center of the long front table, as befits the committee chairman.

All through the hot summer morning the committee had listened to witnesses: John Driver, Roger K. Memo, Alonzo Pencilbeam, and many others. The concept of the supersonic zeppelin unfolded before the newsmen and started to take on definite solidity right there in the rococo-trimmed hearing room.

Senator Goodyear sat there solemnly all morning, listening to the carefully rehearsed testimony, watching the greenery outside the big sunny window. Whenever he thought about the TV cameras, he sat up straighter and tried to look lean and tough, like Gary Cooper.

Goodyear had a drawer full of Gary Cooper movies on video cassettes in his Ohio home.

Now it was his turn to summarize what the witnesses had said. He looked straight at the nearest camera, trying to come across strong and sympathetic, like the sheriff in *High Noon*.

"Gentlemen," he began, immediately antagonizing the eighteen women in the audience, "I believe that what we have heard here today can mark the beginning of a new program that will revitalize the aerospace industry and put America back in the forefront of international commerce . . ."

One of the younger Senators at the far end of the table interrupted:

"Excuse me, Mr. Chairman, but my earlier question about pollution was never answered. Won't the SSZ use the same kinds of jet engines that the SST was going to use? And won't they cause just as much pollution?"

Goodyear glowered at the junior member's impudence, but controlled his temper well enough to say only, "Em . . . , Dr. Pencilbeam, would you care to answer that question?"

Pencilbeam, seated at one of the witness tables, looked startled for a moment. Then he hunched his bony frame around the microphone in front of him and said:

"The pollution arguments about the SST were never substantiated. There were wild claims that if you operated jet engines up in the high stratosphere, you would eventually cause a permanent cloud layer over the whole Earth or destroy the ozone up there and thus let in enough solar ultraviolet radiation to cause millions of cancer deaths. But these claims were never proved."

"But it was never disproved, either, was it?" the junior Senator said.

Before Pencilbeam could respond, Senator Goodyear grabbed his own microphone and nearly shouted, "Rest assured that we are all well aware of the possible pollution problems. At the moment, though, there is no problem because there is no SSZ. Our aerospace industry is suffering, employment is way down, and the whole economy is in a bad way. The SSZ project will provide jobs and boost the economy. As part of the project, we will consult with the English and French and see what their pollution problems are—if any. And our own American engineers will, I assure you, find ways to eliminate any and all pollution coming from the SSZ engines."

Looking rather disturbed, Pencilbeam started to add something to Goodyear's statement. But Memo put a hand over the scientist's microphone and shook his head in a strong negative.

Mark Sequoia was hiking along a woodland trail in Fairmont Park, Philadelphia, when the news reached him.

Once a flaming crusader for ecological salvation and against pollution, Sequoia had made the mistake of letting the Commonwealth of Pennsylvania hire him as the state ecology director. He had spent the past five years earnestly and honestly trying to clean up Pennsylvania, a job that had driven four generations of the original Penn family into early graves. The deeper Sequoia buried himself in the solid wastes and politics of Pittsburgh, Philadelphia, Chester, Erie, and other hopeless cities, the fewer followers and national headlines he attracted.

Now he led a scraggly handful of sullen high school students through the soot-ravaged woodlands of Fairmont Park on a steaming July afternoon, picking up empty beer cans and loaded prophylactics—and keeping a wary eye out for muggers. Even full daylight was no protection against assault. And the school kids with him wouldn't help. Half of them would jump in and join the fun.

Sequoia was broad-shouldered, almost burly. His face had been seamed by weather and press conferences. He looked strong and fit, but lately his back had been giving him trouble, and his old trick knee . . .

He heard someone pounding up the trail behind him.

"Mark! Mark!"

Sequoia turned to see Larry Helper, his last and therefore most trusted aide, running along the gravel path toward him, waving a copy of the *Evening Bulletin* over his head. Newspaper pages were slipping from his sweaty grasp and fluttering off across the grass.

"Littering," Sequoia mumbled in the tone sometimes used by bishops when faced with a case of heresy.

"Some of you men," Sequoia said in his best Lone Ranger voice, "pick up those newspaper pages."

A couple of kids lackadaisically ambled after the fluttering sheets.

"Mark, look here!" Helper skidded to a stop and breathlessly waved the front page of the newspaper. "Look!"

Sequoia grabbed his aide's wrist and took the newspaper from him. He frowned at Helper, he cringed and stepped back.

"I . . . I thought you'd want to see . . ."

Satisfied that he was in control of things, Sequoia turned his attention to the front page headline.

"Supersonic *zeppelin!*"

By nightfall, Sequoia was meeting with a half-dozen men and women in the basement of a prosperous downtown church that specialized in worthy causes capable of filling the pews upstairs.

Sequoia was pacing across the little room in which they were meeting. There was no table, just a few folding chairs scattered around, and a locked bookcase stuffed with books on sex and marriage.

"No, we've got to do something dramatic!" Sequoia pounded a fist into his open palm. "We can't just drive down to Washington and call a press conference . . ."

"Automobiles pollute," said one of the women, a comely redhead, whose eyes never left Sequoia's broad, sturdy-looking figure.

"We could take the train; it's electrical."

"Power stations pollute."

"Airplanes pollute, too."

"What about riding down on horseback? Like Paul Revere!"

"Horses pollute."

"They do?"

"Ever been around a stable?"

"Oh."

Sequoia pounded his fist again. "I've got it!" His hand stung; he had hit it too hard.

"What?"

"A balloon! We'll ride down to Washington in a nonpolluting, helium-filled balloon. That's the dramatic way to emphasize our point!"

"Fantastic!"

"Marvelous!"

The redhead was panting with excitement. "Oh, Mark, you're so clever. So dedicated." There were tears in her eyes.

Helper said softly, "Uh . . . does anybody know where we can get a balloon? And how much they cost?"

Sequoia glared at him.

When the meeting finally broke up, Helper had the task of finding a suitable balloon, preferably for free. Sequoia would spearhead the effort to raise money for a knockdown fight against the SSZ. The redhead volunteered to assist him. They left arm in arm.


The auditorium in Foggy Bottom was crammed with newsmen. TV lights were glaring at the empty podium. The reporters and cameramen shuffled, coughed, talked to each other. Then:

"Ladies and gentlemen, the President of the United States."

They all stood up and applauded politely as the President strode across the stage toward the podium in his usual bunched together, shoulder-first football style. His dark face was somber under its beetling brows.

The President gripped the lectern and nodded, with a perfunctory smile, to a few of his favorites. The newsmen sat down. The cameras started rolling.

"I have a statement to make about the tragic misfortune that has overtaken one of our finest public figures—Mark Sequoia. According to the latest report I have received from the Coast Guard—no more than ten minutes ago—there is still no trace of him or his party. Apparently the balloon they were riding in was blown out to sea two days ago, and nothing has been heard from them since.

"Now let me make this perfectly clear. Mr. Sequoia was frequently on the other side of the political fence from me, your President. He was often a critic of my policies and actions, the policies and actions of your President. He was on his way to Washington to protest our new SSZ project, when this unfortunate accident occurred—to protest the SSZ project despite the fact that it will employ thousands of aerospace engineers who are otherwise unemployable and untrainable. Despite the fact that it will save the American dollar on the international market and salvage American prestige in the technological battleground of the world.

"Now, in spite of the fact that some of us—such as our Vice President, as is well known—feel that Mr. Sequoia carried the constitutional guarantee of free speech a bit too far, despite all this, mind you, I—as your President and Commander-in-Chief—have dispatched every available military, Coast Guard, and Boy Scout plane, ship, and foot patrol to search the entire coastline and coastal waters between Philadelphia and Washington. We will find Mark Sequoia and his brave party of misguided ecology nuts . . . or their remains.

"Are there any questions?"

The Associated Press reporter, a hickory-tough old man with huge, thick glasses and a white goatee, stood up and asked in stentorian tones: "Is it true that Sequoia's balloon was blown off course by a flight of Air

Force fighter planes that buzzed it?"

The President made a smile that looked somewhat like a grimace and said: "I'm glad you asked that question . . ."

Ronald Eames Trafalgar was Her Majesty's Ambassador Plenipotentiary to the Government of the Union of Soviet Socialist Republics.

He sat rather uneasily in the rear seat of the Bentley, watching the white-boled birch trees flash past the car windows. The first snow of autumn was already on the ground, the trees were almost entirely bare, the sky was a pewter gray. Trafalgar shivered with the iron cold of the steppes, even inside his heavy woolen coat.

Next to him sat Sergei Mihailovitch Traktor, Minister of Technology. The two men were old friends, despite their vast differences in outlook, upbringing, and appearance. Trafalgar could have posed for Horatio Hornblower illustrations: he was tall, slim, poised, just a touch of gray at his well-brushed temples. Traktor looked like an automobile mechanic (which he once was): stubby, heavy-faced, shifty eyes.

"I can assure you that this car is absolutely clean," Trafalgar said calmly, still watching the melancholy birch forest sliding by. The afternoon sun was an indistinct bright blur behind the trees, trying to burn its way through the gray overcast.

"And let me assure you," Traktor said in flawless English, a startling octave higher than the Englishman's voice, "that *all* your cars are bugged."

Trafalgar laughed lightly. "Dear man. We constantly find your bugs and plant them next to tape recordings of the Beatles."

"You only find the bugs we want you to find."

"Nonsense."

"Truth." Traktor didn't mention the eleven kilos of electronic gear that had been strapped to various parts of his fleshy anatomy before he had been allowed to visit the British embassy.

"Ah, well, no matter . . ." Trafalgar gave up the argument with an airy wave of his hand." The basic question is quite simple: what are you going to do about this ridiculous supersonic zeppelin idea of the Americans?"

Traktor pursed his lips and studied his friend's face for a moment, like a garage mechanic trying to figure out how much a customer will hold still for.

"Why do you call it ridiculous?" he asked.

"You don't think it's ridiculous?" Trafalgar asked.

They sparred for more than an hour before they both finally admitted that (a) their own supersonic transport planes were financially ruinous, and (b) they were both secretly working on plans to build supersonic zeppelins.

After establishing that confidence, both men were silent for a long, long time. The car drove out to the limit allowed for a British embassy vehicle by diplomatic protocol, then headed back for Moscow. The driver could clearly see the onion-shaped spires of churches before Trafalgar finally broke down and asked quietly:

"Em . . . Sergei, old man, . . . do you suppose that we could work together on this zeppelin thing? It might save us both a good deal of money and time. And it would help us to catch up with the Americans."

"Impossible," said Traktor.

"I'm sure the thought has crossed your mind before this," Trafalgar said.

"Working with a capitalist nation . . ."

"Two capitalist nations," Trafalgar corrected. "The French are in with us."

Traktor said nothing.

"After all, you've worked with the French before. It's . . . difficult, I know. But it can be done. And my own government is now in the hands of the Socialist Party."

"Improbable," said Traktor.

"And you *do* want to overtake the Americans, don't you?"

The President's desk was cleared of papers. Nothing cluttered the broad expanse of redwood except three phones (red, white, and black), a memento from an early Latin America tour (a fist-sized rock), and a Ping-Pong paddle.

The President sat back in the elevated chair behind the desk and fired instructions at his personal staff.

"I want to make it absolutely clear," he was saying to his press secretary, "that we are not in a race with the Russians or anybody else. We're building our SSZ for very sound economic and social reasons, not for competition with the Russians."

"Right, Chief," said the press secretary.

He turned to his top congressional liaison man. "And you'd better make darned certain that the Senate Appropriations Committee votes the extra funds for the SSZ. Tell them that if we don't get the extra funding, we'll fall behind the Reds.

"And I want you," he said to the Director of TURD, "to spend every nickel of your existing SSZ money as fast as you can. Otherwise we won't be able to get Congress to put in more money."

"Yes sir."

"But, Chief," the head of Budget Management started to object.

"I know what you're going to say," the President said to the top BUM. "I'm perfectly aware that money doesn't grow on trees. But we've got to make the SSZ a success . . . and before next November. Take money from education, from poverty, from the space program—anything. I want that SSZ flying by next spring, when I'm scheduled to visit Paris, Moscow, and Peking."

The whole staff gasped in sudden realization of the President's master plan.

"That's entirely correct," he said, smiling slyly at them. "I want to be the first Chief of State to cross the Atlantic, Europe, and Asia in a supersonic aircraft."

The VA hospital in Hagerstown had never seen so many reporters. There were reporters in the lobby, reporters lounging in the halls, reporters bribing nurses, reporters sneaking into elevators and surgical theaters (where they inevitably fainted). The parking lot was a jumble of cars bearing press stickers.

Only two reporters were allowed to see Mark Sequoia on any given day, and they had to share their story with all the other newsmen. Today the two-picked by lot—were a crusty old veteran from UPI and a rather pretty blonde from *Women's Wear Daily*.

"But I've told your colleagues what happened at least

a dozen times," Sequoia mumbled from behind a swathing of bandages.

He was hanging by both arms and legs from four traction braces, his backside barely touching the bed. Bandages covered 80 percent of his body.

The two reporters stood by his bed. UPI looked flinty as he scribbled some notes on a rumpled sheet of paper. The blonde had a tiny tape recorder in her hand.

She looked misty-eyed. "Are . . . are you in much pain?"

"Not really," Sequoia answered bravely, with a slight tremor in his voice.

"Why the damned traction?" UPI asked in a tone reminiscent of a cement mixer riding over a gravel road. "The docs said there weren't any broken bones."

"Splinters," Sequoia said weakly.

"Bone splinters? Oh, how awful!" gasped the blonde.

"No—" Sequoia corrected. "Splinters. When the balloon came down, it landed in a clump of trees just outside of Hagerstown. We all suffered from thousands of splinters. It took the surgical staff here three days to pick all the splinters out of us. The chief of surgery said he was going to save the wood and build a scale model of the *Titanic* with it. . . ."

"Oh, how painful!" The blonde insisted on gasping. She gasped very well, Sequoia noted, watching her blouse.

"And what about your hair?" asked UPI gruffly.

Sequoia felt himself blush. "I . . . I must have been very frightened. After all, we were aloft in an open balloon for six days, without food, without anything to drink except a six pack of beer that one of my aides brought along. We went through a dozen different thunderstorms . . ."

"With lightning?" the blonde asked.

Nodding painfully, Sequoia added, "We all thought we were going to die."

UPI frowned. "So your hair turned white from fright. There was some talk that cosmic rays might have done it."

"Cosmic rays? We weren't that high . . . Cosmic rays don't have any effect until you get to very high altitudes . . . isn't that right?"

"How high did you go?"

"I don't know," Sequoia answered. "We didn't have an altimeter with us. Those thunderstorms pushed us pretty high, the air got kind of thin . . ."

"But not high enough for cosmic-ray damage."

"I doubt it."

"Too bad," said UPI. "Would've made a better story than just being scared. Hair turned white by cosmic rays. Maybe even sterilized."

"Sterilized?"

"Cosmic rays do that, too," UPI said. "I checked."

"Well, we weren't that high."

"You're sure?"

"Yeah . . . well, I don't think we were that high."

"But you could have been."

Shrugging was sheer torture, Sequoia found out.

"Okay, but those thunderstorms could've lifted you pretty damned high . . ."

The door opened and a horse-faced nurse said firmly, "That's all, please. Mr. Sequoia must rest now."

"Okay, I think I got something to hang a story onto,"

UPI said with a happy grin on his seamed face.

The blonde looked shocked and terribly upset. "You . . . you don't think you were really sterilized, do you?"

Sequoia tried to make himself sound worried and brave at the same time. "I don't know. I just . . . don't know."

Late that night the blonde snuck back into his room. If she knew the difference between sterilization and impotence, she didn't tell Sequoia about it. On his part, he forgot about his still-tender skin and his traction braces. The day nurse found him the next morning, unconscious, one shoulder dislocated, his skin terribly inflamed, most of his bandages rubbed off and a silly grin on his face.


"Will you look at this!"

Senator Goodyear tossed the morning *Post* across the breakfast table to his wife. She was a handsome woman: nearly as tall as her husband, athletically lean, shoulder-length dark hair with just a wisp of silver. She always dressed for breakfast just as carefully as for dinner. This morning she was going riding, so she wore slacks and a turtle-neck sweater that outlined her figure.

But the Senator was more interested in the *Post* article. "That Sequoia! He'll stop at nothing to destroy me! Just because the Ohio River melted his houseboat once, years ago, . . . he's been out to crucify me ever since."

Mrs. Goodyear looked up from the newspaper. "Sterilized? You mean that people who fly in the SSZ could be sterilized by cosmic rays?"

"Utter nonsense!" Goodyear snapped.

"Of course," his wife murmured soothingly.

But after the Senator drove off in his chauffeured limousine, Mrs. Goodyear made three phone calls. One was to the Smithsonian Institution. The second was to a friend in the Zero Population Growth movement. The third was to the underground Washington headquarters of the Women's International Terrorist Conspiracy from Hell. Unbeknownst to her husband or any of her friends or associates, Mrs. Goodyear was an undercover agent for WITCH.

The first snow of Virginia's winter was sifting gently past Roger K. Memo's office window. He was pacing across the plastic-tiled floor, his footsteps faintly echoing in the too large room. Copies of the Washington *Post*, New York *Times*, and *Aviation Week* were spread across his desk.

Dr. Pencilbeam sat at one of the unmatched conference chairs, all bony limbs and elbows and knees.

"Relax, Roger," he said calmly. "Congress isn't going to stop the SSZ. It means too many jobs, too much international prestige. And besides, the President has staked his credibility on it."

"That's what worries me," Memo mumbled.

"What?"

But Memo's eye was caught by movement outside his window. He waddled past his desk and looked out at the street below.

"Oh, my God."

"What's going on?" Pencilbeam unfolded like a pocket ruler into a six-foot-long human and hurried to the window.

Outside, in the thin mushy snow, a line of somber men was filing down the street past the TURD building Silently they bore screaming signs:

> STOP THE SSZ
> DON'T STERILIZE THE HUMAN RACE
> SSZ MURDERS UNBORN CHILDREN
> ZEPPELINS, GO HOME

"Isn't that one with the sign about unborn children a priest?" Pencilbeam asked.

Memo shrugged. "Your eyes are better than mine."

"Ah-hah! And look at this!"

Pencilbeam pointed further down the street. A swarm of women was advancing on the building. They also carried signs:

> SSZ FOR ZPG
> ZEPPELINS SI! BABIES NO
> ZEPPELINS FOR POPULATION CONTROL
> UP THE SSZ

Memo visibly sagged at the window. "This . . . this is awful . . ."

The women marched through the thin snowfall and straight into the line of picketing men. Instantly the silence was shattered by shouts and taunts. Shrill female voices battled against rumbling baritones and basses. Signs wavered. Bodies pushed. Someone screamed. One sign struck a skull and then bloody war broke out.

Memo and Pencilbeam watched aghast until the helmeted TAC squad police doused the whole scene with riot gas, impartially clubbed men and women  and dragged everyone off.

The huge factory assembly bay was filled with the skeleton of a giant dirigible. Great aluminum ribs stretched from titanium nosecap back toward the more intricate cagework of the tail fins. Tiny men with flashing laser welders crawled along the ribbing like maggots cleaning the bones of a noble whale.

Even the jet engines sitting on their loading pallets dwarfed human scale. Some of the welders held clandestine poker games inside them. John Driver and Richard Grand stood beside one of them, craning their necks to watch the welding work going on far overhead. The assembly bay rang to the shouts of working men, the hum of electrical machinery, and the occasional clatter of metal against metal.

"It's going to be some Christmas party if Congress cancels the project," Driver said gloomily from behind his inevitable pipe.

"Oh, they wouldn't dare cancel it, now that Women's Liberation is behind it," said Grand with a sardonic little smile.

Driver glared at him. "With those bitches for allies, you don't need any enemies. Half those idiots in Congress will vote against us just to prove that they're not scared of Women's Lib."

"Do you really think so?" Grand asked.

*He always acts as if he knows more than I do*, Driver thought. It had taken him several years to realize that Grand actually knew rather less than most people—but he had a way of hiding this behind protective language.

"Yes, I really think so!" Driver snapped. Then he pulled his pipe out of his mouth and jabbed it in the general direction of Grand's eyeballs. "And listen to me, kiddo. I've been working on that secretary of mine since the last goddamned Christmas party. If this project falls through and the party's a bust, that palpitating hunk of female flesh is going to run home and cry. And so will I!"

Grand blinked several times, then murmured, "Pity."

The banner saying HAPPY HOLIDAYS drooped sadly across one wall of the cafeteria. Outside in the darkness, lights glimmered, cars were moving, and a bright moon lit the snowy peak of Mt. Olympia.

But inside Everett Aircraft's cafeteria there was nothing but gloom. The Christmas party had been a dismal flop, especially so since half the company's employees had received their layoff notices the day before.

The tables had been pushed to one side of the cafeteria to make room for a dance floor. Syrupy music was oozing out of the loud-speakers in the acoustic-tile ceiling. But no one was dancing.

Bob Wisdom sat at one of the tables, propping his aching head on his hands. Ray Kurtz and Tommy Rohr sat with him, equally dejected.

"Why the hell did they have to cancel the project two days before Christmas?" Rohr asked rhetorically.

"Makes for more pathos," Kurtz muttered from inside his beard.

"It's pathetic, all right," Wisdom said. "I've never seen so many secretaries crying at once."

"Even Driver was crying," Rohr said.

"Well," Kurtz said, staring at his half-finished drink on the table before him, "Sequoia did it. He's a big national hero again."

"And we're on the bread line," Rohr said.

"You get laid off?"

"Not yet, . . . but it's coming. This place will be closing its doors before another year is out."

"It's not that bad," said Wisdom. "There's still the Air Force work."

Rohr frowned. "You know what gets me? The way the whole project was scrapped, without giving us a chance to build one of the damned zeps and see how they work. Without a goddam chance!"

Kurtz said, "Congressmen are scared of being sterilized."

"Or castrated by Women's Lib."

"Next time you dream up a project, Bob, make it underground. Something in a lead mine. Then the Congressmen won't have to worry about cosmic rays."

Wisdom started to laugh, then held off. "You know," he said slowly, "you just might have something there."

"What?"

"Where?"

"A supersonic transport—in a tunnel."

"Oh, for Chri . . ."

Wisdom sat up straight in his chair. "No, listen. You could make an air-cushion vehicle go supersonic. If you put it in a tunnel, you get away from the sonic boom and the pollution . . ."

"Hey, the safety aspects would be a lot better, too."

Kurtz shook his head. "You guys are crazy! Who the hell's going to dig tunnels all over the United States?"

But Wisdom waved him down. "Somebody will. Now, the way I see the design of this . . . SSST, I guess we call it."

"SSST?"

"Sure, he answered, grinning. "Supersonic subway train."

# Foeman, Where Do You Flee?

*I've never liked the title to this story, which was supplied by Frederik Pohl, who was editor of* Galaxy *magazine when I wrote it. The only good thing about the title is that it's better than my original title, which was so forgettable that now I can't remember it! This story is the only one I've written in response to a cover drawing, which Pohl supplied together with a request for a "strong lead novelette." Well, it's a novelette and it led that issue of the magazine. You can judge its strength for yourself.*

## I

Deep in cryogenic sleep the mind dreams the same frozen dreams, endlessly circuiting through the long empty years. Sidney Lee dreamed of the towers on Titan, over and again, their smooth blank walls of metal that was beyond metal, their throbbing, ceaseless, purposeful machines that ran at tasks that men could not even guess at. The towers loomed in his darkened dreams, standing menacing and alien above the frozen wastes of Titan, utterly unmindful of the tiny men that groveled at their base. He tried to scale those smooth, steep walls and fell back. He tried to penetrate them and failed. He tried to scream. And in his dreams, at least, he succeeded.

He didn't dream of Ruth, or of the stars, or of the future or the past. Only of the towers, of the machines that blindly obeyed a builder who had left Earth's solar system countless millenia ago.

He opened his eyes.

"What happened?"

Carlos Pascual was smiling down at him, his round dark-skinned face relaxed and almost happy. "We are there . . . here, I mean. We are braking, preparing to go into orbit."

Lee blinked and sat up. "We made it?"

"Yes, yes," Pascual answered softly as his eyes shifted to the bank of instruments on the console behind Lee's shoulder. "The panel claims you are alive and well. How do you feel?"

That took a moment's thought. "A little hungry."

"A common reaction." The smile returned. "You can join the others in the galley."

The expedition's medical chief helped Lee to swing his legs over the edge of the couch, then left him and went to the next unit, where a blonde  woman lay still sleeping. With an effort, Lee recalled her: Doris McNertny, primary biologist, backup biochemist. Lee pulled a deep breath into his lungs and tried to get himself started. The overhead light panels, on full intensity now, made him want to squint.

Standing was something of an experiment. *No shakes*, Lee thought gratefully. The room was large and circular, with no viewports.

Each of the twenty hibernation couches had been painted a different color by some psychology team back on Earth. Most of them were empty now. The remaining occupied ones had their lids off and the lifesystem connections removed as Pascual, Tanaka and May Connearney worked to revive the people. Despite the color scheme, the room looked uninviting, and it smelled clinical.

*The galley*, Lee focused his thoughts, *is in this globe, one flight up.* The ship was built in globular sections that turned in response to g-pulls. With the main fusion engines firing to brake their approach to final orbit, "up" was temporarily in the direction of the engines' thrustors. But inside the globes it did not make much difference.

He found the stairwell that ran through the globe. Inside the winding metal ladderway the rumbling vibrations from the ship's engines were echoing strongly enough to hear as actual sound.

"Sid! Good morning!" Aaron Hatfield had stationed himself at the entrance to the galley and was acting as a one-man welcoming committee.

There were only a half dozen people in the galley. Of course, Lee realized. *The crew personnel are at their stations.* Except for Hatfield, the people were bunched at the galley's lone viewpoint, staring outside and speaking in hushed, subdued whispers.

"Hello, Aaron." Lee didn't feel jubilant, not after a fifteen-year sleep. He tried to picture Ruth in his mind and found that he couldn't.

*She must be nearly fifty by now.*

Hatfield was the expedition's primary biochemist, a chunky, loud-speaking overgrown kid whom it was impossible to dislike, no matter how he behaved. Lee knew that Hatfield wouldn't go near the viewport because the sight of empty space terrified him.

"Hey, here's Doris!" Hatfield shouted to no one. He scuttled toward the entrance as she stepped rather uncertainly into the galley.

Lee dialed for coffee. With the hot cup in his hand he walked slowly toward the viewport.

"Hello Dr. Lee," Marlene Ettinger said as he came up alongside her. The others at the viewport turned and muttered their greetings.

"How close are we?" Lee asked.

Charnovsky, the geologist, answered positively, "Two days before we enter final orbit."

The stars crowded out the darkness beyond their viewport: against the blackness like droplets from a paint spray. In the faint reflection of the port's plastic, Lee could see six human faces looking lost and awed.

Then the ship swung, ever so slightly, in response to some command from the crew and computers. A single star—close and blazingly powerful—slid into view, lancing painfully brilliant light through the polarizing viewport. Lee snapped his eyes shut, but not before the glare burned its afterimage against his closed eyelids. They all ducked back instinctively.

"Welcome to Sirius," somebody said.

Man's fight to the stars was made not in glory, but in fear.

The buildings on Titan were clearly the work of an alien intelligent race. No man could tell exactly how old they were, how long their baffling machines had been running, what their purpose was. Whoever had built them had left the solar system hundreds of centuries ago.

For the first time, men truly dreaded the stars.

Still, they had to know, had to learn. Robot probes were sent to the nearest dozen stars, the farthest that man's technology could reach. Nearly a generation passed on Earth before the faint signals from the probes returned. Seven of the stars had planets circling them. Of these, five possessed Earthlike worlds. On four of them, some indications of life were found. Life, not intelligence. Long and hot were the debates about what to do next. Finally, manned expeditions were dispatched to the Earthlike ones.

Through it all, the machines on Titan hummed smoothly.

"They should have named this ship *Afterthought*," Lee said to Charnovsky. (The ship's official name was *Carl Sagan*.)

"How so?" the Russian muttered as he pushed a pawn across the board between them. They were sitting in the pastel-lighted rec room. A few others were scattered around the semicircular room, reading, talking, dictating messages that wouldn't get to Earth for more than eight years. Soft music purred in the background.

The Earthlike planet—Sirius A-2 swung past the nearest viewport. The ship had been in orbit for nearly three weeks now and was rotating around its long axis to keep a half-g feeling of weight for the scientists.

"We were sent here as an afterthought," Lee continued. "Nobody expects us to find anything. Most of the experts back on Earth didn't really believe there could be an Earthlike planet around a blue star."

"They were correct, " Charnovsky said. "Your move."

Picture our solar system. Now replace the sun with Sirius A, the Dog Star: a young, blue star, nearly twice as hot and big as the sun. Take away the planet Uranus, nearly two billion kilometers from the sun, and replace it with the white dwarf Sirius B, the Pup: just as hot as Sirius A, but collapsed to a hundredth of a star's ordinary size. Now sweep away all the planets between the Dog and the Pup except two: a bald chunk of rock the size of Mercury orbiting some 100 million kilometers from A, and an Earth-sized planet some seven times farther out.

Give the Earth-sized planet a cloud-sprinkled atmosphere, a few large seas, some worn-down mountain chains, and a thin veneer of simple green life clinging to its dusty surface. Finally, throw in one lone gas giant planet, far beyond the Pup, some 200 billion kilometers from A. Add some meteoroids and comets and you have the Sirius system.

Lehman, the psychiatrist, pulled up a webchair to the kibitzer's position between Lee and Charnovsky.

"Mind if I watch?" He was trim and athletic looking, kept himself tanned under the UV lights in the ship's gym booth.

Within minutes they were discussing the chances of finding anything on the planet below them.

"You sound terribly pessimistic," the psychiatrist said.

"The planet looks pessimistic," Charnovsky replied. "It was scoured clean when Sirius B exploded, and life has hardly had a chance to get started again on its surface."

"But it *is* Earthlike, isn't it?"

"Hah!" Charnovsky burst. "To a simple-minded robot it may seem Earthlike. The air is breathable. The chemical composition of the rocks is similar. But no man would call that desert an Earthlike world. There are no trees, no grasses, it's too hot, the air is too dry. . ."

"And the planet's too young to have evolved an intelligent species," Lee added, "which makes me the biggest afterthought of all."

"Well, there might be something down there for an anthropologist to puzzle over," Lehman countered. "Things will look better once we get down to the surface. I think we're all getting a touch of cabin fever in here."

Before Lee could reply, Lou D'Orazio—the ship's geophysicist and cartographer—came bounding through the hatchway of the rec room and, taking advantage of the half-gravity, crossed to their chess table in two jumps.

"Look at this!"

He slapped a still-warm photograph on the chess table, scattering pieces over the floor. Charnovsky swore something Slavic, and everyone in the room turned.

It was one of the regular cartographic photos, crisscrossed with grid lines. It showed the shoreline of one of the planet's mini-oceans. A line of steep bluffs followed the shore.

"It looks like an ordinary . . ."

"*Aspertti un momento* . . . wait a minute . . . see here." D'Orazio pulled a magnifier from his coverall pocket. "Look!"

Lee peered through the magnifier. Fuzzy, wavering, gray. . .

"It looks like—"

Lehman said, "Whatever it is, it's standing on two legs."

"It's a man," Charnovsky said flatly.

## II

Within minutes the whole scientific staff had piled into the rec room and crowded around the table, together with all the crew members except the two on duty in the command globe. The ship's automatic cameras took twenty more photographs of the area before their orbit carried them over the horizon from the spot.

Five of the pictures showed the shadowy figure of a bipedal creature.

The spot was in darkness by the time their orbit carried them over it again. Infrared and radar sensors showed nothing.

They squinted at the pictures, handed them from person to person, talked and argued and wondered through two entire eight-hour shifts. Crewmen left for duty and returned again. The planet turned beneath them, and once again the shoreline was bathed in Sirius's hot glow. But there was no trace of the humanoid. Neither the cameras, the manned telescopes, nor the other sensors could spot anything.

One by one, men and women left the rec room, sleepy and talked out. Finally, only Lee, Charnovsky, Lehman and Captain Rassmussen were left sitting at the chess table with the finger-grimed photos spread out before them.

"They're men." Lee murmered. "Erect bipedal men."

"It's only one creature," the captain said. "And all we know is that it looks like a man."

Rassmussen was tall, hamfisted, rawboned, with a ruddy face that could look either elfin or Viking but nothing in between. His voice, though, was thin and high. To the everlasting applause of all aboard, he had fought to get a five-year supply of beer brought along. Even now, he had a mug tightly wrapped in one big hand.

"All right, they're humanoids," Lee conceded. "That's close enough."

The captain hiked a shaggy eyebrow. "I don't like jumping at shadows, you know. These pictures—"

"Men or not." Charnovsky said, "we must land and investigate closely."

Lee glanced at Lehman, straddling a turned-around chair and resting his arms tiredly on the back.

"Oh, we'll investigate," Rassmussen agreed, "but not too fast. If they are an intelligent species of some kind, we've got to go gingerly. I'm under orders from the Council, you know."

"They haven't tried to contact us," Lee said. "That means they either don't know we're here, or they're not interested, or—"

"Or what?"

Lee knew how it would sound, but he said it anyway. "Or they're waiting to get their hands on us."

Rassmussen laughed. "That sounds dramatic, sure enough."

"Really?" Lee heard his voice as though it were someone else's. "Suppose the humanoids down there are from the same race that built the machines on Titan?"

"Nonsense," Charnovsky blurted. "There are no cities down there, no sign whatever of an advanced civilization."

The captain took a long swallow of beer, then, "There is no sign of Earth's civilization on the planet either, you know. Yet we are here, sure enough."

Lee's insides were fluttering now. "If they are the ones who built on Titan . . ."

"It is still nonsense!" Charnovsky insisted. "To assume that the first extraterrestrial creature resembling a man is a representative of the race that visited the solar system hundreds of centuries ago . . . ridiculous! The statistics alone put the idea in the realm of fantasy."

"Wait, there's more to it," Lee said. "Why would a visitor from another star go to the trouble to build a machine that works for centuries, without stopping?"

They looked at him, waiting for him to answer his own question: Rassmussen with his Viking's craggy face, Charnovsky trying to puzzle it out in his own mind, Lehman calm and half-amused.

"The Titan buildings are more than alien," Lee explained. "They're hostile. That's my belief. Call it an assumption, a hypothesis. But I can't envision an alien race building machinery like that except for an all-important purpose. That purpose was military."

Rassmussen looked truly puzzled now. "Military? But who were they fighting?"

"Us," Lee answered. "A previous civilization on Earth. A culture that arose before the Ice Ages, went into space, met an alien culture and was smashed in a war so badly that there's no trace of it left."

Charnovsky's face was reddening with the effort of

staying quiet.

"I know it's conjecture," Lee went on quietly, "but if there was a war between ancient man and the builders of the Titan machines, then the two cultures must have arisen close enough to each other to make war possible. Widely separated cultures can't make war, they can only contact each other every few centuries or millennia. The aliens had to come from a nearby star . . . like Sirius."

"No, no, no!" Charnovsky slapped a hand on his thigh. "It's preposterous, unscientific! There is not one shred of evidence to support this, this . . . pipe-dream!"

But Rassmussen looked thoughtful.

"Still. . ."

"Still it is no nonsense," Charnovsky repeated. "The planet down there holds no interstellar technology. If there ever was one, it was blasted away when Sirius B exploded. Whoever is down there, he has no cities, no electronic communications, no satellites in orbit, no cultivated fields, no animal herds . . . nothing!"

"Then maybe he's a visitor too," Lee countered.

"Whatever it is," Rassmussen said, "it won't do for us to go rushing in like berserkers. Suppose there's a civilization down there that's so advanced we simply do not recognize it as such?"

Before Charnovsky could reply, the captain went on, "We have plenty of time. We will get more data about surface conditions from the robot landers and do a good deal more studying and thinking about the entire problem. Then, if conditions warrant it, we can land."

"But we don't have time!" Lee snapped. Surprised at

his own vehemence, he continued, "Five years is a grain of sand compared to the job ahead of us. We have to investigate a completely alien culture and determine what its attitude is toward us. Just learning the language might take five years all by itself."

Lehman smiled easily and said, "Sid, suppose you're totally wrong about this, and whoever's down there is simply a harmless savage. What would be the shock to his culture if we suddenly drop in on him?"

"What'll be the shock to our culture if I'm right?"

Rassmussen drained his mug and banged it down on the chess table. "This is getting us nowhere. We have not enough evidence to decide on an intelligent course of action. Personally, I'm in no hurry to go blundering into a nest of unknowns. Not when we can learn safely from orbit. As long as the beer holds out, we go slow."

Lee pushed his chair back and stood up. "We won't learn a damned thing from orbit. Not anything that counts. We've got to go down there and study them close up. And the sooner the better."

He turned and walked out of the rec room. *Rassmussen's spent half his life hauling scientists out to Titan, and he can't understand why we have to make the most of our time here*, he raged to himself.

Halfway down the passageway to his quarters, he heard footsteps padding behind him. He knew who it would be. Turning, he saw Lehman coming along toward him.

"Sacking in?" the psychiatrist asked.

"Aren't you sleepy?"

"Completely bushed, now that you mention it."

"But you want to talk to me," Lee said.

Lehman shrugged. "No hurry."

With a shrug of his own, Lee resumed walking to his room. "Come on. I'm too worked up to sleep anyway."

All the cubicles were more or less the same: a bunk, a desk, a filmspool reader, a sanitary closet. Lee took the webbed desk chair and let Lehman plop on the sighing air mattress of the bunk.

"Do you really believe this hostile alien theory? Or are you just—"

Lee slouched down in his chair and interrupted. "Let's not fool around, Rich. You know about my breakdown on Titan and you're worried about me."

"It's my job to worry about everybody."

"I take my pills every day . . . to keep the paranoia away."

"That wasn't the diagnosis of your case, as you're perfectly well aware."

"So they called it something else. What're you after, Rich? Want to test my reflexes while I'm sleepy and my guard's down?"

Lehman smiled professionally. "Look Sid. You had a breakdown on Titan. You got over it. That's finished."

Nodding grimly, Lee added, "Except that I think there might be aliens down there plotting against me."

"That could be nothing more than a subconscious attempt to increase the importance of the anthropology department," Lehman countered.

"Crap" Lee said. "I came out here expecting something like this. Why do you think I fought my way onto this expedition? It wasn't easy, after my breakdown. I had to push ahead of a lot of former friends."

"And leave your wife."

"That's right. Ruth divorced me for it. She's getting all my accumulated dividends. She'll die in comfort while we're sleeping our way back home."

"But why?" Lehman asked. "Why should you give up everything—friends, wife, family, position—to get out here?"

Lee knew the answer, hesitated about putting it into words, then realized that Lehman knew it too. "Because I had to face it . . . had to do what I could to find out about those buildings on Titan."

"And that's why you want to rush down and contact whoever it is down there? Am I right?"

"Right," Lee said. He almost wanted to laugh. "I'm hoping they can tell me if I'm crazy or not."


### III

It was three months before they landed.

Rassmussen was thorough, patient and stubborn. Unmanned landers sampled and tested surface conditions. Observation satellites crisscrossed the planet at the lowest possible altitudes—except for one thing that hung in synchronous orbit in the longitude of the spot where the first humanoid had been found.

That was the only place where humanoid life was seen, along that shoreline for a grand distance of perhaps five kilometers. Nowhere else on the planet.

Lee argued and swore and stormed at the delay. Rassmussen stayed firm. Only when he was satisfied that nothing more could be learned from orbit did he agree to land the ship. And still he sent clear word back toward Earth that he might be landing in a trap.

The great ship settled slowly, almost delicately, on a
hot tongue of fusion flame, and touched down on the
western edge of a desert some 200 kilometers from the
humanoid site. A range of rugged-looking hills separated them. The staff and crew celebrated that night.
The next morning, Lee, Charnovsky, Hatfield, Doris
McNertny, Marlene Ettinger and Alicia Monteverde
moved to the ship's "Sirius globe." They were to be the
expedition's "outsiders," the specialists who would
eventually live in the planetary environment. They
represented anthropology, geology, biochemistry,
botany, zoology and ecology, with backup specialties in
archeology, chemistry and paleontology.

The Sirius globe held their laboratories, workrooms,
equipment and living quarters. They were quarantined
from the rest of the ship's staff and crew, the "insiders,"
until the captain agreed that the surface conditions on
the planet would be no threat to the rest of the expedition members. That would take two years mini-
mum, Lee knew.

Gradually, the "outsiders" began to expose
themselves to the local environment. They began to
breathe the air, acquire the microbes. Pascual and
Tanaka made them sit in the medical examination
booths twice a day, and even checked them personally
every other day. The two M.D.'s wore disposable biosuits and worried expressions when they entered the Sirius globe. The medical computers compiled miles of
data tapes on each of the six "outsiders," but still Pascual's normally pleasant face acquired a perpetual
frown of anxiety about them.

"I just don't like the idea of this damned armor," Lee grumbled.

He was already encased up to his neck in a gleaming white powersuit, the type that crew members wore when working outside the ship in a vacuum. Aaron Hatfield and Marlene Ettinger were helping to check all the seams and connections. A few feet away, in the cramped "locker room," tiny Alicia Monteverdi looked as though she were being swallowed by an oversized automaton; Charnovsky and Doris McNertny were checking her suit.

"It's for your own protection," Marlene told Lee in a throaty whisper as she applied a test meter to the radio panel on his suit's chest. "You and Alicia won the toss for the first trip outside, but this is the price you must pay. Now be a good boy and don't complain."

Lee had to grin. "*Ja, Fraulein Schluemeisterein.*"

She looked up at him with a rueful smile, "Thank God you never had to carry on a conversation in German."

Finally Lee and Alicia clumped through the double hatch into the airlock. It took another fifteen minutes for them to perform the final checkout, but at last they were ready. The outer hatch slid back, and they started down the long ladder to the planet's surface. The armored suits were equipped with muscle-amplifying power systems, so that even a girl as slim as Alicia could handle their bulk easily.

Lee went down the ladder first and set foot on the ground. It was bare and dusty, the sky a reddish haze.

*The grand adventure*, Lee thought. *All the expected big moments in life are flops.* A hot breeze hummed in his earphones. It was early morning. Sirius had not

cleared the barren horizon yet, although the sky was
fully bright. Despite the suit's air-conditioning, Lee felt
the heat.

He reached up a hand as Alicia climbed warily down
the last few steps of the ladder. The plastic rungs gave
under the suit's weight, then slowly straightened
themselves when the weight was removed.

"Well," he said, looking at her wide-eyed face
through the transparent helmet of her suit, "what do
you think of it?"

"It is hardly paradise, is it?"

"Looks like it's leaning the other way," Lee said.

They explored—Lee and Alicia that first day, then the
other outsiders, shuffling ponderously inside their armor. Lee chafed against the restriction of the power-
suits, but Rassmussen insisted and would brook no argument. They went timidly at first, never out of sight of
the ship. Charnovsky chipped samples from the rock
outcroppings, while the others took air and soil samples,
dug for water, searched for life.

"The perfect landing site," Doris complained after a
hot, tedious day. "There's no form of life bigger than a
yeast mold within a hundred kilometers of here."

It was a hot world, a dry world, a brick-dust world,
where the sky was always red. Sirius was a blowtorch
searing down on them, too bright to look at even
through the tinted visors of their suits. At night there
was no moon to see, but the Pup bathed this world in a
deathly bluish glow far brighter yet colder than moon-
light. The night sky was never truly dark, and only a
few strong stars could be seen from the ground.

Through it all, the robot satellites relayed more pictures of the humanoids along the seacoast. They appeared almost every day, usually only briefly. Sometimes there were a few of them, sometimes only one, once there were nearly a dozen. The highest-resolution photographs showed them to be human in size and build. But what their faces looked like, what they wore, what they were *doing*—all escaped the drone cameras.

The robot landers, spotted in a dozen scattered locations within a thousand kilometers of the ship, faithfully recorded and transmitted everything they were programed to look for. They sent pictures and chemical analyses of plant life and insects. But no higher animals.

Alicia's dark-eyed face took on a perpetually puzzled frown, Lee saw. "It makes no sense," she would say. "There is nothing on this planet more advanced than insects . . . yet there are men. It's as though humans suddenly sprang up in the Silurian period on Earth. They *can't* be here. I wish we could examine the life in the seas . . . perhaps that would tell us more."

"You mean those humanoids didn't originate on this planet," Lee said to her.

She shook her head. "I don't know. I don't see how they could have. . . ."

## IV

Gradually they pushed their explorations further afield, beyond the ship's limited horizon. In the motorized powersuits a man could cover more than a hundred kilometers a day, if he pushed it. Lee always headed toward the grizzled hills that separated them from the seacoast. He helped the others to dig, to collect samples, but he always pointed them toward the sea.

"The satellite pictures show some decent greenery on the seaward side of the hills," he told Doris. "That's where he should go."

Rassmussen wouldn't move the ship. He wanted his base of operations, his link homeward, at least a hundred kilometers from the nearest possible threat. But finally he relaxed enough to allow the scientists to go out overnight and take a look at the hills.

*And maybe the coast*, Lee added silently to the captain's orders.

Rassmussen decided to let them use one of the ship's two air-cushion vehicles. He assigned Jerry Grote, the chief engineer, and Chien Shu Li, electronics specialist, to handle the skimmer and take command of the trip. They would live in biosuits and remain inside the skimmer at all times. Lee, Marlene, Doris and Charnovsky made the trip: Grote did the driving and navigating, Chien handled communications and the computer.

It took a full day's drive to get to the hills. Grote, a lanky, lantern-jawed New Zealander, decided to camp at their base as night came on.

"I thought you'd be a born mountaineer," Lee poked at him.

Grote leaned back in his padded chair and planted a large sandaled foot on the skimmer's control panel.

"I could climb those wrinkles out there in my sleep," he said pleasantly. "But we've got to be careful of this nice, shiny vehicle."

From the driver's compartment, Lee could see Marlene pushing forward toward them, squeezing between the racks of electronics gear that separated the forward compartment from the living and working quarters. Even in the drab coveralls, she showed a nice profile.

"I would like to go outside," she said to Grote. "We've been sitting all day like tourists in a shuttle."

Grote nodded. "I got to wear a hard suit, though."

"But—"

"Orders."

She glanced at Lee, then shrugged. "Very well."

"I'll come with you," Lee said.

Squirming into the armored suits in the aft hatchway was exasperating, but at last they were ready and Lee opened the hatch. They stepped out across the tail fender of the skimmer and jumped to the dusty ground.

"Being inside this is almost worse than being in the car," Marlene said.

They walked around the skimmer. Lee watched his shadow lengthen as he placed the setting Sirius at his back.

"Look . . . *look!*"

He saw Marlene pointing and turned to follow her gaze. The hills rising before them were dazzling with a million sparkling lights: red and blue and white and dazzling, shimmering lights as though a cascade of precious jewels were pouring down the hillside.

"What is it?" Marlene's voice sounded excited, thrilled, not the least afraid.

Lee stared at the shifting multicolored lights, it was like playing a lamp on cut crystal. He took a step toward the hills, then looked down to the ground. From inside the cumbersome suit, it was hard to see the ground close to your feet and harder still to bend down and pick up anything. But he squatted slowly and reached for a small stone. Getting up again, Lee held the stone high enough for it to catch the fading rays of daylight.

The rock glittered with a shower of varicolored sparkles.

"They're made of glass," Lee said.

Within minutes Charnovsky and the other "outsiders" were out of the ship to marvel at it. The Russian collected as many rocks as he could stuff into his suit's thigh pouches. Lee and Grote helped him; the women merely stood by the skimmer and watched the hills blaze with lights.

Sirius disappeared below the horizon at last, and the show ended. The hills returned to being brownish, erosion-worn clumps of rock.

"Glass mountains," Marlene marveled as they returned to the skimmer.

"Not glass," Charnovsky corrected. "Glazed rock. Granitic, no doubt. Probably was melted when the Pup exploded. Atmosphere might have been blown away, and rock cooled very rapidly.

Lee could see Marlene's chin rise stubbornly inside the transparent dome of her suit. "I name them the Glass Mountains," she said firmly.

Grote had smuggled a bottle along with them, part of his personal stock. "My most precious possession," he rightfully called it. But for the Glass Mountains he dug it out of its hiding place, and they toasted both the discovery and the name. Marlene smiled and insisted that

Lee also be toasted, as co-discoverer.

Hours later, Lee grew tired of staring at the metal ceiling of the sleeping quarters a few inches above his top-tier bunk. Even Grote's drinks didn't help him to sleep. He kept wondering about the humanoids, what they were doing, where they were from, how he would get to learn their secrets. As quietly as he could, he slipped down from the bunk. The two men beneath him were breathing deeply and evenly. Lee headed for the rear hatch, past the women's bunks.

The hard suits were standing at stiff attention, flanking both sides of the rear hatch. Lee was in his coveralls. He strapped on a pair of boots, slid the hatch open as quietly as he could, and stepped out onto the fender.

The air was cool and clean, the sky bright enough for him to make out the worn old hills. There were a few stars in the sky, but the hills didn't reflect them.

He heard a movement behind him. Turning, he saw Marlene.

"Did I wake you?"

"I'm a very light sleeper," she said.

"Sorry, I didn't mean—"

"No, I'm glad you did." She shook her head slightly, and for the first time Lee noticed the sweep and softness of her hair. The light was too dim to make out its color, but he remembered it as chestnut.

"Besides," she whispered, "I've been longing to get outside without being in one of those damned suits."

He helped her down from the fender, and they walked a little way from the skimmer.

"Can we see the sun?" she asked, looking skyward.

"I'm not sure, I think maybe ... there. ..." He pointed to a second-magnitude star, shining alone in the grayish sky.

"Where, which one?"

He took her by the shoulder with one hand so that she could see where he was pointing.

"Oh yes, I see it."

She turned, and she was in his arms, and he kissed her. He held onto her as though there was nothing else in the universe.

If any of the others suspected that Lee and Marlene had spent the night outside, they didn't mention it. All six of them took their regular pre-breakfast checks in the medical booth, and by the time they were finished eating in the cramped galley the computer had registered a safe green for each of them.

Lee slid out from the galley's folding table and made his way forward. Grote was slouched in the driver's seat, his lanky frame a geometry of knees and elbows. He was studying the viewscreen map.

"Looking for a pass through these hills for our vehicle," he said absently, his eyes on the slowly-moving photomap.

"Why take the skimmer?" Lee asked, sitting on the chair beside him. We came across these hills in the powersuits."

Grote cocked an eye at him. "You're really set on getting to the coast, aren't you?"

"Aren't you?"

That brought a grin. "How much do you think we ought to carry with us?"

## V

They split the team into three groups. Chien and Charnovsky stayed with the car; Marlene and Doris would go with Lee and Grote to look at the flora and fauna (if any) on the shore side of the hills. Lee and the engineer carried a pair of TV camera packs with them, to set up close to the shoreline.

"Beware of the natives," Charnovsky's voice grated in Lee's earphones as they walked away from the skimmer. "They might swoop down on you with bows and arrows!" His laughter showed what he thought of Lee's worries.

Climbing the hills wasn't as bad as Lee had thought it would be. The powersuit did most of the work, and the glassy rock was not smooth enough to cause real troubles with footing. It was hot though, even with the suit's cooling equipment turned up full bore. Sirius blazed overhead, and the rocks beat glare and heat back into their faces as they climbed.

It took most of the day to get over the crest of the hills. But finally with Sirius edging toward the horizon behind them, Lee saw the water.

The sea spread to the farther horizon, cool and blue, with long gentle swells that steepened into surf as they ran up toward the land. And the land was green here: shrubs and mossy-looking plants were patchily sprinkled around.

"Look! Right here!" Doris' voice.

Lee swiveled his head and saw her clumsily sinking to her knees, like an armor-plated elephant getting down ponderously from a circus trick. She knelt beside a fern like plant. They all walked over and helped her to photograph it, snip a leaf from it, probe its root system.

Might as well sleep here tonight," Grote said. "I'll take the first watch."

"Can't we set the scanners to give an alarm if anything approaches?" Marlene asked. "There's nothing here dangerous enough to—"

"I want one of us awake at all times," Grote said firmly. "And nobody outside of his suits."

"There's no place like home," Doris muttered. "But after a while even your own smell gets to you."

The women lay down, locking the suits into roughly reclining positions. To Lee they looked like oversized beetles that had gotten stuck on their backs. It didn't look possible for them to ever get up again. Then another thought struck him, and he chuckled to himself. *Super chastity belts.*

He sat down, cranked the suit's torso section back to a comfortable reclining angle, and tried to doze off. He was dreaming of the towers on Titan again when Grote's voice in his earphones woke him.

"Is it my turn?" he asked groggily.

"Not yet. But turn off your transmitter. You were groaning in your sleep. Don't want to wake up the girls, do you?"

Lee took the second watch and simply stayed awake until daybreak without bothering any of the others. They began marching toward the sea.

The hills descended only slightly into a rolling plateau that went on until they reached the bluffs that overlooked the sea. A few hundred feet down was a narrow strip of beach, with the breakers surging in.

"This is as far as we go," Grote said.

The women spent the morning collecting plant samples. Marlene found a few insects and grew more excited over them than Doris had been about the shrubbery. Lee and Grote walked along the edge of the cliffs looking for a good place to set up their cameras.

"You're sure this is the area where they were seen?" Lee asked.

The engineer walking alongside him, turned his head inside the plastic helmet. Lee could see he was edgy too.

"I know how to read a map."

"Sorry, I'm just anxious—"

"So am I."

They walked until Sirius was almost directly overhead, without seeing anything except the tireless sea, the beach, and the spongy-looking plants that huddled close to the ground.

"Not even a damned tree," Grote grumbled.

They turned back and headed for the spot where they had left the women. Far up the beach. Lee saw a tiny dark spot.

"What's that?"

Grote stared for a few moments. "Probably a rock." But he touched a button on the chest of his suit.

Lee did the same, and an electro-optical viewpiece slid down in front of his eyes. Turning a dial on the suit's control panel, he tried to focus on the spot. It wavered in the heat currents of the early afternoon, blurred and uncertain. Then it seemed to jump out of view.

Lee punched the button and the lens slid away from his eyes. "It's moving!" he shouted, and started to run.

He heard Grote's heavy breathing as the engineer followed him, and they both nearly flew in their power-suits along the edge of the cliffs.

It was a man! No, not one, Lee saw, but two of them walking along the beach, their feet in the foaming water.

"Get down you bloody fool" he heard Grote shrilling at him.

He dove headlong, bounced, cracked the back of his head against the helmet's plastic, then banged his chin on the soft inner lining of the collar.

"Don't want them to see, do you?" Grote was whispering now.

"They can't hear us, for God's sake," Lee said into his suit radiophone.

They wormed their way to the cliff's edge again and watched. The two men seemed to be dressed in black. *Or are they black-skinned and naked?* Lee wondered.

After a hurried council, they unslung one of the video cameras and its power unit, set it up right there, turned it on and then backed away from the edge of the cliff. Then they ran as hard as they could, staying out of sight of the beach, with the remaining camera. They passed the startled women and breathlessly shouted out their find. The women dropped their work and started running after them.

About a kilometer or so further on they dropped to all fours again and painfully crawled to the edge once more. Grote hissed the women into silence as they hunched up beside him.

The beach was empty now.

"Do you think they saw us?" Lee asked.

"Don't know."

Lee used the electro-optics again and scanned the beach. "No sign of them."

"Their footprints," Grote snapped. "Look there."

The trails of two very human-looking sets of footprints marched straight into the water. All four of them searched the sea for hours, but saw nothing. Finally, they decided to set up the other camera. It was turning dark by the time they finished.

"We've got to get back to the car," Grote said, wearily, when they finished. "There's not enough food in the suits for another day."

"I'll stay here," Lee replied. "You can bring me more supplies tomorrow."

"No. If there's anything to see, the cameras will pick it up. Chien is monitoring them back at the car, and the whole crew of the ship must be watching the view."

Lee saw there was no sense arguing. Besides, he was bone tired. But he knew he'd be back again as soon as he could get there.

## VI

"Well, it settles a three-hundred-year-old argument," Aaron Hatfield said as he watched the viewscreen.

The biochemist and Lee were sitting in the main workroom of the ship's Sirius globe, watching the humanoids as televised by the cameras on the cliffs. Charnovsky was on the other side of the room, at a workbench, flashing rock chips with a laser so that a spectrometer could analyze their chemical composition.

The other outsiders were traveling in the skimmer again, collecting more floral and insect specimens.

"What argument?" Lee asked.

Hatfield shifted in his chair, making the webbing creak. "About the human form . . . whether it's an accident or a result of evolutionary selection. From *them*," he nodded toward the screen, "I'd say it's no accident."

One camera was on wide-field focus and showed a group of three of the men. They were wading hip-deep in the surf, carrying slender rods high above their heads to keep them free of the surging waves. The other camera was fixed on a close-up view of three women standing on the beach, watching their men. Like the men, they were completely naked and black-skinned. They looked human in every detail.

Every morning they appeared on the beach, often carrying the rods, but sometimes not. Lee concluded that they must live in caves cut into the cliffs. The rods looked like simple bone spears but even under the closest focus of the cameras he couldn't be sure.

"They're not Negroid," he muttered, more to himself than anyone listening.

"It's hard to tell, isn't it?" Hatfield asked.

Nodding, Lee said, "They just don't look like terrestrial Negroes . . . except for their skin coloring. And that's an adaptation to Sirius' brightness. Plenty of ultraviolet, too."

Charnovsky came over and pulled up a chair. "So. Have they caught any fish this morning?"

"Not yet," Lee answered.

Jabbing a stubby finger toward the screen, the Russian asked, "Are these the geniuses who built the

machines on Titan? Fishing with bone spears? They
don't make much of an enemy, Lee."

"They could have been our enemy," Lee answered,
forcing a thin smile. He was getting accustomed to
Charnovsky's needling, but not reconciled to it.

The geologist shook his head sadly. "Take the advice
of an older man, dear friend, and disabuse yourself of
this idea. Statistics are a powerful tool, Lee. The
chances of this particular race being the one that built
on Titan are fantastically high. And the chances . . ."

"What're the chances that two intelligent races will
both evolve along the same physical lines?" Lee
snapped.

Charnovsky shrugged. "We have two known races.
They are both human in form. The chances must be excellent."

Lee turned back to watch the viewscreen, then asked
Hatfield, "Aaron, the biochemistry is very similar to
Earth's, isn't it?"

"Very close."

"I mean . . . I could eat local food and be nourished
by it? I wouldn't be poisoned or anything like that?"

"Well," Hatfield said, visibly thinking it out as he
spoke, "as far as the structure of the proteins and other
foodstuffs are concerned . . . yes, I guess you could get
away with eating it. The biochemistry is basically the
same as ours, as nearly as I've been able to tell. But so
are terrestrial shellfish, and they make me deathly ill.
You see, there're all sorts of enzymes, and microbial
parasites, and viruses . . ."

"We've been living with the local bugs for months

now," Lee said. "We're adapted to them, aren't we?"

"You know what they say about visiting strange places: don't drink the water."

One of the natives struck into the water with his spear, and instantly the water began to boil with the thrashing of some sea creature. The other two men drove their spears home, and the thrashing died. They lifted a four-foot-long fish out of the water and started back for the beach, carrying it triumphantly over their heads. The camera's autotracker kept the picture on them. The women on the beach were jumping and clapping with joy.

"Damn," Lee said softly. "They're as human as we are."

"And obviously representative of a high technical civilization," Charnovsky said.

"Survivors of one, maybe," Lee answered. "Their culture might have been wiped out by the Pup's explosion . . . or by war."

"Ah, now it gets even more dramatic: two cultures destroyed, ours *and* theirs."

"All right, go ahead and laugh," Lee said. "I won't be able to prove anything until I get to live with them."

"Until what?" Hatfield said.

"Until I go out there and meet them face to face, learn their language, their culture, live with them."


"Live with them?" Rassmussen looked startled; the first time Lee had seen him jarred. The captain's monomolecular biosuit gave his craggy face a faint sheen, like the beginnings of a sweat.

They were sitting around a circular table in the con-

ference room of the Sirius globe: the six "outsiders,"
Grote, Chien, Captain Rassmussen, Pascual and
Lehman.

"Aren't you afraid they might put you in a pot and
boil you?" Grote asked, grinning.

"I don't think they have pots. Or fire, for that matter," Lee countered.

The laugh turned on Grote.

Lee went on quietly, "I've checked it out with Aaron,
here. There's no biochemical reason why I couldn't survive in the native environment. Doris and Marlene have
agreed to gather the same types of food we've seen the
humanoids carrying, and I'll go on a strictly native diet
for a few weeks before I go to live with them."

Lehman hunched forward, from across the table, and
asked Lee, "About the dynamics of having a representative of our relatively advanced culture step into their
primitive—"

"I won't be representing an advanced culture to
them,"Lee said. "I intend to be just as naked and tool-
less as they are. And just as black. Aaron can inject me
with the proper enzymes to turn my skin black."

"That would be necessary in any event if you don't
want to be sunburned to death," Pascual said.

Hatfield added, "You'll also need contact lenses
that'll screen out the UV and protect your eyes."

They spent an hour discussing all the physical prec-
autions he would have to take. Lee kept glancing at
Rassmussen. *The idea's slipping out from under his control.* The captain watched each speaker in turn,
squinting with concentration and sinking deeper and
deeper into his Viking scowl. Then, when Lee was cer-

tain that the captain could no longer object, Rassmussen spoke up: "One more question. Are you willing to give up an eye for this mission of yours?"

"What do you mean?"

The captain's hands seemed to wander loosely without a mug of beer to tie them down. "Well . . . you seem to be willing to run a good deal of personal risk to live with these . . . eh, people. From the expedition's viewpoint, you will also be risking our only anthropologist, you know. I think the wise thing to do, in that case, would be to have a running record of everything you see and hear."

Lee nodded.

"So we can swap one of your eyes for a TV camera and plant a transmitter somewhere in your skull. I'm sure there's enough empty space in your head to accommodate it." The captain chuckled toothily at his joke.

"We can't do an eye procedure here," Pascual argued. "It's too risky."

"I understand that Dr. Tanaka is quite expert in that field," the captain said. "And naturally we would preserve the eye to restore it afterward. Unless, of course, Professor Lee—" He let the suggestion dangle.

Lee looked at them sitting around the big table: Rassmussen, trying to look noncommittal; Pascual, upset and nearly angry; Lehman, staring intently right back into Lee's eyes.

*You're just trying to force me to back down*, Lee thought of Rassmussen. Then, of Lehman, *And if I don't back down, you'll be convinced that I'm crazy.*

For a long moment there was no sound in the

crowded conference room except the faint whir of the air blower.

"All right," Lee said. "If Tanaka is willing to tackle the surgery, so am I."

## VII

When Lee returned to his cubicle, the message light under the phone screen was blinking red. He flopped on the bunk, propped a pillow under his head, and asked the computer, "What's the phone message?"

The screen lit up: PLS CALL DR. LEHMAN.

*My son, the psychiatrist.* "Okay," he said aloud, "get him."

A moment later Lehman's tanned face filled the screen.

"I was expecting you to call," Lee said.

The psychiatrist nodded. "You agreed to pay a big price just to get loose among the natives."

"Tanaka can handle the surgery," he answered evenly.

"It'll take a month before you are fit to leave the ship again."

"You know what our Viking captain says . . . we'll stay here as long as the beer holds out."

Lehman smiled. *Professional technique*, Lee thought.

"Sid, do you really think you can mingle with these people without causing any cultural impact? Without changing them?"

Shrugging, he answered, "I don't know. I hope so. As far as we know, they're the only humanoid group on the planet. They may have never seen a stranger before."

"That's what I mean," Lehman said. "Don't you feel that—"

"Let's cut the circling, Rich. You know why I want to see them first-hand. If we had the time I'd study them remotely for a good long while before trying any contact. But it gets back to the beer supply. We've got to squeeze everything we can out of them in a little more than four years."

"There will be other expeditions, after we return to Earth and tell them about these people."

"Probably so. But they may be too late."

"Too late for what?"

His neck was starting to hurt; Lee hunched up to a sitting position on the bunk. "Figure it out. There can't be more than about fifty people in the group we've been watching. I've only seen a couple of children. And there aren't any other humanoid groups on the planet. That means they're dying out. This gang is the last of their kind. By the time another expedition gets here, there might not be any of them left."

For once, Lehman looked surprised "Do you really think so?"

"Yes. And before they die, we have to get some information out of them."

"What do you mean?"

"They might not be natives of this planet," Lee said, forcing himself to speak calmly, keeping his face a mask, freezing any emotion inside him. "They probably came from somewhere else. That elsewhere is the home of the people who built the Titan machine . . . their real home. We have got to find out where it is." *Flawless logic.*

Lehman tried to smile again. "That's assuming your theory about an ancient war is right."

"Yes. Assuming I'm right."

"Assume you *are*," Lehman said. "And assume you find what you're looking for. Then what? Do you just take off and go back to Earth? What happens to the people here?"

"I don't know," Lee said, ice-cold inside. "The main problem will be how to deal with the home world of their people."

"But the people here, do we just let them die out?"

"Maybe. I guess so."

Lehman's smile was completely gone now; his face didn't look pleasant at all.

It took much more than a month. The surgery was difficult. And beneath all the pain was Lee's rooted fear that he might never have his sight fully restored again. While he was recovering, before he was allowed out of his infirmary bed, Hatfield turned his skin black with a series of enzyme injections. He was also fitted for a single quartz contact lens.

Once he was up and around, Marlene followed him constantly. Finally she said, "You're even better looking with black skin; it makes you more mysterious. And the prosthetic eye looks exactly like your own. It even moves like the natural one."

Rassmussen still plodded. Long after he felt strong enough to get going again, he was still confined to the ship. When his complaints grew loud enough, they let him start on a diet of native foods. The medics and Hatfield hovered around him while he spent a miserable week with dysentary. Then it passed. But it took a while to build up his strength again; all he had to eat now were fish, insects, and pulpy greens.

After more tests, conferences, a two-week trial run out by the Glass Mountains, and then still more exhaustive physical exams, Rassmussen at last agreed to let Lee go.

Grote took him out in the skimmer, skirting the long way around the Glass Mountains, through the surf and out onto the gently billowing sea. They kept far enough out at sea for the beach to be constantly beyond their horizon.

When night fell, Grote nosed the skimmer landward. They came ashore around midnight, with the engines clamped down to near silence, a few kilometers up the beach from the humanoids' site. Grote, encased in a powersuit, walked with him part way and buried a relay transceiver in the sand, to pick up the signals from the camera and radio imbedded in Lee's skull.

"Good luck." His voice was muffled by the helmet.

Lee watched him plod mechanically back into the darkness. He strained to hear the skimmer as it turned and slipped back into the sea, but he could neither see nor hear it.

He was alone on the beach.

Clouds were drifting landward, riding smoothly overhead. The breeze on the beach, though, was blowing warmly out of the desert, spilling over the bluffs and across the beach, out to sea. The sky was bright with the all-night twilight glow, even though the clouds blotted out most of the stars. Along the foot of the cliffs, though, it was deep black. Except for the wind, there wasn't a sound: not a bird nor a nocturnal cat, not even an insect's chirrup.

Lee stayed near the water's edge. He wasn't cold, even

though naked. Still, he could feel himself trembling.

*Grote's out there*, he told himself. *If you need him, he can come rolling up the beach in ten minutes.*

But he knew he was alone.

The clouds thickened and began to sprinkle rain, a warm, soft shower. Lee blinked the drops away from his eyes and walked slowly, a hundred paces one direction, then a hundred paces back again.

The rain stopped as the sea horizon started turning bright. The clouds wafted away. The sky lightened, first gray, then almost milky white. Lee looked toward the base of the cliffs. Dark shadows dotted the rugged cliff face. Caves. Some of them were ten feet or more above the sand.

Sirius edged a limb above the horizon, and Lee, squinting, turned away from its brilliance. He looked back at the caves again, feeling the warmth of the hot star's might on his back.

The first ones out of the cave were two children. They tumbled out of the same cave, off to Lee's left, giggling and running.

When they saw Lee, they stopped dead. As though someone had turned them off. Lee could feel his heart beating as they stared at him. He stood just as still as they did, perhaps a hundred meters from them. They looked about five and ten years old, he judged. *If their lifespans are the same as ours.*

The taller of the two boys took a step toward Lee, then turned and ran back into the cave. The younger boy followed him.

For several minutes nothing happened. Then Lee heard voices echoing from inside the cave. Angry?

Frightened? *They are not laughing.*

Four men appeared at the mouth of the cave. Their hands were empty. They simply stood there and gaped at him, from the shadows of the cave's mouth.

*Now we'll start learning their customs about strangers,* Lee said to himself.

Very deliberately, he turned away from them and took a few steps up the beach. Then he stopped, turned again, and walked back to his original spot.

Two of the men disappeared inside the cave. The other two stood there. Lee couldn't tell what the expressions on their faces meant. Suddenly other people appeared at a few of the other cave entrances. *They're interconnected.*

Lee tried a smile and waved. There were women among the onlookers now, and a few children. One of the boys who saw him first—at least, it looked like him—started chattering to an adult. The man silenced him with a brusque gesture.

It was getting hot. Lee could feel perspiration dripping along his ribs as Sirius climbed above the horizon and shone straight at the cliffs. Slowly, he squatted down on the sand.

A few of the men from the first cave stepped out onto the beach. Two of them were carrying bone spears. Others edged out from their caves. They slowly drew together, keeping close to the rocky cliff wall, and started talking in low, earnest tones.

*They're puzzled, all right. Just play it cool. Don't make any sudden moves.*

He leaned forward slightly and traced a triangle on the sand with one finger.

When he looked up again, a grizzled, white-haired man had taken a step or two away from the conference group. Lee smiled at him, and the elder froze in his tracks. With a shrug, Lee looked back at the first cave. The boy was still there, with a woman standing beside him, gripping his shoulder. Lee waved and smiled. The boy's hand fluttered momentarily.

The old man said something to the group, and one of the younger men stepped out to join him. Neither held a weapon. They walked to within a few meters of Lee, and the old man said something, as loudly and bravely as he could.

Lee bowed his head. "Good morning. I am Professor Sidney Lee of the University of Ottawa, which is one hell of a long way from here."

They squatted down and started talking, both of them at once, pointing to the caves and then all around the beach and finally out to the sea.

Lee held up his hands and said, "It ought to be clear to you that I'm from someplace else, and I don't speak your language. Now if you want to start teaching me—"

They shook their heads, talked to each other, said something else to Lee.

Lee smiled at them and waited for them to stop talking. When they did, he pointed to himself and said very clearly, "Lee."

He spent an hour at it, repeating only that one syllable, no matter what they said to him or to each other. The heat was getting fierce; Sirius was a blue flame searing his skin, baking the juices out of him.

The younger man got up and, with a shake of his

head, spoke a few final words to the elder and walked back to the group that still stood knotted by the base of the cliff. The old man rose, slowly and stiffly. He beckoned to Lee to do the same.

As Lee got to his feet he saw the other men start to head out for the surf. A few boys followed behind, carrying several bone spears for their—what? Fathers? Older brothers?

*As long as the spears are for the fish and not me,* Lee thought.

The old man was saying something to him. Pointing toward the caves. He took a step in that direction, then motioned for Lee to come along. Lee hesitated. The old man smiled a toothless smile and repeated his invitation.

Grinning back at him in realization, Lee said aloud, "Okay. If you're not scared of me, I guess I don't have to be scared of you."


## VIII

It took more than a year before Lee learned their language well enough to understand roughly what they were saying. It was an odd language, sparse and practically devoid of pronouns.

His speaking of their words made the adults smile, when they thought he couldn't see them doing it. The children still giggled at his speech, but the old man—Ardraka—always scolded them when they did.

They called the planet Makta, and Lee saw to it that Rassmussen entered that as its official name in the expedition's log. He made a point of walking the beach alone one night each week, to talk with the others at the ship and make a personal report. He quickly found that most of what he saw, heard and said inside the caves never got out to the relay transceiver buried up the beach; the cliff's rock walls were too much of a barrier.

Ardraka was the oldest of the clan and the nominal chief. His son, Ardra, was the younger man who had also come out to talk with Lee that first day. Ardra actually gave most of the orders. Ardraka could over-rule him whenever he chose to, but he seldom exercised the right.

There were only forty-three people in the clan, nearly half of them elderly looking. Eleven were pre-adolescent children; two of them infants. There were no obvious pregnancies. Ardraka must have been about fifty, judg-ing by his oldest son's apparent age. But the old man had the wrinkled, sunken look of an eighty-year-old. The people themselves had very little idea of time beyond the basic rhythm of night and day.

They came out of the caves only during the early morning and evening hours. The blazing midday heat of Sirius was too much for them to face. They ate crus-taceans and the small fish that dwelt in the shallows along the beach, insects, and the grubby vegetation that clung to the base of the cliffs. Occasionally they found a large fish that had blundered into the shallows; then they feasted.

They had no wood, no metal, no fire. Their only tools were from the precious bones of the rare big fish, and hand-worked rock.

They died of disease and injury, and aged pre-maturely from poor diet and overwork. They had to search constantly for food, especially since half their day was taken away from them by Sirius' blowtorch heat. They were more apt to be prowling the beach at night, hunting seaworms and crabs, than by daylight. *Grote and I damn near barged right into them*, Lee realized after watching a few of the night gathering sessions.

There were some dangers. One morning he was watching one of the teenaged boys, a good swimmer, venture out past the shallows in search of fish. A sharklike creature found him first.

When he screamed, half a dozen men grabbed spears and dove into the surf. Lee found himself dashing into the water alongside them, empty-handed. He swam out to the youngster, already dead, sprawled face down in the water, half of him gone, blood staining the swells. Lee helped to pull the remains back to shore.

There wasn't anything definite, no one said a word to him about it, but their attitude toward him changed. He was fully accepted now. He hadn't saved the boy's life, hadn't shown uncommon bravery. But he had shared a danger with them, and a sorrow.

*Wheel the horse inside the gates of Troy.* Lee found himself thinking. *Nobody ever told you to beware of men bearing gifts.*

After he got to really understand their language Lee found that Ardraka often singled him out for long talks. It was almost funny. There was something that the old man was fishing for, just as Lee was trying to learn where these people *really* came from.

They were sitting in the cool darkness of the central cove, deep inside the cliff. All the outer caves channeled back to this single large chamber, high-roofed and moss-floored, its rocks faintly phosphorescent. It was big enough to hold four or five times the clan's present number. It was midday. Most of the people were sleeping. A few of the children, off to the rear of the cave, were scratching pictures on the packed bare earth with pointed, fist-sized rocks.

Lee sat with his back resting against a cool stone wall. The sleepers were paired off, man and mate, for the most part. The unmated teenagers slept apart, with the older couples between them. As far as Lee could judge, the couples paired permanently, although the teens played the game about as freely as they could.

Ardraka was dozing beside him. Lee settled back and tried to turn off his thoughts, but the old man said: "Lee is not asleep?"

"No, Lee is not," he answered.

"Ardraka has seen that Lee seldom sleeps," Ardraka said.

"That is true."

"Is it that Lee does not need to sleep as Ardraka does?"

Lee shook his head. "No, Lee needs sleep as much as Ardraka or any man."

"This . . . place . . . that Lee comes from. Lee says it is beyond the sea?"

"Yes, far beyond."

In the faint light from the gleaming rocks, the old man's face looked troubled, deep in difficult thought.

"And there are men and women living in Lee's place, men and women like the people here?"

Lee nodded.

"And how did Lee come here? Did Lee swim around the sea?"

They had been through this many times. "Lee came around the edge of the sea, walking on land just as Ardraka would."

Laughing softly, the old man said, "Ardraka is too feeble now for such a walk. Ardra could make such a walk."

"Yes, Ardra can."

"Ardraka has tried to dream of Lee's place, and Lee's people. But such dreams do not come."

"Dreams are hard to command," Lee said.

"Yes, truly."

"And what of Ardraka and the people here?" Lee asked. "Is this the only place where such men and women live?"

"Yes. It is the best place to live. All other places are death."

"There are no men and women such as Ardraka and the people here living in another place?"

The old man thought hard a moment, then smiled a wrinkled toothless smile. "Surely Lee jokes. Lee knows that Lee's people live in another place."

*We've been around that bush before.* Trying another tack, he asked, "Have Ardraka's people *always* lived in this place? Did Ardraka's father live here?"

"Yes, of course."

"And his father?"

A nod.

"And all the fathers, from the beginning of the people? All lived here, always?"

A shrug. "No man knows."

"Have there always been this many people living here?" Lee asked. "Did Ardraka's people ever fill this cave when they slept here?"

"Oh yes. . . . When Ardraka was a boy, many men and women slept in the outer caves, since there was no room for them here. And when Ardraka's father was young, men and women even slept in the lower caves."

"Lower caves?"

Ardraka nodded. "Below this one, deeper inside the ground. No man or woman has been in them since Ardraka became chief."

"Why is that?"

The old man evaded Lee's eyes. "They are not needed."

"May Lee visit these lower caves?"

"Perhaps," Ardraka said. After a moment's thought, he added, "Children have been born and grown to manhood and died since any man set foot in those caves. Perhaps they are gone now. Perhaps Ardraka does not remember how to find them."

"Lee would like to visit the lower caves."

Late that night he walked the beach alone, under the glowing star-poor sky, giving his weekly report back to the ship.

"He's been cagy about the lower caves," Lee said as the outstretched fingers of surf curled around his ankles.

"Why should he be so cautious?" It was Marlene's voice. She was taking the report this night.

"Because he's no fool, that's why. These people have never seen a stranger before . . . not for generations, at least. Therefore their behavior toward me is original, not instinctive. If he's leery of showing me the caves, it's for some reason that's fresh in his mind, not some hoary tribal taboo."

"Then what do you intend to do?"

"I'm not sure yet—" Lee turned to head back down the beach and saw Ardra standing twenty paces behind him.

"Company," he snapped. "Talk to you later. Keep listening."

Advancing toward him, Ardra said, "Many nights, Ardra has seen Lee leave the cave and walk on the beach. Tonight Lee was talking, but Lee was alone. Does Lee speak to a man or woman that Ardra cannot see?"

His tone was flat, factual, neither frightened nor puzzled. It was too dark to really make out the expression on his face, but he sounded almost casual.

"Lee is alone," he answered as calmly as he could. "There is no man or woman here with Lee. Except Ardra."

"But Lee speaks and then is silent. And then Lee speaks again."

*He knows a conversation when he hears one, even if it's only one side of it and in a strange language.*

Ardra suggested, "Perhaps Lee speaks to men and women from Lee's place, which is far from the sea?"

"Does Ardra believe that Lee can speak to men and women far away from this place?"

"Ardra believes that is what Lee does at night on the beach. Lee speaks with the *Karta*."

"*Karta*? What is the meaning of *karta*?"

"It is an ancient word. It means men and women who live in another place."

*Others*, Lee translated to himself. "Yes," he said to Ardra, "Lee speaks to the others."

Ardra's breath seemed to catch momentarily, then he said with deliberate care, "Lee speaks with the Others." His voice had an edge of steel to it now.

*What have I stepped into?*

"It is time to be sleeping, not walking the beach," Ardra said, in a tone that Lee knew was a command. And he started walking toward the caves.

Lee outweighed the chief's son by a good twenty pounds and was some ten centimeters taller. But he had seen the speed and strength in Ardra's wiry frame and knew the difference in reaction times that the fifteen years between them made. So he didn't run or fight; he followed Ardra back to the caves and obediently went to sleep. And all the night Ardra stayed awake and watched over him.

## IX

The next morning, when the men went out to fish and the women to gather greens, Ardra took Lee's arm and led him toward the back of the central cave. Ardraka and five other elders were waiting for them. They all looked very grim. Only then did Lee realize that Ardra was carrying a spear in his other hand.

They were sitting in a ragged semicircle, their backs to what looked like a tunnel entrance, their eyes hard on Lee. He sat at their focus, with Ardra squatting beside him.

"Lee," Ardraka began without preliminaries, "why is

it that Lee wishes to see the lower caves?''

The question caught him by surprise. "Because . . . Lee wishes to learn more about Ardraka's people. Lee comes from far away, and knows little of Ardraka's people."

"Is it true," one of the elders asked, "that Lee speaks at night with the Others?" His inflection made the word sound special, fearful, ominous.

"Lee speaks to the men and women of the place where Lee came from. It is like the way Ardraka speaks to Ardraka's grandfather . . . in a dream."

"But Ardraka sleeps when doing this. Lee is awake."

Ardra broke in, "Lee says Lee's people live beyond the sea. Beyond the sea is the sky. Do Lee's people live in the sky?"

*Off the edge of the world, just like Columbus.* "Yes," he admitted. "Lee's people live in the sky—"

"*See!*" Ardra shouted. "Lee is of the Others!"

The councilmen physically backed away from him. Even Ardraka seemed shaken.

"Lee is of the Others," Ardra repeated. "Lee must be killed, before he kills Ardraka's people!"

"Kill?" Lee felt stunned. He had never heard any of them speak of violence before.

"Why should Lee kill the people here?"

They were all babbling at once. Ardraka raised his hand for silence.

"To kill a man is very serious," he said painfully. "It is not certain that Lee is of the Others."

"Lee says it with Lee's own mouth!" Ardra insisted. "Why else did Lee come here? Why does Lee want to see the lower caves?"

Ardraka glowered at his son, and the younger man stopped. "The council must be certain before it acts."

Struggling to keep his voice calm, Ardra ticked off on his fingers, "Lee says Lee's people live in the sky . . . the Others live in the sky. Lee wishes to see the lower caves. Why? To see if more of Ardraka's people are living there, so that he can kill *all* the people!"

The council members murmured and glanced at him fearfully. *Starting to look like a lynch jury.*

"Wait," Lee said. "There is more to the truth than what Ardra says. Lee's people live in the sky . . . that is true. But that does not mean that Lee's people are the Others. The sky is wide and larger . . . wider than the sea, by far. Many different peoples can live in the sky."

Ardraka nodded, his brows knitted in concentration. "But, Lee, if both Lee's people and the Others live in the sky, why have not the Others destroyed Lee's people as they destroyed Ardraka's ancestors?"

Lee felt his stomach drop out of him. *So that's it!*

"Yes," one of the councilmen said. "The Others live far from this land, yet the Others came here and destroyed Ardraka's forefathers and all the works of such men and women."

"Tell Lee what happened," he said, stalling for time to work out answers. "Lee knows nothing about the Others." *Not from your side of the war, anyway.*

Ardraka glanced around at the council members sitting on both sides of him. They looked uncertain, wary, still afraid. Ardra, beside Lee, had the fixed glare of a born prosecutor.

"Lee is not of Ardraka's people," the younger man

said, barely controlling the fury in his voice. "Lee must be of the Others. There are no people except Ardraka's people and the Others!"

"Perhaps that is not so." Ardraka said. "True, Ardraka has always thought it to be this way, but Lee looks like an ordinary man, not like the Others."

Ardra huffed. "No living man has seen the Others. How can Ardraka say . . ."

"Because Ardraka has seen pictures of the Others," the chief said quietly.

"Pictures?" They were startled.

"Yes. In the deepest cave, where only the chief can go . . . and the chief's son. Ardraka had thought for a long time that soon Ardra should see the deepest cave. But no longer. Ardra must see the cave now."

The old man got up, stiffly, to his feet. His son was visibly trembling with eagerness.

"May Lee also see the pictures?" Lee asked.

They all began to protest, but Ardraka said firmly, "Lee has been accused of being of the Others. Lee stands in peril of death. It is right that Lee should see the pictures."

The council members muttered among themselves. Ardra glowered, then bent down and reached for the spear he had left at his feet. Lee smiled to himself. *If those pictures give you the slightest excuse, you're going to ram that thing through me. You'd made a good sheriff: kill first, then ask questions.*

Far from having gotten his way to the deeper caves, Ardraka threaded through a honeycomb of tunnels and chambers, always picking the path that slanted downward. Lee sensed that they were spiraling deeper and deeper into the solid rock of the cliffs, far below the sea level. The walls were crusted, and a thick mat of dust clung to the ground. But everything shone with the same faint luminosity as the upper caves, and beneath the dust the footing felt more like pitted metal than rock.

Finally Ardraka stopped. They were standing in the entryway to a fairly small chamber. The lighting was very dim. Lee stood behind Ardraka and felt Ardra's breath on his back.

"This is the place," Ardraka said solemnly. His voice echoed slightly.

They slowly entered the chamber. Ardraka walked to the farthest wall and wordlessly pointed to a jumble of lines scrawled at about eye level. The cave was dark, but the lines of the drawing glowed slightly brighter than the wall itself.

Gradually, Lee pieced the picture together. It was crude, so crude that it was hard to understand. But there were stick figures of men that seemed to be running, and rough outlines of what might be buildings, with curls of smoke rising up from them. Above them all were circular things, ships, with dots for ports. Harsh jagged lines were streaking out of them and toward the stick figures.

"Men and women," Ardraka said, in a reverent whisper as he pointed to the stick drawings. "The men and women of the time of Ardraka's farthest ancestors. And *here—*" his hand flashed to the circles— "are the Others."

Even in the dim light, Lee could see Ardra's face

gaping at the picture. "The Others," he said, his voice barely audible.

"Look at Lee," Ardraka commanded his son. "Does Lee look like the Others, or like a man?"

Ardra seemed about to crumble. He said shakily, "Lee . . . Ardra has misjudged Lee. . . . Ardra is ashamed."

"There is no shame," Lee said. "Ardra has done no harm. Ardra was trying to protect Ardraka's people." *And besides, you were right.*

Turning to Ardraka, Lee asked. "Is this all that you know of the Others?"

"Ardraka knows that the Others killed the people of Ardraka's forefathers. Before the Others came, Ardraka's ancestors lived in splendor: their living places covered the land everywhere; they swam the seas without fear of any creature of the deep; they leaped through the sky and laughed at the winds and storms; every day was bright and good and there was no night. Then the Others came and destroyed everything. The Others turned the sky to fire and brought night. Only the people in the deepest cave survived. This was the deepest cave. Only the people of Ardraka escaped the Others."

*We destroyed this world,* Lee told himself. *An interstellar war, eons ago. We destroyed each other old man. Only you've been destroyed for good, and we climbed back.*

"One more thing remains," Ardraka said. He walked into the shadows on the other end of the room and pushed open a door. *A door!* It was metal, Lee could feel as he went past it. There was another chamber, larger.

A storeroom! Shelves lined the walls. Most of them empty, but here and there were boxes, containers, machinery with strange writing on it.

"These belonged to Ardraka's oldest ancestors," the chief said. "No man today knows why these things were saved here in the deepest cave. They have no purpose. They are dead. As dead as the people who put them here."

It was Lee who was trembling as they made their way up to the dwelling caves.

## X

It was a week before he dared stroll the beach at night again, a week of torment, even though Ardra never gave him the slightest reason to think that he was still under suspicion.

They were just as stunned as he was when he told them about it.

"We killed them," he whispered savagely at them, back in the comfort of the ship. "We destroyed them. Maybe we even made the Pup explode, to wipe them out completely."

"That's . . . farfetched," Rassmussen answered. But his voice sounded lame.

"What do we do now?"

"I want to see those artifacts."

"Yes, but how?"

Lee said, "I can take you down to the cave, if we can put the whole clan to sleep for a few hours. Maybe gas. . ."

"That could work," Rassmussen agreed.

"A soporific gas?" Pascual's soft tenor rang

incredulously in Lee's ears. "But we haven't the faintest idea of how it might affect them."

"It's the only way," Lee said. "You can't dig your way into the cave . . . even if you could, they would hear it, and you'd be discovered."

"But gas . . . it could kill them all."

"They're all dead right now," Lee snapped. "Those artifacts are the only possible clue to their early history."

Rassmussen decided. "We'll do it."

Lee slept less than ever the next few nights, and when he did he dreamed, but no longer about the buildings on Titan. Now he dreamed of the ships of an ancient Earth, huge round ships that spat fire on the cities and people of Makta. He dreamed of the Pup exploding and showering the planet with fire, blowing off the atmosphere, boiling the oceans, turning mountains into glass slag, killing every living thing on the surface of the world, leaving the planet bathed in a steam cloud, its ground ruptured with angry new volcanoes.

It was a rainy dark night when you could hardly see ten meters beyond the cave's mouth that they came. Lee heard their voices in his head as they drove the skimmer up onto the beach and clambered down from it and headed for the caves. Inside the caves, the people were asleep, sprawled innocently on the damp musty ground.

Out of the rain a huge, bulky metal shape materialized, walking with exaggerated caution.

"Hello, Sid," Jerry Grote's voice said in his head, and the white metal shape raised a hand in greeting.

*The Others*, Lee thought as he watched four more

powersuited figures appear in the dark rain.

He stepped out of the cave, the rain a cold shock to his body. "Bring the stuff?"

Grote hitched a gauntleted thumb at one of the others. "Pascual's got it. He's insisting on administering the gas himself."

"Okay, but let's get it done quickly, before somebody wakes up and spots you. Who else is with you?"

"Chien, Tanaka and Stek. Tanaka can help Carlos with the anesthetic. Chien and Stek can look over the artifacts."

Lee nodded agreement.

Pascual and Tanaka spent more than an hour seeping the mildest soporific they know of through the sleeping cave. Lee fidgeted outside on the beach, in the rain, waiting for them to finish. When Tanaka finally told them it was safe to go through, he hurried past the sprawled bodies, scarcely seeing Pascual—still inside his cumbersome suit—patiently recording medical analyses of each individual.

Even with the suit lamps to light the corridors, it was hard to retrace his steps down to the lowest level of the ancient shelter. But when he got to the storeroom, Lee heard Stek break into a long string of Polish exultation at the sight of the artifacts.

The three suited figures holographed, x-rayed, took radiation counts, measured, weighed, every piece on the ancient shelves. They touched nothing directly, but lifted each piece with loving tenderness in a portable magnetic grapple.

"This one," Stek told Lee, holding a hand-size, oddly

angular instrument in mid-air with the grapple, "we must take with us."

"Why?"

"Look at it," the physicist said. "If it's not an astronautical sextant or something close to it, I'll eat Charnovsky's rocks for a month."

The instrument didn't look impressive to Lee. It had a lens at one end, a few dials at the other. Most of it was just an angular metal box, with strange printing on it.

"You want to know where these people orignally came form?" Stek asked. "If they came from somewhere other than this planet, the information could be inside this instrument."

Lee snapped his gaze from the instrument to Stek's helmeted face.

"If it is a sextant, it must have a reference frame built into it. A tape, perhaps, that lists the stars that these people wanted to go to."

"Okay," Lee said. "Take it."

By the time they got back up to the main sleeping cave and out to the beach again, it was full daylight.

"We'll have to keep them sleeping until almost dawn tomorrow," Lee told Pascual. "Otherwise they might suspect that something unusual's happened."

The doctor's face looked concerned but not worried. "We can do that without harming them, I think. But Sid, they'll be very hungry when they awake."

Lee turned to Grote. "How about taking the skimmer out and stunning a couple of big fish and towing them back here to the shallows?"

Grinning, Grote replied, "Hardly fair sport with the equipment I've got." He turned and headed for the car.

"Wait," Stek called to him. "Give me a chance to get this safely packed in a magnetic casing." And the physicist took the instrument off toward the skimmer.

"Sid," Pascual said gently, "I want you to come back with us. You need a thorough medical check."

"Medical?" Lee flashed. "Or are you fronting for Lehman?"

Pascual's eyes widened with surprise. "If you had a mirror, you would see why I want to check you. You're breaking out in skin cancers."

Instinctively, Lee looked at his hands and forearms. There were a few tiny blisters on them. And more on his belly and legs.

"It's from overexposure to the ultraviolet. Hatfield's skin-darkening didn't fully protect you."

"Is it serious?"

"I can't tell without a full examination."

*Just like a doctor.* "I can't leave now," Lee said. "I've got to be here when they wake up and make sure that they don't suspect they've been visited by the . . . by us."

"And if they do suspect?"

Lee shrugged. "That's something we ought to know, even if we can't do anything about it."

"Won't it be dangerous for you?"

"Maybe."

Pascual shook his head. "You mustn't stay out in the open any longer. I won't be responsible for it."

"Fine. Do you want me to sign a release form?"

Grote brought the skimmer back around sundown, with two good-size fish aboard. The others got aboard around midnight, and with a few final radioed words of parting, they drove off the beach and out to sea.

At dawn the people woke up. They looked and acted completely normally, as far as Lee could tell. It was one of the children who noticed the still-sluggish fish that Grote had left in a shallow pool just outside the line of breakers. Every man in the clan splashed out, spear in hand, to get them. They feasted happily that day.

The dream was confusing. Somehow the towers on Titan and the exploding star got mixed together. Lee saw himself driving a bone spear into the sleeping form of one of the natives. The man turned on the ground, with the spear run through his body, and smiled bloodily at him. It was Ardraka.

"Sid!"

He snapped awake. It was dark, and the people were sleeping, full-bellied. He was slouched near one of the entryways to the main sleeping cave, at the mouth of a tunnel leading to the openings in the cliff wall.

"Sid, can you hear me?"

"Yes," he whispered so low that he could only feel the vibration in his throat.

"I'm up the beach about three kilometers from the relay unit. You've got to come back to the ship. Stek thinks he's figured out the instrument."

Wordlessly, silently, Lee got up and padded through the tunnel and out onto the beach. The night was clear and bright. Dawn would be coming in another hour, he judged. The sea was calm, the wind a gentle crooning as it swept down from the cliffs.

"Sid, did you hear what I said? Stek thinks he knows what the instrument is for. It's part of a pointing system for a communications setup."

"I'm on my way." He still whispered and turned to see if anyone was following him.

Grote was in a biosuit, and no one else was aboard the skimmer. The engineer jabbered about Stek's work on the instrument all the way back to the ship.

Just before they arrived, Grote suggested, "Uh, Sid, you do want to put on some coveralls, don't you?"

Two biosuited men were setting up some electronics equipment at the base of the ship's largest telescopes dangling in a hoist sling overhead, the fierce glow of Sirius glinting off its metal barrel.

"Stek's setting up an experiment," Grote explained.

Lee was bundled into a biosuite and ushered into the physicist's workroom as soon as he set foot inside the ship. Stek was a large, round, florid man with thinning red hair. Lee had hardly spoken to him at all, except for the few hours at the cave, when the physicist had been encased in a powersuit.

"It's a tracker, built to find a star in the sky and lock onto it as long as it's above the horizon," Stek said, gesturing to the instrument hovering in a magnetic grapple a few inches above his work table.

"You're sure of that?" Lee asked.

The physicist glanced at him as though he had been insulted. "There's no doubt about it. It's a tracker, and it probably was used to aim a communication antenna at their home star."

"And where is that?"

"I don't know yet. That's why I'm setting up the experiment with the telescope."

Lee walked over to the work table and stared at the instrument. "How can you be certain that it's what you say it is?"

Stek flushed, then controlled himself. With obvious patience, he explained, "X-ray probes showed that the instrument contained a magnetic memory tape. The tape was in binary code, and it was fairly simple to transliterate the code, electronically, into the ship's main computers. We didn't even have to touch the instrument physically . . . except with electrons."

Lee made an expression that showed he was duly impressed.

Looking happier, Stek went on, "The computer crosschecked the instrument's coding and came up with correlations: altitude references were on the instrument's tape, and astronomical ephemerides, timing data and so forth. Exactly what we'd put into a communications tracker."

"But this was made by a different race of people—"

"It makes no difference," Stek said sharply. "The physics are the same. The universe is the same. The instrument can only do the job it was designed to do, and that job was to track a single star."

"Only one star?"

"Yes, that's why I'm certain it was for communicating with their home star."

"So we can find their home star after all." Lee felt the old dread returning, but with it something new, something deeper. *Those people in the caves were our enemy. And maybe their brothers, the ones who built the machines on Titan, are still out there somewhere looking for them—and for us.*

## XI

Lee ate back at the Sirius globe, but Pascual insisted on his remaining in a biosuit until they had thoroughly checked him out. And they wouldn't let him eat Earth food, although there was as much local food as he wanted. He didn't want much.

"You've thinned out too much," Marlene said. She was sitting next to him at the galley table.

"Ever see a fat Sirian?" He meant it as a joke; it came out waspish. Marlene dropped the subject.

The whole ship's company gathered around the telescope and the viewscreen that would show an amplified picture of the telescope's field of view. Stek bustled around, making last-minute checks and adjustments of the equipment. Rassmussen stood taller than everyone else, looking alternately worried and excited. Everyone, including Lee, was in a biosuit.

Lehman showed up at Lee's elbow. "Do you think it will work?"

"Driving the telescope from the ship's computer's version of the instrument's tape? Stek seems to think it'll go all right."

"And you?"

Lee shrugged. "The people in the caves told me what I wanted to know. Now this instrument will tell us where they came from originally."

"The home world of our ancient enemies?"

"Yes."

For once, Lehman didn't seem to be amused. "And what happens then?"

I don't know," Lee said. "Maybe we go out and see if they are still there. Maybe we re-open the war."

"If there was a war."

"There was. It might still be going on, for all we know. Maybe we're just a small part of it, a skirmish."

"A skirmish that wiped out the life on this planet," Lehman said.

"And also wiped out Earth, too."

"But what about the people on this planet, Sid? What about the people in the caves?"

Lee couldn't answer.

"Do we let them die out, just because they might have been our enemies a few millennia ago."

"They would still be our enemies, if they knew who we are," Lee said tightly.

"So we let them die?"

Lee tried to blot their faces out of his mind, to erase the memory of Ardraka and the children and Ardra apologizing shamefully and the people fishing in the morning . . .

"No," he heard himself say. "We've got to help them. They can't hurt us any more, and we ought to help them."

Now Lehman smiled.

"It's ready," Stek said, his voice pitched high with excitement.

Sitting at the desk-size console that stood beside the telescope, he thumbed the power switch and punched a series of buttons.

The viewscreen atop the desk glowed into life, and a swarm of stars appeared. With a low hum of power, the telescope slowly turned, slowly, to the left. The scene in the viewscreen shifted. Beside the screen was a smaller display, an astronomical map with a bright luminous dot showing where the telescope was aiming.

The telescope stopped turning, hesitated, edged slightly more to the left and then made a final, barely discernible correction upward.

"It's locked on."

The viewscreen showed a meager field of stars, with a single bright pinpoint centered exactly in the middle of the screen.

"What is it, what star?"

Lee pushed forward, through the crowd that clustered around the console.

"My God," Stek said, his voice sounding hollow. "That's . . . the sun."

Lee felt his knees wobble. "They're from Earth!"

"It can't be," someone said.

Lee shoved past the people in front of him and stared at the map. The bright dot was fixed on the sun's location.

"They're from Earth!" he shouted. "They're part of us!"

"But how could . . ."

"They were a colony of *ours*," Lee realized. "The Others were an enemy . . an enemy that nearly wiped them out and smashed Earth's civilization back into a stone age. The Others built those damned machines on Titan, but Ardraka's people did not. And we didn't destroy the people here . . . we're the same people!"

"But that's—"

"How can you be sure?"

"He is right," Charnovsky said, his heavy bass rumbling above the other voices. They all stopped to hear him. "There are too many coincidences any other way.

These people are completely human because they came from Earth. Any other explanation is extraneous."

Lee grabbed the Russian by the shoulders. "Nick, we've got work to do! We've got to help them. We've got to introduce them to fire and metals and cereal grains—"

Charnovsky laughed. "Yes, yes, of course. But not tonight, eh? Tonight we celebrate."

"No," Lee said, realizing where he belonged. "Tonight I go back to them."

"Go back?" Marlene asked.

"Tonight I go back with a gift," Lee went on. "A gift from my people to Ardraka's. A plastic boat from the skimmer. That's a gift they'll be able to understand and use."

Lehman said, "You still don't know who built the machinery on Titan."

"We'll find out one of these days."

Rassmussen broke in, "You realize that we will have to return Earthward before the next expedition could possibly get anywhere near here."

"Some of us can wait here for the next expedition. I will, anyway."

The captain nodded and a slow grin spread across his face. "I knew you would even before we found out that your friends are really our brothers."

Lee looked around for Grote. "Come on, Jerry. Let's get moving. I want to see Ardraka's face when he sees the boat."

# The Sightseers

*Some stories are little more than gags, but despite the brevity of this one, there's a bit more to it than the punch line at the end. (No fair peeking!)*

*Incidentally, this shortie led to my writing a short novel called CITY OF DARKNESS, which takes up where this tale ends.*

My heart almost went into fibrillation when I saw the brown cloud off on the horizon that marked New York City. Dad smiled his wiser-than-thou smile as I pressed my nose against the plane's window in an effort to see more. By the time we got out of the stack over LaGuardia Airport and actually landed, my neck hurt.

The city's fantastic! People were crowding all over, selling things, buying, hurrying across the streets, gawking. And the noise, the smells, all those old gasoline-burning taxis rattling around and blasting horns. Not like Sylvan Dell, Michigan!

"It's vacation time," Dad told me as we shouldered our way through the crowds along Broadway. "It's always crowded during vacation time."

And the girls! They looked back at you, right straight at you, and smiled. They knew what it was all about, and they liked it! You could tell, just the way they looked back at you. I guess they really weren't any prettier than the girls at home, but they dressed . . . wow!

"Dad, what's a bedicab?"

He thought it over for a minute as one of them, long and low, with the back windows curtained, edged through traffic right in front of the curb where we were standing.

"You can probably figure it out for yourself," he said uncomfortably. "They're not very sanitary."

Okay, I'm just a kid from the north woods. It took me a couple of minutes. In fact, it wasn't until we crossed the street in front of one—stopped for a red light—and I saw the girl's picture set up on the windshield that I realized what it was all about. Sure enough, there was a meter beside the driver.

But that's just one of the things about the city. There were old movie houses where we saw real murder films. Blood and beatings and low-cut blondes. I think Dad watched me more than the screen. He claims he thinks I'm old enough to be treated like a man, but he acts awfully scared about it.

We had dinner in some really crummy place, down in a cellar under an old hotel. With live people taking our orders and bringing the food!

"It's sanitary," Dad said, laughing when I hesitated about digging into it. "It's all been inspected and approved. The didn't put their feet in it."

Well, it didn't hurt me. It was pretty good, I guess . . . too spicy, though.

We stayed three days altogether. I managed to meet a couple of girls from Maryland at the hotel where we stayed. They were okay, properly dressed and giggly and always whispering to each other. The New York girls were just out of my league, I guess. Dad was pretty careful about keeping me away from them . . . or them away from me. He made sure I was in the hotel room every night, right after dinner. There were plenty of really horrible old movies to watch on the closed-circuit TV; I stayed up past midnight each night. Once I was just drifting off to sleep when Dad came in and flopped on his bed with all his clothes on. By the time I woke up in the morning, though, he was in his pajamas and sound asleep.

Finally we had to go. We rented a sanitary car and decontaminated ourselves on the way out to the airport. I didn't like the lung-cleansing machine. You had to work a tube down one of your nostrils.

"It's just as important as brushing your teeth," Dad said firmly.

If I didn't do it for myself, he was going to do it for me.

"You wouldn't want to bring billions of bacteria and viruses back home, would you?" he asked.

Our plane took off an hour and a half late. The holiday traffic was heavy.

"Dad, is New York open every year . . . just like it is now?"

He nodded. "Yes, all during the vacation months. A lot of the public health doctors think it's very risky to keep a city open for more than two weeks out of the year, but the tourist industry has fought to keep New York going all summer. They shut it down right after Labor Day."

   As the plane circled the brown cloud that humped
over the city, I made up my mind that I'd come back
again next summer. Alone, maybe. That'd be great!
   My last glimpse of the city was the big sign painted
across what used to be The Bronx:

   NEW YORK IS A SUMMER FESTIVAL OF FUN!

# To Be or Not

*When it comes to making science fiction films, Hollywood has two big shortcomings: (1) no understanding of the scientific concepts that underlie science fiction, and (2) no originality. Here's a story that makes full use of both.*

Year: 2007 A.D.

NOBEL PRIZE FOR PHYSICAL ENGINEERING: Albert Robertus Leoh, for application of simultaneity effect to interstellar flight

OSCAR/EMMY AWARD: Best dramatic film, "The Godfather, Part XXVI"

PULITZER PRIZE FOR FICTION: Ernestine Wilson, "The Devil Made Me"

Al Lubbock and Frank Troy shared an office. Not the largest in Southern California's entertainment industry, but adequate for their needs. Ankle-deep carpeting. Holographic displays instead of windows. Earthquake-proof building.

Al looked like a rangy, middle-aged cowboy in his rumpled blue jumpsuit. Frank wore a traditional Wall Street vested suit of golden brown, neat and precise as an accountant's entry. His handsome face was tanned; his body had the trimness of an inveterate tennis player.

Al played tennis, too, but he won games instead of losing weight.

The walls of their office were covered with plaques and shelves bearing row after row of awards—a glittering array of silver and gold plated statuettes. But as they slumped in the foam chairs behind their double desk, they stared despondently at each other.

"Ol' buddy," Al said, still affecting a Texas drawl, "I'm fresh out of ideas, dammit."

"This whole town's fresh out of ideas," Frank said sadly.

"Nobody's got any creativity anymore."

"I'm awfully tired of having to write our own scripts," Frank said. "You'd think there would be at least one creative writer in this industry."

"I haven't seen a decent script in three years," Al grumbled.

"Or a treatment."

"An *idea*, even." Al reached for one of his nonhallucinogenic cigarettes. It came alight the instant it touched his lips.

"Do you suppose," he asked, blowing out blue smoke, "that there's anything to this squawk about pollution damaging people's brains?"

Frowning, Frank reached for the air-circulation control knob on his side of the desk and edged it up a bit. "I don't know," he answered.

"It'd effect the lower income brackets most," Al said.

"That *is* where the writers come from," Frank admitted slowly.

For a long moment they sat in gloomy silence.

"Damn!" Al said at last. "We've just *got* to find some

creative writers."

"But where?"

"Maybe we could make a few . . . you know, clone one of the old-timers who used to be good."

Frank shook his head carefully, as if he was afraid of making an emotional investment. "That doesn't work. Look at the Astaire clone they tried. All it does is fall down a lot."

"Well, you can't raise a tap dancer in a movie studio," Al said. "They should have known that. It takes more than an exact copy of his genes to make an Astaire. They should have reproduced his environment, too. His whole family. Especially his sister."

"And raised him in New York City during World War I?" Frank asked. "You know no one can reproduce a man's whole childhood environment. It just can't be done."

Al gave a loose-jointed shrug. "Yeah. I guess cloning won't work. That Brando clone didn't pan out either."

Frank shuddered. "It just huddles in a corner and picks its nose."

"But where can we get writers with creative talent?" Al demanded.

There was no answer.

Year: 2012 A.D.

NOBEL PRIZE FOR SCIENCE AND/OR MEDICINE: Jefferson Muhammed X, for developing technique of re-creating fossilized DNA

OSCAR/EMMY/TONY AWARD: Best entertainment series, "The Plutonium Hour"

PULITZER PRIZE FOR FICTION OR DRAMA: No award

It was at a party aboard the ITT-MGM orbital station that Al and Frank met the real estate man. The party was floating along in the station's zero-gravity section, where the women had to wear pants but didn't need bras. A thousand or so guests drifted around in three dimensions, sucking drinks from plastic globes, making conversation over the piped-in music, standing in mid-air up, down, or sideways as they pleased.

The real estate man was a small, owlish-looking youngster of thirty, thirty-five. "Actually, my field is astrophysics," he told Al and Frank. Both of them looked quite distinguished in iridescent gold formal suits and stylishly graying temples. Yet Al still managed to appear slightly mussed, while Frank's suit had creases even on the sleeves.

"Astrophysics, eh?" Al said, with a happy-go-lucky grin. "Gee', way back in college I got my Ph.D. in molecular genetics."

"And mine in social psychology," Frank added. "But there weren't any jobs for scientists then."

"That's how we became TV producers," Al said.

"There still aren't any jobs for scientists," said the astrophysicist–real estate man. "And I know all about the two of you. I looked you up in the *IRS Who's Who*. That's why I inveigled my way into this party. I just *had* to meet you both."

Frank shot Al a worried glance.

"You know the Heinlein Drive has opened the stars to humankind," asked the astro-realtor rhetorically. "This means whole new worlds are available to colonize. It's the biggest opportunity since the Louisiana Purchase. Dozens of new Earthlike planets, unoccupied, uninhabited, pristine! Ours for the taking!"

"For a few billion dollars apiece," Frank said.

"That's small potatoes for a whole world!"

Al shook his head, a motion that made his whole weightless body start swaying. "Look fella . . . we're TV producers, not land barons. Our big problem is finding creative writers."

The little man clung to Al tenaciously. "But you'd have a whole new *world* out there! A fresh, clean, unspoiled new world!"

"Wait a minute," Frank said. "Psychologically, . . maybe a new world is what we need to develop new writers."

"Sure," the astro-realtor agreed.

A gleam lit Al's eye. "The hell with new writers. How about re-creating old writers?"

"Like Schulberg?"

"Like Shakespeare."

> Year: 2037A.D.
> NOBEL PRIZE FOR SCI-MED: Cobber McSwayne, for determining optimal termination time for geriatrics patients
> OSCAR/EMMY/TONY/HUGO/EDGAR/ET AL. AWARD: The California Earthquake
> PULITZER PRIZE FOR WRITING: Krissy Jones, "Grandson of Captain Kangaroo"

Lubbock & Troy was housed in its own satellite now. The ten-kilometer-long structure included their offices, living quarters, production studios, and the official Hollywood Hall of Fame exhibit hall. Tourists paid for the upkeep, which was a good thing because hardly anyone except children watched new dramatic shows.

"Everything's reruns," Frank complained as he floated weightlessly in their foam-walled office. He was nearly sixty years old, but still looked trim and distinguished. Purified air and careful diet helped a lot.

Al looked a bit older, a bit puffier. His heart had started getting cranky, and the zero-gravity they lived in was a necessary precaution for his health.

"There aren't any new ideas," Al said from up near the office's padded ceiling. "The whole human race's creative talents have run dry." His voice had gotten rather brittle with age. Snappish.

"I know I can't think of anything new anymore," Frank said. He began to drift off his desk chair, pushed himself down and fastened the lap belt.

"Don't worry, ol' buddy. We'll be hearing from New Stratford one of these days."

Frank looked up at his partner. "We'd better. The project is costing us every cent we have."

"I know," Al answered. "But the Shakespeare World exhibit is pulling in money, isn't it? The new hotels, the entertainment complex. . ."

"They're all terribly expensive. They're draining our capital. Besides, that boy in New Stratford is a very expensive proposition. All those actors and everything."

"Willie?" Al's youthful grin broke through his aging face. "He'll be okay. Don't worry about him. I supervised that DNA reconstruction myself. Finally got a chance to use my ol' college education."

Frank nodded thoughtfully.

"That DNA's perfect," Al went on, "right down to the last hydrogen atom." He pushed off the ceiling with one hand and settled slowly down toward Frank, at the desk. "We've got an exact copy of William Shakespeare—at least, genetically speaking."

"That doesn't guarantee he'll write Shakespeare-level plays," Frank said. "Not unless his environment is a faithful reproduction of the original Shakespeare's. It takes an *exact* reproduction of both genetics and environment to make an exact duplicate of the original."

"So?" Al said, a trifle impatiently. "You had a free hand. A whole damned planet to play with. Zillions of dollars. And ten years' time to set things up."

"Yes, but we knew so little about Shakespeare's boyhood when we started. The research we had to do!"

Al chuckled to himself. It sounded like a wheezing cackle. "Remember the look on the lawyers' faces when we told 'em we had to sign the actors to lifetime contracts?"

Frank smiled back at his partner. "And the construction crews, when they found out that their foremen would be archeologists and historians?"

Al perched lightly on the desk and worked at catching his breath. Finally he said, more seriously, "I wish the kid would hurry up with his new plays, though."

"He's only fifteen," Frank said. "He won't be writing anything for another ten years. You know that. He's got to be apprenticed, and then go to London and get a job with. . . ."

"Yeah, yeah." Al waved a bony hand at his partner.

Frank muttered, "I just hope our finances will hold

out for another ten years."

"What? Sure they will."

Frank shrugged. "I hope so. This project is costing us every dollar we take from the tourists on Shakespeare's World, and more. And our income from reruns is dropping out of sight."

"We've got to hang on," Al said. "This is bigger than anything we've ever done, ol' buddy. It's the biggest thing to hit the industry since . . . since 1616. New plays. New originals, written by Shakespeare. Shakespeare! All that talent and creativity working for us!"

"New dramatic scripts." Frank's eyes glowed. "Fresh ideas. Creativity reborn."

"By William Shakespeare," Al repeated.

Year: 2059 A.D.

NOBEL PRIZE FOR THINKING: Mark IX of Tau Ceti Computer Complex, for correlation of human creativity index with living space

ALL-INCLUSIVE SHOWBIZ AWARD: *The Evening News*

PULITZER PRIZE FOR REWRITING: *The Evening News*

Neither Al nor Frank ever left their floater chairs anymore, except for sleeping. All day, every day, the chairs buoyed them, fed them intravenously, monitored their aging bodies, pumped their blood, worked their lungs, reminded them of memories that were fading from their minds.

Thanks to modern cosmetic surgery their faces still looked reasonably handsome and taut. But underneath their colorful robes they were more machinery than functional human bodies.

Al floated gently by the big observation port in their old office, staring wistfully out at the stars. He heard the door sigh open and turned his chair slowly around.

There was no more furniture in the office. Even the awards they had earned through the years had been pawned to the Hall of Fame, and when their creditors took over the Hall, the awards went with everything else.

Frank glided across the empty room in his chair. His face was drawn and pale.

"They're still not satisfied?" Al asked testily.

"Thirty-seven grandchildren, between us," Frank said. "I haven't even tried to count the great-grandchildren. They all want a slice of the pie. Fifty-eight lawyers, seventeen ex-wives . . . and the insurance companies! They're the worst of the lot."

"Don't worry, ol' buddy. They can't take anything more from us. We're bankrupt."

"But they still . . ." Frank's voice trailed off. He looked away from his old friend.

"What? They still want more? What else is there? You haven't told them about Willie, have you?"

Frank's spine stiffened. "Of course not. They took Shakespeare World, but none of them know about Will himself, and his personal contract with us."

"Personal *exclusive* contract."

Frank nodded, but said, "It's not worth anything, anyway. Not until he gets some scripts to us."

"That ought to be soon," Al said, forcing his old optimistic grin. "The ship is on its way here, and the

courier aboard said he's got ten plays in his portfolio.
Ten plays!"

"Yes. But in the meantime. . ."

"What?"

"It's the insurance companies," Frank explained.
"They claim we've both exceeded McSwayne's Limit
and we ought to be terminated."

"Pull our plugs? They can't force. . ."

"They can, Al. I checked. It's legal. We've got a
month to settle our debts, or they turn off our chairs
and . . . we die."

"A month?" Al laughed. "Hell, Shakespeare's plays
will be here in a month. Then we'll show 'em!"

"If . . ." Frank hesitated uncertainly. "If the project
has been a success."

"A success? Of course, it's a success! He's writing
plays like mad. Come on, ol' buddy. With your
reproduction of his environment and my creation of his
genes, how could he be anybody else except William
goddam' Shakespeare? We've got it made, just as soon
as that ship docks here."

The ship arrived exactly twenty-two days later. Frank
and Al were locked in a long acrimonious argument
with an insurance company's computer-lawyer over the
legal validity of a court-ordered termination notice,
when their last remaining servo-robot brought them a
thick portfolio of manuscripts.

"Buzz off, tin can!" Al chortled happily and flicked
the communicator switch off before the computer could
object.

With trembling hands, Frank opened the portfolio.

Ten neatly bound manuscripts floated out weightlessly. Al grabbed one and opened it. Frank took another one.

"*Henry VI, Part One.*"

"*Titus Andronicus!*"

"*The Two Gentlemen from Verona . . .*"

Madly they thumbed through the scripts, chasing them all across the weightless room as they bobbed and floated through the purified air. After fifteen frantic minutes they looked up at each other, tears streaming down their cheeks.

"The stupid sonofabitch wrote the same goddam' plays all over again!" Al bawled.

"We reproduced him exactly," Frank whispered, aghast. "Heredity, environment . . . exactly."

Al pounded the communicator button on his chair's armrest.

"What . . . what are you doing?" Frank asked.

"Get me the insurance company's medics," Al yelled furiously. "Tell 'em to come on up here and pull my goddam' plug!"

"Me too!" Frank shouted with unaccustomed vehemence. "And tell them not to make any clones of us, either!"

# The Lieutenant and the Folksinger

*Chet Kinsman is a character I've been living with for more than a quarter-century. This is the last short story I wrote about him. Paradoxically enough, it depicts a key event at the very beginning of his adult life, when he was (is?) eighteen years old.*

From the rear seat of the T-38 jet, San Francisco Bay was a sun-glittering mirror set among the brown California hills. Fog was still swirling around the stately towers of the Golden Gate Bridge, but the rest of the Bay was clear and brilliant, the late morning sky brazen, the city on the hills far enough below them so that it looked shining white and clean.

"Like it?" asked the pilot.

Chet Kinsman heard his voice as a disembodied crackle in his helmet earphones over the shrill whine of the turbojet engines.

"Love it!" he answered to the bulbous white helmet in the seat in front of him.

The cockpit was narrow and cramped; Kinsman could barely move in his seat without bumping his own helmet into the plexiglass canopy that covered them both. The straps of his safety harness cut into his shoulders. He had tugged the harness on too tightly. But he felt no discomfort.

*This is flying!* he said to himself. *Five hundred knots at the touch of a throttle.*

"How high can we go?" he asked into his helmet microphone.

A pause. Then, "Oh, she'll do fifty thousand feet easy enough."

Kinsman grinned. "A lot better than hang gliders."

"I like hang gliding," the pilot said.

"Yeah, but it doesn't compare to this . . . this is *power*, man."

"Right enough."

It had been a disappointing week. Kinsman had flown to California on impulse. Life at the Air Force Academy was rigid, cold, and a first-year man was expected to obey everyone's orders rather than make friends. So when the first week-long break in the semester came, he dashed to La Jolla with his roommate.

While his fellow cadet was engulfed by his family, Kinsman wandered alone through the beautiful but friendless La Jolla area. His own family was a continent away and would have no part of a son of theirs stooping to the military life, no matter what his reason. Finally Kinsman rented a car and drove north along the spectacular coast highway, up into the Bay area. Alone.

Then on Friday night, at a topless bar in North Beach, where he had to wear his uniform to avoid the hassle of E.D. checks, he bumped into a Navy flier in the midst of the naked dancers and their bouncing, jiggling breasts.

Now he was flying. And happy.

Suddenly the plane's nose dropped, and Kinsman's stomach disappeared somewhere over his right

shoulder. The pilot rolled the plane, wingtips making
full circles in the empty air, as they dived toward the
water—which now looked steel hard. Kinsman swallowed hard and felt his pulse racing in every part of his
body.

"Try a low-level run. Get a real sensation of speed,"
the pilot said.

Kinsman nodded, then realized he couldn't be seen.
"Okay. Great."

In less than a minute they were skimming across the
water, engines howling, going so fast that Kinsman
could not see individual waves on the choppy Bay, only
a blur of blue-gray whizzing just below them. The roar
of the engines filled his helmet and the whole plane was
shaking, bucking, as if eager to get back up into the
thinner air where it was designed to fly.

He thought he saw the International Airport along the
blur of hills and buildings off to his left. He knew the
Bay Bridge was somewhere up ahead.

"Whoops! Freighter!"

The control stick between Kinsman's knees yanked
back toward his crotch. The plane stood on her tail,
afterburners screaming, and a microsecond's flicker of a
ship's masts zipped past the corner of his eye. He felt
the weight of death pressing on his chest, flattening him
into the contoured seat, turning it into an invalid's
couch. He couldn't lift his arms from his lap or even cry
out. It was enough to try to breathe.

They leveled off at last, and Kinsman sucked in a
great sighing gulp of oxygen.

"Damned sun glare does that sometimes," the pilot
was saying, sounding half-annoyed and half-apologetic.

"Damned water looks clear, but there's a whole damned fleet hidden by the glare off the water. That's why I'd rather fly under a high overcast—overwater, anyway."

"That was a helluva ride," Kinsman said at last.

The pilot chuckled. "I'll bet there's some damned pissed sailors down there. Probably on the horn now, trying to get our tail number."

They headed back to Moffett Field. The pilot let Kinsman take the controls for a few mintues, directing him toward the Navy base where the airfield and the NASA research station were.

"You got a nice steady touch, kid. Make a good pilot."

"Thanks. I used to fly my father's plane. Even the business jet, once."

"Got your license?"

"Not yet. I figure I'll qualify at the Academy."

The pilot said nothing.

"I'm going in for astronaut training as soon as I qualify," Kinsman went on.

"Astronaut, huh? Well . . . I'd rather fly a plane. Damned astronauts are like robots. Everything's done by remote control for those rocket jockeys."

"Not everything," Kinsman said.

He could sense the pilot shaking his head in disagreement. "Hell, I'll bet they have machines to do their screwing for them."

They called it a coffee shop, but the bar served mainly liquor. *Irish coffee is what they mean*, Kinsman told himself as he hunched over a cold beer and listened to the girl with the guitar singing.

> "Jack of diamonds, queen of spades, Fingers
> tremble and the memory fades, And it's a foolish
> man who tries to bluff the dealer . . ."

Through the coffee shop's big front window, Kinsman could see the evening shadows settling over the Berkeley streets. Students, loungers, street people eased along the sidewalks, most of them looking shabby in denims and faded Army fatigues. Kinsman felt out of place in his sky-blue uniform; he had worn it to the Navy base to help get past the security guards for his meeting with the pilot.

But now as he sat in the coffee shop and watched the night come across the clapboard buildings, and the lights on the Bay Bridge form a twinkling arch that led back to San Francisco, he was just as alone as he had been at the Academy, or back home, or all week long here in California, except for that one hour's flight in the jet.

> "You can't win,
> And you can't break even,
> You can't get out of the game . . .

*She has a lovely voice*, all right, he realized. *Like a silver bell. Like water in the desert.*

It was a haunting voice. And her face, framed by long midnight-black hair, had a fine-boned dark-eyed ascetic look to go with it. She sat on a high stool, under a lone spotlight, blue-jeaned legs crossed and guitar resting on one knee.

As Kinsman was trying to work up the nerve to introduce himself to her and tell her how much he enjoyed her singing, a dozen kids his own age shambled into the place. The singer, just finished her song, smiled and called to them. They bustled around her.

Kinsman turned his attention to his beer. By the time he had finished it, the students had pushed several tables together and were noisily ordering everything from Sacred Cows to Diet 7-Up. The singer had disappeared. It was full night outside now.

"You alone?"

He looked up, startled, and it was her. The singer.

"Uh . . . yeah." Clumsily he pushed the chair back and got to his feet.

"Why don't you come over and join us?" She gestured toward the crowd of students.

"Sure. Great. Love to."

She was tall enough to be almost eye level with Kinsman, and as slim and supple as a young willow. She wore a black long-sleeved turtleneck pullover atop the faded denims.

"Hey, everybody, this is . . ." She turned to him with an expectant little smile. All the others stopped their conversation and looked up at him.

"Kinsman," he said. "Chet Kinsman."

Two chairs appeared out of the crowd, and Kinsman sat down between the singer and a chubby blonde girl who was intently rolling a joint for herself.

Kinsman felt out of place. They were all staring at him, except for the rapt blonde, without saying a word. *Wrong uniform,* he told himself. He might as well have been wearing a Chicago policeman's riot suit.

"My name's Diane," the singer said to him, as the bar's only waitress placed a fresh beer in front of him.

"That's Shirl, John, Carl, Eddie, Delores . . . She made a circuit of the table and Kinsman forgot the names as soon as he heard them. Except for Diane's.

They were still eying him suspiciously.

"You with the National Guard?"

"No," Kinsman said. "Air Force Academy."

"Going to be a flyboy?"

"A flying pig!" said the blonde on his left.

Kinsman stared at her. "I'm going in for astronaut training."

"An orbiting pig," she muttered.

"That's a stupid thing to say."

"She's upset," Diane told him. "We're all on edge after what happened at Kent State today."

"Kent State?"

"You haven't heard?" It was an accusation.

"No. I was flying this afternoon and . . ."

"They gunned down a dozen students."

"The National Fuckin' Guard."

"Killed them!"

"Where?"

"At Kent State. In Ohio."

"The students were demonstrating against the Cambodian invasion and the National Guard marched onto the campus and shot them down."

"Christ, don't they let you see the newspapers?"

"Or TV, even?"

Kinsman shook his head weakly. It was like they were blaming him for it.

"We'll show them, those friggin' bastards!" said an intense, waspish little guy sitting a few chairs down from Kinsman. *Eddie?* he tried to remember. The guy was frail-looking, but his face was set in a smoldering angry mold, tight-lipped. The thick glasses he wore made his eyes look huge and fierce.

"Right on," said the group's one black member. "We gonna tear the campus apart."

"How's that going to help things in Cambodia?" Kinsman heard his own voice asking. "Or in Kent State?"

"How's it gonna *help?*" They looked aghast at his blasphemy.

"Yeah," Kinsman answered, wanting to bounce some of their hostility back at them. "You guys tear up the campus. Big deal. What do you accomplish? Maybe the National Guard shoots you. You think Nixon or anybody else in Washington will give a damn? They'll just call you a bunch of Commies and tell everyone we've got to fight harder over in 'Nam because the whole country's full of subversives."

"That doesn't make any sense," Eddie said.

"Neither does ripping up the campus."

"But you don't understand," Diane said. "We've got to do *something*. We can't let them kill students and draft us into a war we never declared. We've got to show them that we'll fight against them!"

"I'd go after my Congressmen and Senators and tell them to get us out Vietnam."

They laughed at him. All but Eddie, who looked angrier still.

"You don't understand anything about how the political process works, do you?" Eddie asked.

*Now I've got you!* "Well," Kinsman answered, "An uncle of mine is a U.S. Senator. My grandfather was

Governor of the Commonwealth of Pennsylvania. And a cousin is in the House of Representatives. I've been involved in political campaigns since I was old enough to hold a poster."

Silence. As if a leper had entered their midst.

"Jesus Christ," said one of the kids at last. "He's with the Establishment."

"Your kind of politics," Diane said to him, "doesn't work for us. The Establishment won't listen to us."

"We've got to fight for our rights."

"Demonstrate."

"Fight fire with fire!"

"Action!"

"Bullshit," Kinsman snapped. "All you're going to do is give the cops an excuse to mash your heads in—or worse."

The night, and the argument, wore on. They swore at each other, drank, smoked, talked until they started to get hoarse. Diane had to get up and sing for the other customers every hour, but each time she finished she came back and sat beside Kinsman.

And still the battle raged. The bar finally closed and Kinsman found that his legs had turned rubbery. But he went with them along the dark Berkeley streets to someone's one-room pad, four flights up the back stairs of a dark old house, yammering all the way, arguing with them all, one against ten. And Diane was beside him.

They started drifting away from the apartment. Kinsman found himself sitting on the bare wooden floor, halfway between the stained kitchen sink and the new-looking waterbed, telling them: "Look, I don't like it any more than you do. But violence is their game. You can't win that way. Blow up the whole damned campus, and they'll blow up the whole damned city to get even with you."

One of the students, a burly shouldered kid with a big beefy face and tiny squinting eyes, was sitting on the floor in front of Kinsman.

"You know your trouble flyboy? You're chicken."

Kinsman shrugged at him and looked around the floor for the can of beer he had been working on.

"You hear me? You're all talk. But you're scared to fight for your rights."

Kinsman looked up and saw that Diane, the blonde girl, and two of the guys were the only ones left in the room.

"I'll fight for my rights," Kinsman said, very carefully because his tongue wasn't always obeying his thoughts. "And I'll fight for your rights, too. But not in any stupid-ass way."

"You callin' me stupid?" The guy got to his feet.

*A weight lifter*, Kinsman told himself. *And he's going to show off his muscles on me.*

"I don't know you well enough to call you anything," he said.

"Well I'm callin' you chicken. A gutless motherfuck-in' coward."

Slowly Kinsman got to his feet. It helped to have the wall behind him to lean against.

"I take that, sir, to be a challenge to my honor," he said, letting himself sound drunk. It took very little effort.

"Goddam' right it's a challenge. You must be some goddam' pig—secret police or something."

"That's why I'm wearing this inconspicuous uniform."

"To throw us off guard."

"Don't be silly."

"I'm gonna break your head, wise-ass."

Kinsman raised one finger. "Now hold on. You challenged me. I get the choice of weapons. That's the way it works in the good ol' *code duello*."

"Choice of weapons?" The guy looked confused.

"You challenged me to a duel, didn't you? You have impeached my honor. I have the right to choose the weapons."

The guy made a fist the size of a football. "This is all the weapon I need."

"But that's not the weapon I choose," Kinsman countered. "I believe that I'll choose sabers. I won a few medals back East with my saber fencing. Now where can we find a pair of sabers at this hour of the morning . . .?"

The guy grabbed Kinsman's shirt. "I'm gonna knock that fuckin' grin off your face."

"You probably will. But not before I kick your kneecaps off. You'll never see the inside of a gym again, muscleman."

"That's enough, both of you," Diane snapped.

She stepped between the two of them, forcing the big student to let go of Kinsman.

"You'd better get back to your place, Ray," she said, her voice iron hard. "You're not going to break up my pad and get me thrown out on the street."

Ray pointed a thick, blunt finger at Kinsman. "He's a narc. Or something. Don't trust him."

"Go home, Ray. It's late."

"I'll get you, blue-suit," Ray said. "I'll get you."

Kinsman said, "When you find the sabers, let me know."

"Shut up!" Diane hissed at him. But she was grinning.

She half pushed the lumbering Ray out of the door. The others left right after him, and suddenly Kinsman was alone with Diane.

"I guess I ought to get back to my hotel," Kinsman said, his insides shaking now that the danger had passed.

"Where's that?"

"The Stanhope . . . in the city."

"God, you *are* Establishment!"

"Born with a silver spoon in my ear. To the manner born. Rich or poor, it pays to have money. Let 'em eat cake. Or was it coke?"

"You're drunk!"

"How can you tell?"

"Well, for one thing, your feet are standing in one place, but the rest of you is swaying like a tree in the breeze."

"I am drunk with your beauty . . . and a ton and a half of beer."

Diane laughed. "I can believe the second one."

Looking around for a phone, Kinsman asked, "How do you get a cab around here?"

"You won't. Not at this hour. No trains, either.

"I'm stuck here?"

She nodded.

"A fate worse than death." Kinsman saw that the room's furnishings consisted of a bookshelf crammed with sheet music, the waterbed, a formica-topped table and two battered wooden chairs that didn't match, the waterbed, a pile of books in one corner of the floor, a few pillows strewn around here and there, and the waterbed.

"You can share the bed with me," Diane said.

He felt his face turning red. "Are your intentions honorable?"

She grinned at him. "The condition you're in, we'll both be safe enough."

"Don't be too sure."

But he fell asleep as soon as he sank into the soft warmth of the bed.

It was sometime during the misty, dreaming light of earliest dawn that he half awoke and felt her body cupped next to his. Still half in sleep, they moved together, slowly, gently, unhurried, alone in a pearly gray fog, feeling without thinking, caressing, making love.

Kinsman lay on his back, smiling dazedly at the cracked ceiling.

"Was that your first time?" Diane asked. Her head was resting on his chest.

He suddenly felt embarrassed. "Well, uh, yeah . . . it was."

She stroked the flat of his abdomen.

Awkwardly, he said, "I guess . . . I was pretty clumsy, wasn't I?"

"Oh no. You were fine"

"You don't have to humor me."

"I'm not. It was marvelous. Terrific."

*It wasn't your first time*, he knew. But he said nothing.

"Go to sleep," Diane said. "Get some rest and we can do it again."

It was almost noon by the time Kinsman had showered in the cracked tub and gotten back into his wrinkled uniform. He was looking into the still-steamy bathroom mirror, wondering what to do about his stubby chin, when Diane called through the half open door:

"Tea or coffee?"

"Coffee."

Kinsman came out of the tiny bathroom and saw that she had set up toast and a jar of Smuckers grape jelly on the table by the window. A teakettle was on the two-burner stove, with a pair of chipped mugs and a jar of instant coffee alongside.

They sat facing each other, washing down the crunchy toast with the hot, strong coffee. Diane watched the people moving along the street below them. Kinsman stared at the clean sky.

"How long can you stay?" she asked.

"I've got a date with this guy to go flying this afternoon . . . then I leave tonight."

"Oh."

"Got to report back to the Academy tomorrow morning."

"You have to."

He nodded. "Wish I didn't."

She gave him a *so do I* look. "But you're free this afternoon?"

"I'm supposed to meet this Navy guy; he's going to take me up with him . . .

"Come down to the campus with me instead," Diane said, brightening. "The demonstration'll be starting around two and you can help us.

"Me?"

"Sure! You're not going to let them get away with it, are you? They'll be sending *you* to Cambodia or someplace to get killed."

"Yeah, maybe, but . . ."

She reached across the table and took his free hand in both of hers. "Chet . . . please. Not for me. Do it for yourself. I don't want to think of you being sent out there to fight a war we shouldn't be fighting. Don't let them turn you into a robot."

"But I'm going into astronaut training."

"You don't believe they'll give you what you want, do you? They'll use you for cannon fodder, just like all the others."

"You don't understand . . ."

"No, *you* don't understand!" she said earnestly. Kinsman saw the intensity in her eyes, the devotion. *Is she really worried that much about me?*

"We've got to stop them, Chet. We've got to use every ounce of courage we can muster to stop this war and stop the killing."

"Tearing up the campus isn't going to do it."

"I know. This is going to be a peaceful demonstration. It's the pigs that start the violence."

He shook his head.

"Come and see, if you don't believe me! Come with me."

"In my uniform? Your friends would trash me."

"No they won't. It'd make a terrific impact for somebody in uniform to show up with us. We've been trying to get some of the Vietnam veterans to show themselves in uniform."

"I can't," Kinsman said. "I've got a date with a guy to go flying this afternoon."

"That's more important than freedom? More important than justice?"

He had no answer.

"Chet . . . please. For me. If you don't want to do it for yourself, or for the people, then do it for me. Please."

He looked away from her and glanced around the shabby, unkempt room. At the stained, cracked sink. The faded wooden floor. The unframed posters scotch-taped to the walls. The waterbed, with its roiled sheet trailing onto the floor.

He thought of the Academy. The cold gray mountains and ranks of uniforms marching mechanically across the frozen parade ground. The starkly functional classrooms, the remorsely efficient architecture devoid of all individual expression.

And then he turned back, looked past the woman across the table from him, and saw the sky once again.

"I can't go with you," he said quietly, finally. "Somebody's got to make sure you don't get bombed while you're out there demonstrating for your rights."

For a moment Diane said nothing. Then, "You're trying to make a joke out of something that's deadly serious."

"I'm being serious," he said. "You'll have plenty of demonstrators out there. Somebody's got to protect and defend you while you're exercising your freedoms."

"It's our own government we need protection from!"

"You've got it. You just have to exercise it a little better. I'd rather be flying. There aren't so many of us up there."

"Diane shook her head. "You're hopeless."

He shrugged.

"I was going to offer to let you stay here . . . if you wanted to quit the Air Force."

"Resign?"

"If you needed a place to hide . . . or you just wanted to stay here, with me."

He started to answer, but his mouth was dry. He swallowed, then in a voice that almost cracked, "I can't. I . . . I'm sorry, Diane, but I just can't." He pushed his chair back and got to his feet.

At the door, he turned back toward her. She was at the table still. "Sorry I disappointed you. And, well, thanks . . . for everything."

She got up, walked swiftly across the tiny room to him, and kissed him lightly on the lips.

"It was my pleasure, General."

"Lieutenant," he quickly corrected. "I'll be a lieutenant when I graduate."

"You'll be a general someday."

"I don't think so."

"You could have been a hero today," she said.

"I'm not very heroic."

"Yes you are." She was smiling at him now. "You just don't know it yet."


That afternoon, forty thousand feet over the Sacramento Valley, feeling clean and free and swift, Kinsman wondered briefly if he had made the right choice.

"Sir?" he asked into his helmet microphone. "Do you really think astronaut training turns men into robots?"

The man's chuckle told him the answer. "Son, any kind of training is aimed at turning you into a robot. Just don't let 'em get away with it. The main thing is to get up and flying . . . up here they can't really touch us. Up here we're free."

"They're pretty strict over at the Academy," Kinsman said. "They like things done their way."

"Tell me about it. I'm an Annapolis man, myself. You can still hold onto your own soul, boy. You have to do things their way on the outside, but you be your own man inside. Isn't easy, but it can be done."

Nodding to himself, Kinsman looked up and through the plane's clear plastic canopy. He caught sight of a pale ghost of the Moon, riding high in the afternoon sky.

*I can do it*, he said to himself. *I can do it.*

# The Secret Life of Henry K.

*This is a pure romp, not to be taken seriously. Obviously, any relation between the characters in this story and real ex-Secretaries of State, movie stars, heiresses, et al. is purely . . . well, would you believe it's an alternate universe maybe?*

This late at night, even the busiest corridors of the Pentagon were deserted. Dr. Young's footsteps echoed hollowly as he followed the mountainous, tight lipped, grim-faced man. Another equally large and steely-eyed man followed behind him, in lockstep with the first.

They were agents, Dr. Young knew that without being told. Their clothing bulged with muscles trained in murderous Oriental arts, other bulges in unlikely places along their anatomy were various pieces of equipment: guns, two-way radios, stilettos, Bowie knives . . . Young decided his imagination wasn't rich enough to picture all the equipment these men might be carrying.

After what seemed like an hour's walk down a constantly curving corridor, the agent in front stopped abruptly before an inconspicuous, unmarked door.

"In here," he said, barely moving his lips.

The door opened by itself, and Dr. Young stepped into

what seemed to be an ordinary receptionist's office. It was no bigger than a cubicle, and even in the dim lighting—from a single desk lamp, the overhead lights were off—Young could see that the walls were the same sallow depressing color as most Pentagon offices.

"The phone will ring," the agent said, glancing at a watch that looked absolutely dainty on his massive hairy wrist, "In exactly one minute and fifteen seconds. Sit at the desk. Answer when it rings."

With that, he shut the door firmly, leaving Dr. Young alone and bewildered in the tiny anteroom.

There was only one desk, cleared of papers. It was a standard government-issue battered metal desk. IN and OUT boxes stood empty atop it. Nothing else on it but a single black telephone. There were two creaky-looking straight-backed metal chairs in front of the desk, and a typist's swivel chair behind it. The only other things in the room were a pair of file cabinets, side by side, with huge padlocks and red SECURE signs on them, and a bulletin board that had been miraculously cleared of everything except the little faded fire-emergency instruction card.

Dr. Young found that his hands were trembling. He wished that he hadn't given up cigarettes: after all, oral eroticism isn't all that bad. He glanced at the closed hallway door and knew that both the burly agents were standing outside, probably with their arms folded across their chest in unconscious imitation of the eunuchs who guarded sultans' harems.

He took a deep breath and went around the desk and sat on the typist's chair.

The phone rang as soon as his butt touched the chair.

He jumped, but grabbed the phone and settled himself before it could ring again.

"Dr. Carlton Young speaking." His voice sounded an octave too high, and quavery, even to himself.

"Dr. Young, I thank you for accompanying the agents who brought you there without questioning their purpose. They were instructed to tell you who sent them, and nothing else."

He recognized the voice at once. "You—you're welcome, Mr. President."

"Please! No names! This is a matter of utmost security."

"Ye—yessir."

"Dr. Young, you have been recommended very highly for the special task I must ask of you. I know that, as a loyal, patriotic American, you will do your best to accomplish this task. And as the most competent man in your highly demanding and complex field, your efforts will be crowned with success. That's the American way, now isn't it?"

"Yessir. May I ask, just what is the task?"

"I'm glad you asked that. I have a personnel problem that you are uniquely qualified to solve. One of my closest and most valued aides—a man I depend on very heavily—has gone into a tailspin. I won't explian why or how. I must ask you merely to accept the bald statement. This aide is a man of great drive and talent, high moral purpose, and enormous energy. But at the moment, he's useless to himself, to this Administration, and to the Nation. I need you to help him find himself."

"Me? But all I do is—"

"You run the best computer dating service in the

nation, I know. Your service has been checked out thoroughly by the FBI, the Secret Service, and the Defense Intelligence Agency—"

"Not the CIA?"

I don't know, they won't tell me."

"Oh."

"This aide of mine—a very sincere and highly motivated man—needs a girl. Not just any girl. The psychiatrists at Walter Reed tell me that he must find the woman who's perfect for him, his exact match, the one mate that can make him happy enough to get back to the important work he should be doing. As you know, I have a plan for stopping inflation, bridging the generation gap, and settling the Cold War. But to make everything perfectly clear, Dr. Young, none of these plans can be crowned with success unless this certian aide can do his part of the job, carry his share of the burden, pull his share of the load."

Dr. Young nodded in the darkness. "I understand, sir. He needs a woman to make him happy. So many people do." A fleeting thought of the bins upon bins of punchcards that made up his files passed through Dr. Young's mind. "Even you, sir, even you need a woman."

"Dr. Young! I'm a married man!"

"I know—that's what I meant. You couldn't be doing the terrific job you're doing without your lovely wife, your lifetime mate, to support and inspire and you."

"Oh, I see what you mean. Yes, of course. Well, Dr. Young, my aide is in the office there with you, in the inner office. I want you to talk with him, help him, find him the woman he truly needs. Then we can end the war in Indochina, stop inflation, bridge—well, you know."

"Yes sir. I'll do my best."

"That will be adequate for the task, I'me sure. Good night, and God bless America!"

Dr. Young found that he was on his feet, standing at ramrod attention, a position he hadn't assumed since his last Boy Scout jamboree.

Carefully he replaced the phone in its cradle, then turned to face the door that led to the inner office. Who could be in there? The Vice President? No, Young told himself with a shake of his head; that didn't fit the description the President had given him.

Squaring his shoulders once again, Dr. Young took the three steps that carried him to the door and knocked on it sharply.

"Come in," said an equally sharp voice.

The office was kept as dark and shadowy as the anteroom, but Dr. Young recognized the man sitting rather tensely behind the desk.

"Dr. Kiss—!"

"No names! Please! Absolute security, Dr. Young."

"I under—no, come to think of it, I don't understand. Why keep the fact that you're using a computer-dating service so secret? What do the Russians and Chinese care—"

The man behind the desk cut him short with a gesture. "It's not the Russians or Chinese. It's the Democrats. If *they* find out—" He waggled both hands in the air—a semitic gesture of impending doom.

Dr. Young took one of the plush chairs in front of the desk. "But Dr. K—"

"Just call me Henry," the other man said, "But don't get personal about it."

"All right, Henry. I still don't see what's so terrible about a man in your position using a computer dating service. After all, some of the top Senators and Congressmen on the Democratic side of the aisle have been clients of mine."

"I know, I saw it all in the FBI report. Or was it the DIA report? Well, never mind." He fixed Dr. Young with a penetrating stare. "How would it look if the Dems knew that the President's most trusted and valued aide couldn't get a girl for himself? Eh?"

"Oh, I'm sure you could—"

"I can't!" The penetrating stare melted into something more pathetic. "I can't, the God our forefathers knows I've tried. But I'm a failure, a flop. There are times when I can't even talk to a woman."

Dr. Young sat there in shocked silence. Even his advanced degrees in psychology might not be enough for this task, he began to realize.

"It's my mother's fault!" Henry all but sobbed. "My pushy mother! Why do you think I took this job in the White House? Because she pushed me into it, and because I thought it might help me to get girls. Well, it hasn't. I can tell the President when to invade Cambodia. I can eat shark's fin with Chou En-lai, but I get totally tongue-tied when I try to talk to an attractive woman! My momma—what can I do?"

Henry started to bury his head in his hands, then with an obvious effort of great willpower, he straightened up in his chair. "Sorry," he said. "I shouldn't get emotional like that."

"No, it's good for you," Dr. Young soothed. "You can't keep everything bottled up all the time."

"Well I have been," Henry retorted sourly, "and I'm getting very uptight about it."

"*Uptight*?" thought Dr. Young "and everyone thinks he's a man of the world. I've got to help him."

"Listen," he said, "you tell me the kind of girl you like, and I'll comb my computer files until I find her—"

Henry smiled faintly, stoically. "So what good will that do? I'll take one look at her and collapse like a pricked balloon, you should excuse the expression."

But Dr. Young expected that response and was ready for it. "You don't understand, Henry. The girl that I'll find for you will be special. She'll be anxious to make you happy: she'll know that the future of the nation—of the whole world—depends on her pleasing you."

"How can you be sure that she'll really want to?"

"Leave it to me," Dr. Young said, with his best professional smile of assurance. "Just tell me what you'd like, and I'll get my computer cracking on it before the sun comes up."

Henry gave a little shrug, as if he didn't really believe what he was hearing but was desperate enough to give it a try anyway.

"I've already taken the liberty," he said, "of coding my—" he smiled bashfully. "—my dream girl onto these punchcards. And you won't have to use your own computer. Too risky, security-wise, for one thing. Besides, the FBI computer has *everybody* on it."

Dr. Young gasped. "The FBI computer?"

Henry nodded.

Then it hit!

For the first time, it struck home to Dr. Young that he was really playing in the big leagues. Was he ready for it?

The room was sumptuous, with thick carpeting and rich drapes framing the full-length windows that looked out over Manhattan's glittering skyline. A thousand jewels gleamed in the skyscrapers and across the graceful bridges, outshining by far the smogged-over stars of heaven.

Henry swallowed his nervousness as he stood at the doorway with the famous movie star.

"Um, nice room you've got here," he managed to say.

She smiled at him and slid out of her coat. "The studio arranged it. It's mine until the premiere tomorrow night."

Her dress glittered more than the view outside. And showed more, too. Henry worked a finger into his shirt collar, it was starting to feel uncomfortably tight, and warm.

"Here, let me help you," she purred, still showing her perfectly capped teeth in a smile that earned a thousand letters per week, most of them obscene.

She undid his tie and popped the collar button open. "Make yourself comfortable and tell me all about those nasty Russians you outsmarted."

"I—uh—um—"

Taking him by the wrist, she led Henry to the plushest couch he had ever seen and pulled him down into it, right next to her lush, lascivious body.

"You're not going to be shy with me, are you? After all, I'm just a lonely little girl far from my home, and I need a big strong daddy to look after me."

He could smell her musky perfume, feel the brush of her beautiful plasticized hair against his cheek.

"I, uh, I've got to catch a plane for—for Ulan Bator in one hour!" As the words popped out of his mouth, Henry sat up stiffly on the edge of the couch. He looked at his wristwatch. "Yes. One hour, to Ulan Bator. That's in Mongolia, you know."

She stared at him, pouting. "But what about our date tomorrow night? The premiere of my new movie!"

"I'm sorry. You'll have to go with someone else. The President needs me in Mongolia. Top secret negotiations. You mustn't say a word about this—any of this! To any one!"

With a shrug that nearly popped her breasts out of the low-cut gown, she said, "Okay. Okay. But tell those creepy friends of yours that I've done my patriotic duty, and dont' come around here looking for more!"

"But she liked you," Dr. Young said. He felt surprised and slightly hurt as he sat in the same dimly lit office in the Pentagon. Again it was late at night, and again Henry sat nervously behind the desk.

"It was all an act. She's an actress, you know."

"Of course, I know. But she genuinely liked you. It was no act. Take my word for it."

"How can you be sure?"

"Well—" Dr. Young hesitated, but then realized he'd find out anyway. "We had her room bugged. She cried for twenty minutes after you left."

Instead of getting angry, Henry looked suddenly guilty. "She did?"

A kaleidoscope of emotions played across Henry's face. Dr. Young saw surprise, guilt, pride, anxiety, and then he stopped watching.

At length Henry shook himself, as if getting rid of something unpleasant. "She was too—flighty. A silly kid."

"She was what you programmed into the computer." Dr. Young retorted. "I checked out the characteristics myself, mathematically, of course."

"Well, the computer goofed!"

"No, Henry. That's not possible. You simply didn't give us a descritpion of what you really want in a woman. You told us what you *think* you want, you gave us some idealizations. But that's not what your heart's really set on."

"You're trying to tell me I don't know what I want?"

"Not consciously, you don't. Now with a team of psychiatrists and possibly hypnosis therapy—"

"No!" Henry slammed a hand on the desktop. "Too risky! Remember our need for absolute security."

"But your conscious mind has only a very hazy idea of what your dream woman should be. The very term 'dream woman' indicates—"

"Never mind," Henry siad firmly. "Just add a few points to the computer program. I want someone just like Jill, but tougher, more intelligent. Better able to stand on her own feet."

Dr. Young nodded. Another week of computer programming ahead.

"This is my pad, Hank. What do you think of it?"

Henry surveyed the crumbling plaster, the dirt-caked

floor, the stacks of books strewn across the room covering the sink and the range, the desk, the drawing board, the sofa, the coffee table. The only piece of furniture in the filthy place that wasn't covered with books or papers of one sort or another was the bed. And *that* looked like something out of a Hong Kong brothel—a slimy, grimy, wrinkled mess that seemed to be writhing by itself even as he stared at it.

"It's efficient looking," he said. Actually, it looked like the storage room in the cellar of a Village tenement. Which it had been, until recently.

"Efficient, huh?" Gloria tossed her head slightly, a motion that spilled her long sun-bleached hair over one T-shirted shoulder.

"It's efficient, all right," she said. "This is where I do my writing, my illustrating, my editing, and my fucking."

Henry blinked. His glasses seemed to be getting steamed up. Or maybe it was dirt.

"You like to fuck, Hank?" she asked, grinning at him.

He squeezed his eyes shut and heard his voice utter a choked, "Yes."

"Good. Me too. But no sexual chauvinism. I get on top the same number of times you do," she said, starting toward the bed and pulling off the T-shirt. "No oral stuff unless we go together, and," she stepped out of her ragged jeans, "say, how many times can you pop off in one—"

She turned and saw that she was talking to the empty air. Henry had fled, and left the door open behind him.

"She was a monster!" Henry babbled to Dr. Young.

"That computer is trying to destroy me. I'm going to have it investigated! And you too!"

"Now, now," Dr. Young said as soothingly as he could. "No one's tampered with anything. I've done all the programming myself, taken the printouts myself, done it *all* by myself. I haven't slept a full night since our first meeting. I'm losing business because of you."

"She was a monster," Henry repeated.

"If you'd only let the psychiatrists probe your subconcious—"

"No! I went through all that months ago. All they ever said was that it's all my mother's fault. I know that!"

Dr. Young made a helpless shrug. "But if you can't verbalize your real desires—can't tell me what you're really looking for—how can I help you?"

Clenching his hands into fists and frowning mightily Henry said, "Just find me the girl I'm looking for. Someone who's beautiful, intelligent, patient, patriotic—but not agressive!"

"Back to the computer," Dr. Young thought wearily. But something in the back of his mind made him smile inwardly. "There might be—yes, that might work."


The Baroness's yacht rode easily at anchor in the soft swells of the sheltered cove. The coast of Maine was dark, just a jagged blackness against the softer star-scattered darkness of the sky.

"I've never seen the stars look so beautiful," Henry said. Then, sneaking a peek at the notes on his shirt cuff, he added. "They're almost as beautiful as you."

The Baroness smiled. And she was truly beautiful as she stood by the rail of the yacht, almost close enough to

touch her warm and thrilling body to his. Her long
midnight hair, always severely combed back and
pinned up during the day, was now sweeping free and
loose to her lovely bare shoulders.

"I would offer you another drink, Henri, but the
servants have gone ashore."

"Oh?" He gripped the rail a bit tighter. "All of
them?"

"Yes, I sent them away. I wanted to be alone with
you."

Henry took a deep breath. All through the evening—
the ballet recital, the dinner, the dizzying private jet
ride to this cove, the dancing on the deck—he had been
steeling himself for the supreme moment. He had no
intention of muffing it this night.

"Maybe," he suggested slyly, "we can go back inside
and find something for ourselves."

She put a hand to his close-shaven, lime-scented
cheek. "What an admirable idea, Henri. No wonder
your *President* depends on you so heavily.

Half an hour later they were sitting in the salon on a
leather couch, discussing international relations.
Gradually, Henry began to realize that the subject had
drifted into the super romantic areas of spies and
espionage.

She was leaning against him, as closely as her
extensive bosom would allow. "You must have known
many spies—clever, dangerous men and deceptive,
beautiful women."

"Uh, well, yes," he lied. His hands were starting to
tremble.

Suddenly she slid off the couch and kneeled at his feet.

"Pretend I'm a spy! Pretend you've caught me and have me at your mercy. Tie me up! Beat me! Torture me! Rape me!"

With a strangled scream, Henry leaped to his feet, dropped his glasses, bolted for the hatch, pounded up the ladder to the deck, and leaped into the water. For the first time since his last full summer at camp, he swam for his life. And his sanity.

"It's useless, it'll never work. It's just no good." Henry was muttering as Dr. Young led him down a long antiseptically white corridor.

"It might work. It could work."

For a moment the doctor thought he would have to take Henry by the hand and march him through the corridor like a stern schoolteacher with a recalcitrant child. Studying his "customer," Dr. Young realized that Henry was going down the drain. His physical condition was obviously deteriorating: his hands trembled, there were bags under his eyes, he had lost weight, and his face was starting to break out in acne. And his mental state! Poor Henry kept muttering things like, "Peeking—must get the Ping-Pong people to Peeking—"

Dr. Young felt desperate. And he knew that if *he* felt desperate, Henry must be on the verge of collapse.

Henry said, "You're sure nobody else knows—"

"It's two in the morning. This is my own building, my company owns it and occupies it exclusively. The guard couldn't possibly have recognized you with that false beard and the sunglasses. I laid off every known or suspected Democrat in my company weeks ago. Stop worrying.

They came at last to Room X. Dr. Young opened the door and motioned Henry to follow him inside.

The room was well lit, neat, and orderly. There was a comfortable couch along one wall, a modest desk of warm mahogany with a deep leather chair behind it, and a panel of lights and grillwork on the farthest wall. The panel was set into the wall so that someone reclining on the couch couldn't see it.

Henry balked at the doorway. "I'm not sure—"

"Come on," Dr. Young coaxed. "It won't hurt you. The President himself authorized nearly a million dollars to allow me to build this system. You wouldn't want him to feel that the money was wasted, would you?"

As he said that, Dr. Young almost laughed out loud. This system was going to make him the king of the computer selection business. And all built at government expense.

Henry took a hesitant step into the room. "What do I have to do?" he asked suspiciously.

"Just lie on the couch. I attach these two little electrodes to your head." Dr. Young pulled a small plastic bag from his jacket pocket, inside was something that looked rather like the earphones that are handed out on airplanes for listening to the movie or stereo tapes.

"It won't hurt a bit," Dr. Young promised.

Henry just glared at him sullenly.

"I'll explain it again," Dr. Young said, as calmly as he could manage. It was like coaxing a four-year-old: "You don't want to talk to psychiatrists or anyone else—for security reasons. So I've programmed my own company's computer with the correlations determined by six of the nation's leading psychiatrists. All you have to do is answer a few questions that I'll ask you, and the computer will be able to translate your answers into an understanding of your subconscious desires—your real wishes, the dream girl that your conscious mind is too repressed to verbalize.

"I'm not sure I like this."

"It's harmless."

"What are the electrodes for?"

Dr. Young tried to make his reply sound casual, airy. "Oh, they're just something like lie detectors, not that you're consciously lying, of course. But they'll compare your brain's various electrical waves with your conscious words and allow the computer to determine what's really on your mind."

"A computer that can read minds?" Henry took a half-step back toward the door.

"Not at all," Dr. Young assured him and grabbed him by the shoulder of his jacket. "It doesn't read your mind. How could it? It's only a computer. It merely correlates your spoken words with your brain waves, that's all. Then it's up to a human being—me, in this case—to interpret those correlations."

As he half dragged Henry to the couch, Dr. Young wondered if he should tell him that the computer does most of the correlation work itself. And thanks to the clandestine link between his company's computer here in this building and the FBI's monster machine, the correlations will come out as specific names and addresses.

"You really think this will work?" Henry asked as Dr.

Young pushed him down onto the couch.

"Not only do I think it will work, but the President thinks it will. Now we wouldn't want to disappoint the President, would we?"

Henry lay back and closed his eyes. "No, I suppose not."

"Fine," said Dr. Young. He pulled the electrodes from the bag. "Now this isn't going to hurt at all." Henry jumped when the soft rubberized pads touched his temples.

"And if it doesn't work?" the President's voice sounded darkly troubled. "How can I get Chou to meet me at the airport if Henry isn't available to set things up?"

"It will work, Mr. Pre-Uh, sir. I'm sure of it," Dr. Young said into the phone. "It better work," he said to himself. "Tonight's the night. We'll find out for sure tonight."

"I don't like it. I want to make that perfectly clear. I don't like this one little bit."

"It's scientific, sir. You can't argue with science."

"It had better be worth the money we've spent," was the President's only reply.

Henry was strangely calm as he stepped out of the limousine and walked up the steps to the plain, red brick house in Georgetown. It was barely dusk, not dark enough to worry about muggers yet.

There was only one bell button at the door. Usually these homes were split into several apartments. This one was not. He and his dream girl would have it all to themselves.

He sighed. He had waited so long, been through so much. And now some computer-designated girl was waiting for him. Well, maybe it would work out all right. All he had ever wanted was a lovely, sweet woman to make him feel wanted and worthwhile.

He pressed the button. A buzzer sounded gratingly and he pushed the front door open and stepped inside.

The hallway led straight to the back of the house.

"In the kitchen!" a voice called out.

Briefly he wondered whether he should stop here and take off his topcoat. He was holding a bouquet of gladiolas in one hand, stiffly wrapped in green paper. Squaring his shoulders manfully, he strode down the hallway to the kitchen.

The lights were bright, the radio blaring, and the kitchen was filled with delicious warm aromas and sizzlings. The woman was standing at the range with her back to him.

Without turning, she said:

"Put the flowers on the table and take off your coat. Then wash your hands and we'll eat."

With a thrill that surpassed understanding, Henry said, "Yes, Momma."

# The Man Who Saw
# "Gunga Din" Thirty Times

*I've seen "Gunga Din"
more than thirty times, and I have the feeling that unless
you've seen the film often enough, or recently enough,
to remember it well, this story may not hit you as hard
as it could. But it says something to me about the
Zarathustrian dichotomy between the Forces of Light
and the Froces of Darkness, a conflict that was very
much in evidence when you worked for a military-
oriented research laboratory during the strife-torn
Sixties.*

N osing the car through the growling traffic down
Memorial Drive, autos clustered thick and sullen
as bombay thieves, the Charles River looking clear in
the morning sunlight, the golden dome of the Capitol
sparkling up on Beacon Hill, the sky a perfect Indian
blue.

The temple of gold.
—What?—
Charlie's a perfect Higgenbottom type: capable in a
limited way, self-centered, basically stupid.
The golden temple, I repeat.
—Oh, the Capitol. It's a wonder the goddam
politicians haven't stolen *that* yet—

A Fiat bulging with bearded Harvard Square types cuts in front of us. I hit the brakes and Charles lurches and grumbles—Goddam hippies. They oughtta get a job—

They're in the morning traffic. Maybe they have jobs.

—Yeah. Undercutting some guy who's been working twenty years and has a family to support—

It was on the Late Show again last night, did you see it?

—See what?—

*Gunga Din.* The movie. Cary Grant. Doug Fairbanks, Jr., Victor McLaglen . . .

—What? They have that on again?—

It's the best movie Hollywood ever made. It has everything: golden temple, elephants, cavalry charges, real heroes. They don't make movies like that any more. Can't.

—They must have it on the Late Show every week—

No, it's been months since they showed it. I check *TV Guide* every week to make sure.

Charlie looks a little surprised, startled. Just like Higgenbottom when Cary Grant dropped that kilted Scottie corporal out the window.

I'll bet I've seen that movie thirty times, at least. I know every line of it, just about. They cut it terribly on television. Next time there's a Cary Grant film festival in New York I'm going down to see it. All of it. Without cuts.

Charlie says nothing.

We inch along, crawling down the Drive as slowly as the waterboy himself. I can seen him, old Sam Jaffe all blacked over, heavy goatskin waterbag pulling one shoulder down, twisting his whole skinny body. White turban, white breechcloth. Staggering down the grassy walk alongside the Drive, keeping pace with us. If they made the movie now, they'd have to use a real Negro for the part. Or an Indian. For the guru's part, too. No Eduardo Cianelli.

We turn off at the lab. There are guards at the gates and more guards standing around in the parking lot. The lab building is white and square and looming, like Army headquarters—an oasis of science and civilization in the midst of the Cambridge slum jungles.

Even in uniform the guards look sloppy. They ought to take more pride in themselves. We drive past them slowly, like the colonel reviewing the regiment. The regimental bank is playing *Bonnie Charlie*. The wind is coming down crisply off the mountains, making all the pennants flutter.

—Stockhodlers' meeting today. They're worried about some of these hippie students kicking up a rumpus.—

McLaglen would straighten them out. That's what they need, a tough sergeant major.

This time Charlie really looks sour.—McLaglen! You'd better come back into the real world. It's going to be a long day.—

For you, I say to myself. Accountant, paper shuffler. Money juggle The stockholders will be after you. Not me. They don't care what I do, as long as it makes money. They don't care who it kills, as long as it works right and puts number in the right columns of your balance sheets.

The air-conditioning in my office howls like a wind tunnel. It's too cold. Be nice to have one of those big lazy fans up on the ceiling.

—Got a minute?—

Come on in, Elmer. What's the matter, something go wrong downstairs?

—Naw, the lab's fine. Everything almost set up for the final series. Just got to calibrate the spectrometer.—

But something's bothering you.

—I was wondering if I could have some time off to attend the stockholders meeting—

Today? I didn't know you were a stockbroker.

—Five shares.—

He's black. He's always seemed like a good lab technician, a reasonable man. But could he be one of them?

—I never been to a stockholders' meeting.—

Oh sure. You can go. But . . . we're not allowed to talk about PMD. Understand?

—Yeah, I know.—

Not that it's anything we're ashamed of—military security.

—Yeah I know.—

Good military form. Good regimental attitude. We've got to stand together against the darkness.

Elmer nods as he leaves, but I don't think he really understands. When the time comes, when the Thugees rise in rebellion, which side will he join?

I wonder how I'd look in uniform? With one of those stiff collars and a sergeant's stripes on my sleeves. I'm about as tall as Grant, almost. Don't have his shoulders, though. And this flabby middle—ought to exercise more.

Through my office window I can see the world's
ugliest water twower, one of Cambridge's distin-
guishing landmarks. Mountains, that's what should be
out there. The solid rock walls of the Himalayas. And
the temple of gold is tucked in them somewhere. Pure
gold! Din was telling the truth. It's all gold. And I'm
stuck here, like Cary Grant in the stockade. Get me out
of here, Din. Get me out.

—Please, sahib, don't take away bugle. Bugle only joy
for poor *bhisti*.—

He only wants to be one of us. Wants to be a soldier,
like the rest of us. A bugler. McLagen would laugh at
him. Fairbanks would be sympathetic. Let him keep the
bugle. He's going to need it.

—Tonight, when everyone sleeping. I go back to
temple.—

Not now, Din. Not now. Got some soldiering to do.
Down in the lab. Test out the new batch of PMD. A
soldier's got to do his duty.

The phone. Don't answer it. It's only some civilian
who wants to make trouble. Leave it ringing and get
down to the lab. Wife, sister, mother, they're all alike.
Yes, I'm a man, but I'm a soldier first. You don't want a
man, you want a coward who'd run out on his friends.
Well, that's not me and never was . . . No, wait—that's
Fairbanks' speech. He's Ballantine. And who was the
girl? Olivia de Haviland or her sister?

The halls are crawling with stockholders. Fat and old.
Civilians. Visiting the frontier, inspecting the troops.
We're the only thing standing between you and the
darkness, but you don't know it. Or if you do, you
wouldn't dare admit it.

The lab's always cold as ice. Got to keep it chilled down. If even a wiff of PMD gets out . . .

Elmer, hey, why isn't the spectrometer ready to go?

—You said I could go to the stockholders' meeting.—

Yes, but we've still got work to do. When does the meeting start?

—Ten sharp.—

Well, we've still got lots of time. . .

—It's ten of ten.—

What? Can't be. . . Is that clock right?

—Yep.—

He wouldn't have tampered with the clock; stop being so suspicious. O.K., go on to the meeting. I'll set it up myself.

—O.K., thanks.—

But I'm not by myself, of course. Good old grinnin' gruntin' Gunga Din. You lazarushin leather Gunga Din. He's not much help, naturally. What does an actor know about biochemistry? But he talks, and I talk, and the work gets done.

—Satisfactory, sahib?—

Very regimental, Din. Very regimental.

He glows with pride. White teeth against black skin. He'll die for us. They'll kill him, up there atop the temple of gold. The Thugees, the wild ones. The cult of death, worshippers of heathen idols. Kali, the goddess of blood.

Up to the roof for lunch. The stockholders are using the cafeteria. Let them. It's better up here, alone. Get the sun into your skin. Let the heat sink in and the glare dazzle your eyes.

My god, there they are! The heathens, the Thugees.

Swarms of them grumbling outside the gate. Dirty, unkempt. Stranglers and murderers. Already our graves
are dug. Their leader, he't too young to be Cianelli. And
he's bearded; the guru should be clean-shaven. The
guards look scared.

He's got a bullhorn. He's black enough to be the guru,
all right. What's he telling the crowd? I know what he's
saying, even though he tries to disguise the words. Cianelli didn't hide it, he said it straight out: Kill lest you be
killed yourselves. Kill for the love of killing. Kill for the
love of Kali. Kill! Kill! Kill!

They howl and rush the gate. The guards are bowled
over. Not a chance for them. The swarming heathen
boil across the parking lot and right into the lab building itself. They're all over the place. Savages. I can smell
smoke. Glass is shattering somewhere down there. People screaming.

One of the guards comes puffing up here. Uniform
torn and sweaty, face red.

—Hey, Doc, better get down the emergency stairs
right away. It ain't safe up here. They're burning your
lab.—

I'm a soldier of her Majesty the Queen. I don't bow
before no heathen!

His eyes go wide. He's scared. Scared of rabble, of
heathen rabble.

—I'll. . .I'll get somebody to help you, Doc. The fire
engines oughtta be here any minute.—

Let him run. We can handle it. The Scotties will be
here soon. I can hear their bagpipes now, or is it just the
heat singing in my ear?

They'll be here. Get up on top of the temple dome,

Din. Warn them. Sound your trumpet. The colonel's got to know! These dark incoherent forces of evil can't be allowed to win. You know that. Snake worshippers, formless, nameless shadows of death. The Forces of Light and Order have to win out in the end. Western organization and military precision always triumph. It will kill you, Din, I know. But that's the price of admission. We'll make you an honorary corporal in the regiment, Din. Your name will be written on the rolls of our honored deal.

They're coming; I know they're coming. The whole bloomin' regiment! Climb the golden dome and warn them. Warn them. Warn them!

# The Man Who . . .

*There's not much I can say about this tale except that it triggered a novel called* The Multiple Man. *Political campaigning in America has become a combination of the Olympics, the World Series and the Super Bowl. Too often, the man who is the better campaigner turns out to be mediocre or worse at governing after he is elected. But in American politics nowadays, the campaign's the important part.*

He doesn't have cancer!"

Les Trotter was a grubby little man. He combed his hair forward to hide his baldness, but now as I drove breakneck through the early Minnesota morning, the wind had blown his thinning hair every which way, leaving him looking bald and moon-faced and aging.

And upset as hell.

"Marie, I'm telling you, he doesn't have cancer." He tried to make it sound sincere. His voice was somewhere between the nasality of an upper-register clarinet and its Moog synthesis.

"Sure," I said sweetly. "That's why he's rushed off to a secret laboratory in the dead of night."

Les' voice went up still another notch. "It's not a secret lab! It's the Wellington Memorial Laboratory. It's world famous. And . . . goddammit, Marie, you're *enjoying* this!"

"I'm a reporter, Les." Great line. Very impressive. It hadn't kept him from making a grab for my ass, when we had first met. "It's my job."

He said nothing.

"And if your candidate has cancer . . ."

"He doesn't."

"It's news."

We whipped past the dead bare trees with the windows open to keep me from dozing. It had been a long night, waiting for Halliday at the Twin Cities Airport. A dark horse candidate, sure, but the boss wanted *all* the presidential candidates covered. So we drew lots and I lost. I got James J. Halliday, the obscure. When his private jet finally arrived, he whisked right out to this laboratory in the upstate woods.

I love to drive fast. And the hours around dawn are the best time of the day. The world's clean. And all yours . . . a new day coming. This day was starting with a murky gray as the sun tried to break through a heavy late winter overcast.

"There's ice on the road, you know," Les sulked.

I ignored him. Up ahead I could see lighted buildings.

The laboratory was surrounded by a riot-wire fence. The guard at the gate refused to open up and let us through. It took fifteen minutes of arguing and a phone call from the guard shack by Les before the word came back to allow us in.

"What'd you tell them?" I asked Les as I drove down the crunchy gravel driveway to the main laboratory building.

He was still shivering from the cold. "That it was

either see you or see some nasty scare headlines."

The lab building was old and drab, in the dawning light. There were a few other buildings farther down the driveway. I pulled up behind a trio of parked limousines, right in front of the main entrance.

We hurried through the chilly morning into the lobby. It was paneled with light mahogany, thickly carpeted, and *warm*. They had paintings spotted here and there— abstracts that might have been amateurish or priceless. I could never figure them out.

A smart-looking girl in a green pantsuit came through the only other door in the lobby. She gave me a quick, thorough inspection. I had to smile at how well she kept her face straight. My jeans and jacket were for warmth, not looks.

"Governor Halliday would like to know what this is all about," she said tightly. Pure efficiency: all nerves and smooth makeup. Probably screws to a metronome beat. "He is here on a personal matter; there's no news material in this visit."

"That depends on his X-rays, doesn't it?" I said.

Her eyes widened. "Oh." That's all she said. Nothing more. She turned and made a quick exit.

"Bright," I said to Les. "She picks up right away."

"His whole staff's bright."

"Including his advance publicity man?" *With the overactive paws*, I added silently.

"Yes, including my advance publicity man."

I turned back toward the door. Walking toward me was James J. Halliday, Governor of Montana, would-be President of these United States: tall-cowboy-lean, tanned, goodlooking. He was smiling at me, as if he knew my suspicions and was secretly amused by them. The smile was dazzling. He was a magnetic man.

"Hello, Les," Halliday said as he strode across the lobby toward us. "Sorry to cause you so much lost sleep." His voice was strong, rich.

And Les, who had always come on like a lizard, was blooming in the sunshine of that smile. He straightened up and *his* voice deepened. "Perfectly okay, Governor. I'll sleep after your inauguration."

Halliday laughed outright.

He reached out for my hand as Les introduced, "This is Marie Kludjian of. . ."

"I know," Halliday said. His grip was firm. "Is *Now's* circulation falling off so badly that you have to invent a cancer case for me?" But he still smiled as he said it.

"Our circulation's fine," I said, trying to sound unimpressed. "How's yours?"

He stayed warm and friendly. "You're afraid I'm here for a secret examination or treatment, is that it?"

I wasn't accustomed to frankness from politicians. And he was just radiating warmth. Like the sun. Like a flame.

"You . . . well. . ." I stammered. "You come straight to the point, at least."

"It saves a lot of time," he said. "But I'm afraid you're wasting yours. I'm here to visit Dr. Corio, the new director of the lab. We went to school together back East. And Les has such a busy schedule arranged for me over the next week that this was the only chance I had to see him."

I nodded, feeling as dumb as a high school groupie.

"Besides," he went on, "I'm interested in science. I

think it's one of our most important national resources.
Too bad the current administration can't seem to
recognize a chromosome from a clavicle."

"Uh-huh." My mind seemed to be stuck in neutral.
*Come on!* I scolded myself. *Nobody can have that
powerful an effect on you! This isn't a gothic novel.*

He waited a polite moment for me to say something
else, then cracked, "The preceding was an unpaid
political announcement."

We laughed, all three of us together.

Halliday ushered Les and me inside the lab, and we
stayed with him every minute he was there. He introduced me to Dr. Corio—a compactly built intense
man of Halliday's age, with a short, dark beard and
worried gray eyes. I spent a yawn- provoking two hours
with them, going through a grand tour of the lab's
facilities. There were only five of us: Halliday, Corio,
the girl in the green suit, Les and me. All the lab's offices
and workrooms were dark and unoccupied. Corio spent
half the time feeling along the walls for light switches.

Through it all something buzzed in my head.
Something was out of place. Then it hit me. *No staff. No
flunkies. Just the appointments secretary and
Les . . . and I dragged Les here.*

It was a small thing. But it was different. *A politician
without pomp?* I wondered.

By seven in the morning, while Corio lectured to us
about the search for carcinoma antitoxins or some such,
I decided I had been dead wrong about James J.
Halliday.

By seven-thirty I was practically in love with him. He
was intelligent. And concerned. He had a way of

looking right at you and turning on that dazzling smile. Not phony. Knee-watering. *And unattached,* I remembered. *The most available bachelor in the presidential sweepstakes.*

By eight-thirty I began to realize that he was also as tough as a grizzled mountain man. I was out on my feet, but he was still alert and interested in everything Corio was showing me.

He caught me in mid-yawn, on our way back to the lobby. "Perhaps you'd better ride with us, Marie," he said. "I'll have one of Corio's guards drive your car back to the airport."

I protested, but feebly. I *was* tired. And, after all, it's not every day that a girl gets a lift from a potential President.

Halliday stayed in the lobby for a couple of minutes while Les, the appointments girl and I piled into one of the limousines. Then he came out, jogged to the limo, and slid in beside me.

"All set. They'll get your car back to the Airport."

I nodded. I was too damned sleepy to wonder what had happened to the people who had filled the other two limousines. And all the way back to Minneapolis, Halliday didn't smile at me once.

Sheila Songard, the managing editor at *Now*, was given to making flat statements, such as: "You'll be back in the office in two weeks, Marie. He won't get past the New Hampshire primary."

You don't argue with the boss. I don't anyway. Especially not on the phone. But after Halliday grabbed off an impressive 43% of the fractured New Hampshire vote, I sent her a get well card.

All through those dark, cold days of winter and early spring I stayed with Jim Halliday, got to know him and his staff, watched him grow. The news and media people started to flock in after New Hampshire.

The vitality of the man! Not only did he have sheer animal magnetism in generous globs, he had more energy than a half-dozen flamenco dancers. He was up and active with the sunrise every day and still going strong long after midnight. It wore out most of the older newsmen trying to keep up with him.

When he scored a clear victory in Wisconsin, the Halliday staff had to bring out extra busses and even arrange a separate plane for the media people to travel in, along with The Man's private 707 jet.

I was privileged to see the inside of his private jetliner. I was the only news reporter allowed aboard during the whole campaign, in fact. He never let news or media people fly with him. Superstition, I thought. Or just a desire to have a place that can be really private—even if he has to go 35,000 feet above the ground to get the privacy. Then I'd start daydreaming about what it would be like to be up that high with him. . .

The day I saw the plane, it was having an engine overhauled at JFK in New York. It was still cold out, early April, and the hangar was even colder inside than the weakly sunlit out-of-doors.

The plane was a flying command post. The Air Force didn't have more elaborate electronics gear. Bunks for fifteen people. *There goes the romantic dream*, I thought. No fancy upholstery or decorations. Strictly, utilitarian. But row after row of communication stuff:

even picturephones, a whole dozen of them.

I had known that Jim was in constant communication with his people all over the country. But picturephones—it was typical of him. He wanted to be *there*, as close to the action as possible. Ordinary telephones or radios just weren't good enough for him.

"Are you covering an election campaign or writing love letters?" Sheila's voice, over the phone, had that bitchy edge to it.

"What's wrong with the copy I'm sending in?" I yelled back at her.

"It's too damned laudatory, and you know it," she shrilled. "You make it sound as if he's going through West Virginia converting the sinners and curing the lepers."

"He's doing better than that," I said. "And I'm not the only one praising him."

"I've watched his press conferences on TV," Sheila said. "He's a cutie, all right. Never at a loss for an answer."

"And he never contradicts himself. He's saying the same things here that he did in New York . . . and Denver . . . and Los Angeles."

"That doesn't make him a saint."

"Sheila, believe it. He's *good*. I've been with him nearly four months now. He's got it. He's our next President."

She was unimpressed. "You sound more like you're on his payroll than *Now's*."

Les Trotter had hinted a few days earlier that Jim

wanted me to join his staff for the California primary
campaign. I held my tongue.

"Marie, listen to Momma," Sheila said, softer,
calmer. "No politician is as good as you're painting
him. Don't let your hormones get in the way of your
judgement.

"That's ridiculous!" I snapped.

"Sure . . . sure. But I've seen enough of Halliday's
halo. I want you to find his clay feet. He's got them,
honey. They all do. It might hurt when you discover
them, but I want to see what The Man's standing on.
That's your job."

She meant it. And I know she was right. But if Jim had
clay feet, nobody had been able to discover it yet. Not
even the nastiest bastards Hearst had sent out.

And I knew that I didn't want to be the one who did
it.

So I joined Jim's staff for the California campaign.
Sheila was just as glad to let me go. Officially I took a
leave of absence from *Now*. I told her I'd get a better
look inside The Man's organization this way. She sent
out a lank-haired slouchy kid who couldn't even work a
dial telephone, she was that young.

But instead of finding clay feet on The Man, as we
went through the California campaign, I kept coming
up with gold.

He was beautiful. He was honest. Everyone of the
staff loved him and the voters were turning his rallies
into victory celebrations.

And he was driving me insane. Some days he'd be
warm and friendly and . . . well, it was just difficult to

be near him without getting giddy. But then there were times—sometimes the same day, even—when he'd just turn off. He'd be as cold and out-of-reach as an Antarctic iceberg. I couldn't understand it. The smile was there, his voice and manners and style were unchanged, but the vibrations would be gone. Turned off.

There were a couple of nights when we found ourselves sitting with only one or two other people in a hotel room, planning the next day's moves over unending vats of black coffee. We made contact then. The vibes were good. He wanted me, I know he did, and I certainly wanted him. Yet somehow we never touched each other. The mood would suddenly change. He'd go to the phone and come back . . . different. His mind was on a thousand other things.

*He's running for President*, I raged at myself. *There's more on his mind than shacking up with an oversexed ex-reporter.*

But while all this was going on, while I was helping to make it happen, I was also quietly digging into the Wellington Memorial Laboratory, back in Minnesota. And its director, Dr. Corio. If Jim did have feet of clay, the evidence was there. And I had to know.

I got a friend of a friend to send me a copy of Corio's doctoral thesis from the Harvard library, and while I waited for it to arrive in the mail, I wanted more than anything to be proved wrong.

Jim was beautiful. He was so much more than the usual politician. His speech in Denver on uniting the rich and poor into a coalition that will solve the problems of the nation brought him as much attention for its style as its content. His position papers on R&D, the economy, tax reform, foreign trade, were all called "brilliant" and "pace setting." A crusty old economist from Yale, no less, told the press, "That man has the mind of an economist." A compliment, from him. A half- dozen of Nader's Raiders joined the Halliday staff because they felt, "He's the only candidate who gives a damn about the average guy."

A political campaign is really a means for the candidate to show himself to the people. And *vice versa.* He must get to know the people, all the people, their fears, their prides, their voices and touch and smell. If he can't feel for them, can't reach their pulse and match it with his own heartbeat, all the fancy legwork and lovely ghostwriting in the universe can't help him.

Jim had it. He grew stronger every minute. He kept a backbreaking pace with such ease and charm that we would have wondered how he could do it, if we had had time enough to catch our own breaths. He was everywhere, smiling, confident, energetic, *concerned.* He identified with people and they identified with him. It was uncanny. He could be completely at ease with a Missouri farmer and a New York corporation chairman. And it wasn't phony; he could *feel* for people.

And they felt for him.

And I fell for him; thoroughly, completely, hopelessly. He realized it. I was sure he did. There were times when the electric current flowed between us so strongly that I could barely stand it. He'd catch my eye and grin at me, and even though there were ninety other people in the room, for that instant everything else went blank.

But then an hour later, or the next day, he'd be

completely cold. As if I didn't exist . . . or worse yet, as if I was just another cog in his machine. He'd still smile, he'd say the same things and look exactly the same. But the spark between us just wasn't there.

It was driving me crazy. I put it down to the pressures of the campaign. He couldn't have any kind of private life in this uproar. I scolded myself, *Stop acting like a dumb broad!*

Corio's thesis arrived three days before the California primary. I didn't even get a chance to unwrap it.

Jim took California by such a huge margin that the TV commentators were worriedly looking for something significant to say by ten that evening. It was no contest at all.

As we packed up for the last eastern swing before the National Convention, I hefted Corio's bulky thesis. Still unopened. I was going to need a translator, I realized; his doctoral prose would be too technical for me to understand. We were heading for Washington, and there was a science reporter there that I knew would help me.

Besides, I needed to get away from Jim Halliday for a while, a day or so at least. I was on an emotional rollercoaster, and I needed some time to straighten out my nerves.

The phone was ringing as the bellman put my bags down in my room at the Park Sheraton. It was Sheila.

"How are you?" she asked.

She never calls for social chatter. "What do you want, Sheila?" I asked wearily. It had been a long, tiring flight from the coast, and I knew my time zones were going to be mixed up thoroughly.

"Have you found anything . . . clay feet, I mean?"

The bellman stood waiting expectantly beside me. I started fumbling with my purse while I wedged the phone against my shoulder.

"Listen, Marie," Shiela was saying. "He's too good to be true. *Nobody* can be a masterful politician *and* a brilliant economist *and* a hero to both the ghetto and the suburbs. Its physically impossible."

I popped a handful of change from my wallet and gave it over to the bellman. He glanced at the coins without smiling and left.

"He's doing it," I said into the phone. "He's putting it all together."

"Marie," she said with a great patience, as I flopped on the bed, "he's a puppet. A robot that gets wound up every morning and goes out spouting whatever they tell him to say. Find out who's running him, who's making all those brilliant plans, who's making his decisions for him."

"He makes his own decisions," I said, starting to feel a little desperate. If someone as intelligent as Sheila couldn't *believe* in him, if politics had sunk so low in the minds of the people that they couldn't recognize a knight in brilliant armor when he paraded across their view . . . then what would happen to this nation?

"Marie," she said again, with her *Momma knows best* tone, "listen to me. Find out who's running him. Break the story in *Now*, and you'll come back on the staff as a full editor. With a raise. Promise."

I hung up on her.

She was right in a way. Jim was superman. More than

human. *If only he weren't running for President! If only we could. . .* I shut off that line of thought. Fantasizing wasn't going to help either one of us. Laying there on the hotel bed, I felt a shiver go through me. It wasn't from the air conditioning.

Even with translation into language I could understand, Corio's thesis didn't shed any light on anything. It was all about genetics and molecular manipulation. I didn't get a chance to talk with the guy who had digested it for me. We met at National Airport, he sprinting for one plane and me for another.

My flight took me to San Francisco, where the National Convention was due to open in less than a week.

The few days before a National Convention opens are crazy in a way nothing else on Earth can match. It's like knowing you're going to have a nervous breakdown and doing everything you can to make sure it comes off on schedule. You go into a sort of masochistic training, staying up all night, collaring people for meetings and caucuses, yelling into phones, generally behaving like the world is going to come to an end within the week— and you've got to help make it happen.

Jim's staff was scattered in a half-dozen hotels around San Francisco. I got placed in the St. Francis, my favorite. But there wasn't any time for enjoying the view.

Jim had a picturephone network set up for the staff. For two solid days before the Convention officially convened, I stayed in my hotel room and yet was in immediate face-to-face contact with everyone I had to work with. It was fantastic, and it sure beat trying to drive through those jammed, hilly streets.

Late on the eve of the Conventions' opening gavel— it was morning, actually, about two- thirty—I was restless and wide awake. The idea wouldn't have struck me, I suppose, if Sheila hadn't needled me in Washington. But it *did* hit me, and I was foolish enough to act on the impulse.

*None of Jim's brain trusters are here*, I told myself. *They're all safe in their homes, far from this madhouse. But what happens if we need to pick at one of their mighty intellects at some godawful hour? Can we reach them?*

If I hadn't been alone and nervous and feeling sorry for myself, sitting in that hotel room with nothing but the picturephone to talk to, I wouldn't have done it. I knew I was kidding myself as I punched out the number for Professor Marvin Carlton, down in La Jolla. I could hear Sheila's *listen to Momma* inside my head.

To my surprise, Carlton's image shaped up on the phone's picture screen.

"Yes?." he asked pleasantly. He was sitting in what looked like a den or study—lots of books and wood. There was a drink in his hand and a book in his lap.

"Professor. . ." I felt distinctly foolish. "I'm with Governor Halliday's staff. . ."

"Obviously. No one else has the number for this TV phone he gave me."

"Oh."

"What can I do for you . . . or the Governor? I was just about to retire for the night."

Thinking with the speed of a dinosaur, I mumbled,

"Oh well, we were just . . . um, checking the phone connection . . . to make certain we can reach you when we have to. . .

He pursed his lips. "I'm a bit surprised. The Governor had no trouble reaching me this afternoon."

"This afternoon?"

"Yes. We went over the details of my urban restructuring program."

"Oh—of course." I tried to cover up my confusion. I had been with Jim most of the afternoon, while he charmed incoming delegates at various caucuses. We had driven together all across town, sitting side by side in the limousine. He had been warm and outgoing and . . . and then he had changed, as abruptly as putting on a new necktie. *Was it something I said? Am I being too obvious with him?*

"Well?" the professor asked, getting a bit testy. "Are you satisfied that I'm at my post and ready for instant service?.

"Oh, yes . . . yes sir. Sorry to have disturbed you."

"Very well."

"Um—professor? One question? How long did you and the Governor talk this afternoon? For our accounting records you know. The phone bill, things like that."

His expression stayed sour. "Lord, it must have been at least two hours. He dragged every last detail out of me. The man must have an eidetic memory."

"Yes," I said. "Thank you."

"Good night."

I reached out and clicked the phone's off switch. If Jim had spent two hours talking with Professor Carlton, it couldn't have been that afternoon. He hadn't been out of my sight for more than fifteen minutes between lunch and dinner.

I found myself biting my tongue and punching another number. This time it was Rollie O'Malley, the guy who ran our polling services. He was still in New York.

And sore as hell. "Goin' on five o'clock in the motherin' morning and you wanna ask me what?"

"When's the last time you talked with The Man?"

Rollie's face was puffy from sleep, red-eyed. His skin started turning red, too. "You dizzy broad . . . why in the hell. . ."

"It's important!" I snapped. "I wouldn't call if it wasn't."

He stopped in mid-flight. "Whassamatter? What's wrong?"

"Nothing major . . . I hope. But I need to know when you talked to him last. And for how long."

"Christ." He was puzzled, but more concerned than angry now. "Lessee . . . I was just about to sit down to dinner here at the apartment . . . musta been eight, eight-thirty. 'Round then."

"New York time?" That would put it around five or so our time. *Right when Jim was greeting the Texas delegation.*

"No! Bangkok time! What the hell is this all about, Marie?"

"Tell you later," and I cut him off.

I got a lot of people riled. I called the heads of every one of Jim's think-tank teams: science, economics, social welfare, foreign policy, taxation, even some of his

Montana staff back in Helena. By dawn I had a crazy story: eleven different people had each talked *personally* with The Man that afternoon for an average of an hour and a half apiece, they claimed. Several of them were delighted that Jim would spend so much time with them just before the Convention opened.

That was more than sixteen hours of face-to-face conversation on the picturephones. All between noon and 7 p.m., Pacific Daylight Time.

And for most of that impossible time, Jim was in my presence, close enough to touch me. And never on the phone once.

I watched the sun come up over the city's mushrooming skyline. My hands were shaking. I was sticky damp with a cold sweat.

*Phony.* I wanted to feel anger, but all I felt was sorrow. And the beginnings of self-pity. *He's a phony. He's using his fancy electronics equipment to con a lot of people into thinking he's giving them his personal attention. And all the while he's just another damned public relations robot.*

And his smiles, his magnetism, the good vibes that he could turn on or off whenever it suited him. *I hate him!*

And then I asked myself the jackpot question: *Who's pulling his strings?* I had to find out.

But I couldn't.

I tried to tell myself that it wasn't just my emotions. I told myself that, puppet or not, he was the best candidate running. And God knows we needed a good President, a man who could handle the job and get the nation back on the right tracks again. But, at that

bottom line, was the inescapable fact that I loved him.
As wildly as any schoolgirl loved a movie star. But this
was real. I wanted Jim Halliday . . . I wanted to be *his*
First Lady.

I fussed around for two days, while the Convention
got started and those thousands of delegates from all
over this sprawling nation settled preliminary matters
like credentials and platform and voting procedures.
There were almost as many TV cameras and news
people as there were delegates. The convention hall, the
hotels, the streets were crawling with people asking
each other questions.

It was a streamroller. That became clear right at the
outset when all the credentials questions got ironed out
so easily. Halliday's people were seated with hardly a
murmur in every case where an argument came up.

Seeing Jim privately, where I could ask him about the
phony picturephone conversations, was impossible. He
was surrounded in his hotel suite by everybody from
former party chieftans to movie stars.

So I boiled in my own juices for two days, watching
helplessly while the Convention worked its way toward
the inevitable moment when The Man would be
nominated. There was betting down on the streets that
there wouldn't even be a first ballot: he'd be nominated
by acclamation.

I couldn't take it. I bugged out. I packed my bag and
headed for the airport.


I arrived at Twin Cities Airport at 10 p.m., local time.
I rented a car and started out the road toward the
Wellington Lab.

It was summer now, and the trees that had been bare that icy morning, geologic ages ago, were now full-leafed and rustling softly in a warm breeze. The moon was high and full, bathing everything in cool beauty.

I had the car radio on as I pushed the rental Dart up Route 10 toward the laboratory. Pouring from the speaker came a live interview with James J. Halliday, from his hotel suite in San Francisco.

". . . and we're hoping for a first-ballot victory," he was saying smoothly, with that hint of earnestness and boyish enthusiasm in his voice. *I will not let myself get carried away*, I told myself. *Definitely not.*

"On the question of unemployment. . ." the interviewer began.

"I'd rather think of it as a mismatch between. . . ."

I snapped it off. I had written part of that material for him. But dammit, he had dictated most of it, and he never said it the same way twice. He always added something or shaded it a little differently to make it easier to understand. If he was a robot, he was a damnably clever one.

The laboratory gate was coming up, and the guard was already eyeing my car as I slowed down under the big floodlights that lined the outer fence.

I fished in my purse for my Halliday staff ID card. The guard puzzled over it for a second or two, then nodded.

"Right, Ms. Kludjian. Right straight ahead to the reception lobby."

No fuss. No questions. As if they were expecting me.

The parking area was deserted as I pulled up. The lobby was lit up, and there was a girl receptionist sitting at the desk, reading a magazine.

She put the magazine down on the kidney- shaped
desk as I pushed the glass door open. I showed her my
ID and asked if Dr. Corio was in.

"Yes he is," she said, touching a button on her phone
console. Nothing more. Just the touch of a button.

I asked, "Does he always work this late at night?"

She smiled very professionally. "Sometimes."

"And you too?"

"Sometimes."

The speaker on her phone console came to life. "Nora,
would you please show Ms. Kludjian to Room A-14?"

She touched the button again, then gestured toward
the door that led into the main part of the building.
"Straight down the corridor," she said sweetly, "the last
door on your right."

I nodded and followed instructions. She went back to
her magazine.

Jim Halliday was waiting for me inside Room A-14.

My knees actually went weak. He was sitting on the
corner of the desk that was the only furniture in the
little, tile-paneled room. There was a mini-TV on the
desk. The Convention was roaring and huffing through
the tiny speaker.

"Hello, Marie." He reached out and took my hand.

I pulled it away, angrily. "So that 'live' interview
from your hotel was a fake, too. Like all your taped
phone conversations with your think-tank leaders."

He smiled at me. Gravely. "No, Marie. I haven't
faked a thing. Not even the way I feel about you."

"Don't try that. . ." But my voice was as shaky as
my body.

"That was James J. Halliday being interviewed in San Francisco, live, just a few minutes ago. I watched it on the set here. It went pretty well, I think."

"Then . . . who the hell are you?"

"James J. Halliday," he answered. And the back of my neck started to tingle.

"But. . ."

He held up a silencing hand. From the TV set, a florid speaker was bellowing, "This party *must* nominate the man who has swept all the primary elections across this great land. The man who can bring together all the elements of our people back into a great, harmonious whole. The man who will lead us to *victory* in November . . ." The roar of applause swelled to fill the tiny bare room we were in. ". . . The man who will be our next President!" The cheers and applause were a tide of human emotion. The speaker's apple-round face filled the little screen: "James J. Halliday, of Montana!"

I watched as the TV camera swept across the thronged convention hall. Everybody was on their feet, waving Halliday signs, jumping up and down. Balloons by the thousands fell from the ceiling. The sound was overpowering. Suddenly the picture cut to a view of James J. Halliday sitting in his hotel room in San Francisco, watching *his* TV set and smiling.

James J. Halliday clicked off the TV in the laboratory room and we faced each other in sudden silence.

"Marie," he said softly, kindly, "I'm sorry. If we had met another time, under another star. . ."

I was feeling dizzy. "How can you be there . . . and here. . ."

"If you had understood Corio's work, you'd have

realized that it laid the basis for a practical system of cloning human beings."

"Cloning. . ."

"Making exact replications of a person from a few body cells. I don't know how Corio does it—but it worked. He took a few patches of skin from me, years ago, when we were in school together. Now there are seven of us, all together."

"Seven?" My voice sounded like a choked squeak.

He nodded gravely. "I'm the one that fell in love with you. The others . . . well, we're not *exactly* alike, emotionally."

I was glancing around for a chair. There weren't any. He put his arms around me.

"It's too much for one man to handle," he said, urgently, demandingly. "Running a presidential campaign takes an inhuman effort. You've got to be able to do everything—either that or be a complete fraud and run on slogans and gimmicks. I didn't want that. I want to be the best President this nation can elect."

"So . . . you. . . ."

"Corio helped replicate six more of me. Seven exactly similar James J. Hallidays. Each an expert in one aspect of the presidency such as no presidential candidate could ever hope to be, by himself."

"Then that's how you could talk on the picturephones to everybody at the same time."

"And that's how I could know so much about so many different fields. Each of us could concentrate on a few separate problem areas. It's been tricky shuffling us back and forth—especially with all the news people

around. That's why we keep the 707 strictly off-limits.
Wouldn't want to let the public see seven of us in
conference together. Not yet, anyway."

My stomach started crawling up toward my throat.

"And me . . . us . . .?"

His arms dropped away from me. "I hadn't planned
on something like this happening. I really hadn't. It's
been tough keeping you at arm's length."

"What can we do?" I felt like a little child—helpless,
scared.

He wouldn't look at me. Not straight-on. "We'll have
to keep you here for a while, Marie. Not for long. Just
'til after the Inauguration. 'Til I . . . we . . . are safely in
office. Corio and his people will make you comfortable
here."

I stood there, stunned. Without another word Jim
suddenly got up and strode out of the room, leaving me
there alone.

He kept his promises. Corio and his staff have made
life very comfortable for me here. Maybe they're
putting things in my food or something, who can tell?
Most likely it's for my own good. I do get bored. And so
lonely. And frightened.

I watched his Inauguration on television. They let me
see TV. I watch him every chance I get. I try to spot the
tiny difference that I might catch among the seven of
them. So far, I haven't been able to find any flaw at all.

He said they'd let me go to him after the Inauguration. I hope they remember. His second Inauguration is coming up soon. I know.

Or is it his third?

# Priorities

*After spending nearly a dozen years trying to convince skeptical government and business bureaucrats that funding research is necessary, valuable and esthetically pleasing, this little story just bubbled up to the surface—during a particularly nasty budgetary cutback, of course.*

**D**r. Ira Lefko sat rigidly nervous on the edge of the plastic-cushioned chair. He was a slight man, thin, bald, almost timid-looking. Even his voice was gentle and reedy, like the fine thin tone of an English horn.

And just as the English horn is a sadly misnamed woodwind, Dr. Ira Lefko was actually neither timid nor particularly gentle. At this precise moment he was close to mayhem.

"Ten years of work," he was saying, with a barely controlled tremor in his voice. "You're going to wipe out ten years of work with a shake of your head."

The man shaking his head was sitting behind the metal desk that Lefko sat in front of. His name was Harrison Bower. His title and name were prominently displayed on a handsome plate atop the desk. Harrison Bower kept a very neat desktop. All the papers were primly stacked and both the IN and OUT baskets were empty.

"Can't be helped," said Harrison Bower, with a tight smile that was supposed to be sympathetic and understanding. "Everyone's got to tighten the belt. Reordering priorities, you know. There are many research programs going by the boards—New times, new problems, new priorities. You're not the only one to be affected."

With his somber face and dark suit Bower looked like a funeral director—which he was. In the vast apparatus of Government, his job was to bury research projects that had run out of money. It was just about the only thing on Earth that made him smile.

The third man in the poorly ventilated little Washington office was Major Robert Shawn, from the Air Force Cambridge Research Laboratories. In uniform, Major Shawn looked an awful lot like Hollywood's idea of a jet pilot. In the casual slacks and sportcoat he was wearing now, he somehow gave the vague impression of being an engineer, or perhaps even a far-eyed scientist.

He was something of all three.

Dr. Lefko was getting red in the face. "But you *can't* cancel the program now! We've tentatively identified six stars within twenty parsecs of us that have . . ."

"Yes. I know, it's all in the reports," Bower interrupted, "and you've told me about it several times this afternoon. It's interesting, but it's hardly practical, now is it?"

"Practical? Finding evidence of high technology on other planets, not practical?"

Bower raised his eyes toward the cracked ceiling, as if in supplication to the Chief Bureaucrat. "Really, Dr.

Lefko. I've admitted that it's interesting. But it's not within our restructured priority rating. You're not going to help ease pollution or solve population problems, now are you?"

Lefko's only answer was a half-strangled growl.

Bower turned to Major Shawn. "Really, Major, I would have thought that you could make Dr. Lefko understand the realities of the funding situation."

Shaking his head, the major answered, "I agree with Dr. Lefko completely. I think his work is the most important piece of research going on in the world today."

"Honestly!" Bower seemed shocked. "Major, you know that the Department of Defense can't fund research that's not directly related to a military mission."

"But the Air Force owns all the big microwave equipment!" Lefko shouted. "You can't get time on the university facilities, and they're too small anyway!"

Bower waggled a finger at him. "Dr. Lefko, you can't have DOD funds. Even if there were funds for your research available, it's not pertinent work. You must apply for research support from another branch of the government."

"I've tried that every year! None of the other agencies have any money for new programs. Damnit, you've signed the letters rejecting my applications!"

"Regrettable," Bower said stiffly. "Perhaps in a few years, when the foreign situation settles down and the pollution problems are solved."

Lefko was clenching his fists when Major Shawn put a hand on his frail-looking shoulder. "It's no use, Ira.

We've lost. Come on, I'll buy you a drink."

Out in the shabby corridor that led to the underground garage, Lefko started to tremble in earnest.

"A chance to find other intelligent races in the heavens. Gone. Wiped out . . . The richest nation in the world . . . Oh my God . . ."

The major took him by the arm and towed him to their rented car. In fifteen minutes they were inside the cool shadows of the airport bar.

"They've reordered the priorities," the major said as he stared into his glass. "For five hundred years and more, Western civilization has made the pursuit of knowledge a respectable goal in its own right. Now it's got to be practical."

Dr. Lefko was already halfway through his second rye and soda. "Nobody asked Galileo to be practical," he muttered. "Or Newton. Or Einstein."

"Yeah, people did. They've always wanted immediate results and practical benefits. But the system was spongy enough to let guys like Newton and Plank and even little fish we never hear about—let 'em tinker around on their own, follow their noses, see what they could find."

" 'Madam, of what use is a newborn baby?' " Lefko quoted thickly.

"What?"

"Faraday."

"Oh."

"Six of them." Lefko whispered. "Six point sources of intense microwave radiation. Close enough to separate from their parent stars. Six little planets, orbiting around their stars, with higher technology microwave equipment on them."

"Maybe the Astronomical Union will help you get more funding."

Lefko shook his head. "You saw the reception my paper got. They think we're crazy. Not enough evidence. And worse still. I'm associated with the evil Air Force. I'm a pariah . . . and I don't have enough evidence to convince them. It takes more evidence when you're a pariah."

"I'm convinced," Major Shawn said.

"Thank you, my boy. But you are an Air Force officer, a mindless napalmer of Oriental babies, by definition. Your degrees in astronomy and electronics notwithstanding."

Shawn sighed heavily. "Yeah."

Looking up from the bar, past the clacking color TV, toward the heavily draped windows across the darkened room, Lefko said, "I know they're there. Civilizations like ours. With radios and televisions and radars, turning their planets into microwave beacons. Just as we must be an anomalously bright microwave object to them. Maybe . . . maybe they'll find us! Maybe they'll contact us!"

The major started to smile.

"If only it happens in our lifetime, Bob. If only they find us! Find us . . . and blow us to Hell! We deserve it for being so stupid!"

Tor Kranta stood in the clear night chill, staring at

the stars. From inside the sleeping chamber his wife called, "Tor . . . stop tormenting yourself."

"The fools," he muttered. "To stop the work because of the priests' objections. To prevent us from trying to contact another intelligent race, circling another star. Idiocy. Sheer idiocy."

"Accept what must be accepted. Tor: Come to bed."

He shook his blue-maned head. "I only hope that the other intelligent races of the universe aren't as blind as we are."

# Those Who Can

*Some stories go their own way, despite the conscious volition of the writer. This one was inspired by a funny incident at a metting of a major corporation's board of directors. But the story didn't want to be funny. Not at all.*

*I* get all the kooks, William Ransom thought to himself as he watched the intent young man set up his equipment.

They were in Ransom's office, one of the smaller suites in the management level of Larrimore, Swain & Tucker, seventy-three stories above the crowded Wall Street sidewalk. As the firm's least senior executive (a mere fifty-three years old) Ransom's duties included interviewing intent young inventors who claimed to have new products that would revolutionize industries.

The equipment that the intent young man was assembling looked like a junkpile of old stereo sets, computer consoles, and the insides of Ticktok of Oz. It spread across the splashy orange-brown Rya carpet, climbed over the conversation corner's genuine llama-hide coches, covered the coffee table between the couches and was now encroaching on the teak bar behind them.

"I'll be finished in a minute," said the intent young

inventor. He had said the same thing ten minutes earlier, and ten minutes before *that*. But he continued to pull strange-looking racks of printed circuits and oddly glowing metallic cylinders from the seemingly bottomless black trunk that he had dragged into the office with him.

*If I had known it would take him this long,* Ransom thought, *I would have told him to set up after I'd gone for the day, and let me see it tomorrow morning.*

But it was a half hour too late for that decision. Ransom glanced at the neatly typed note his secretary had efficiently placed on his immaculate desktop. James Brightcloud, it said. Inventor. From Santa Fe, N.Mex. Representing self.

Ransom shook his head and suppressed a sigh. He was going to be stuck with this madman for the rest of the afternoon, he knew it, while Mr. Larrimore and other executives repaired to the rooftop sauna and the comforts of soothing ministrations by this week's bevy of masseuses. It was a fine accomplishment to be the youngest member of the executive board, career-wise. But it also meant that you were low man on the executive totem pole. Ransom had been dreaming about deaths in high places lately. Two nights ago, he had found himself reading *Julius Caesar* and enjoying it.

"Just about done," James Brightcloud muttered. He pulled a slim rod from the trunk and touched it to the last piece of equipment he had set up, atop the bar. Sparks leaped, hissing. Ransom almost jumped out of his seat.

"There," Brightcloud said. "Ready to go."

The inventor looked Hispanic, but without the

easygoing smile that Ransom always associated with
Latins. He couldn't have been more than thirty. Darkish
skin, much darker eyes that brooded. Straight black
hair. Stocky build, almost burly. Lots of muscles under
that plain denim leisure suit. Ransom thought briefly
about the *Puerto Rico Libre* movement that had been
bombing banks and office buildings. He laid his hands
on the edge of his very solid teak desk and pictured
himself ducking under it at the first sign of a detonation.

"I can demonstrate it for you now," James
Brightcloud said. He neither smiled nor frowned. His
face was a mask of stoic impassivity.

"Er . . . before you do," Ransom said, stroking the
smooth solid wood of his desk unobtrusively, wondering
just how much shrapnel it would stop, "just what *is* it? I
mean, what does your invention do?"

"It's a therapeutic device."

Ransom blinked at the young inventor. "A what?"

Brightcloud stepped around the machinery he had
assembled and walked toward Ransom's desk. Pulling
up a chair, he said, "Therapeutic. It makes you feel
better. It heals soreness in the muscles, stiffness caused
by tension. It can even get rid of stomach ulcers for
you."

Ransom's eyes rolled toward the ceiling, and he
thought of the sauna on the top floor. He could feel the
steam and hear the giggling, almost.

"I suppose," he said, "it also cures cancer."

"We've had a couple of remissions in the field tests,"
Brightcloud answered straightfaced, "but we don't like
to emphasize them. They might have been spontaneous,
and it wouldn't be right for us to get peoples' hopes up."

"Of course." Ransom made a mental note to fire his secretary. The woman must be getting soft in the head. "Er . . . how does this device of yours work? Or are the operating principles a secret?"

"No secret . . . if you understand enough biochemistry and radiation therapy principles." ▪

"I don't."

The inventor nodded. "Well . . . to put it simply, the device emits a beam of radiant energy that interacts with the parasympathetic nervous system. It has a variety of effects, and by controlling the frequency of the emitted radiation we can achieve somatic effects in the patient . . . muscular relaxation, easing of tension, of headaches. That sort of thing."

"Radiation?" Ransom was suddenly alert. "You mean like microwaves? The stuff the Russians have been beaming at our embassy in Moscow?"

Unruffled, Brightcloud said, "The same principle, yes. But entirely different wave lengths and entirely different somatic effects."

"Somatic . . . ?"

"Microwave radiation can be harmful," the inventor explained. "The radiation from my device is beneficial. It can even be curative." He hesitated a moment, then, in a lowered voice, added, "Our first sale has been to the government. I don't know this for a fact, but I'm pretty sure it's going to be installed in our Moscow embassy."

Ransom felt his eyebrows climb. "Really?"

"To counteract the Russian machine's effects."

"Is that so?"

"It's unofficial, but that's what I've been led to believe."

"But . . . if your device is curative. . ."

"Therapeutic," Brightcloud corrected. "Therapeutic is the proper term."

"All right, therapeutic. If it's good for your health, why aren't you dealing with a medical organization? Or one of the ethical pharmaceutical houses?"

A trace of disappointment crossed Brightcloud's features. "Two reasons. First, as soon as we get into a medical or pharmaceutical situation, the Federal government gets involved in a major way. Food and Drug Administration, National Institutes of Health, HEW, the Surgeon General. It would be a long, costly mess."

"I see."

"Secondly, this device is not inexpensive. The drug companies are geared to mass marketing. Even the medical technology outfits want to be able to sell their products to all the hospitals and clinics. This device is too costly for that kind of marketing. It can only be sold to the highest levels of corporate management. Nobody else could afford it."

"Really?"

"And no one else needs it so badly." Brightcloud quickly added. "Secretaries and street cleaners can take aspirin for their headaches and pains. It's good enough for them. But top-level executives, such as yourself, have different problems, different kinds of tensions, constant pressure and strain. That's where this device works best."

Ransom almost believed him.

"And frankly," the inventor went on, "it will be much easier for me to market my device as a sort of executive's relaxation gadget, rather than go through the entire government red-tape mill that they use on medical devices."

"But how do I know it's not harmful?" Ransom asked.

Brightcloud shrugged. "I've used it on myself thousands of times. We've run more than five hundred controlled laboratory tests with it and several hundred more field tests. No harmful effects whatsoever."

"Still . . ."

"You've been bathing in its radiation for the past two and a half minutes," the inventor said. "So have I."

Ransom grabbed at the desk's edge. "What!"

"Do you feel anything? Any pain or dizziness?"

"Why . . . er . . . no."

"Just how do you feel?" Brightcloud asked.

Ransom thought about it. "Er . . . fine, as a matter of fact. A little warm, perhaps."

"That's from the stimulation effect on your blood circulation. Here." Brightcloud took a small oblong black box from his shirtjacket pocket. It looked rather like a hand calculator. "Let me adjust the frequency just a bit."

He turned a tiny knob on the box. Ransom relaxed back in his swivel chair. He was about to say that he didn't feel any change when, suddenly, he *did*. A decided change. A growing, warming, magnificent change.

He felt his jaw drop open as he stared at Brightcloud, who merely stretched his legs comfortably, clasped his hands behind his head, and grinned boyishly at him.

As president of Larrimore, Swain & Tucker, Robert Larrimore was accustomed to saying *no*. It had been the hallmark of his long career, a thoroughly negative attitude that had given him the reputation for being the toughest, shrewdest businessman in Lower Manhattan. When others rhapsodized over new products, Larrimore frowned. When junior executives cooed over ideas from their creative staffs and chorused, "Love it! I love it!" Larrimore shook his head and walked in the other direction. When politicians towed in their newest toothpaste-clean candidate, Larrimore would enumerate all the weaknesses of the candidate that his cigar-chomping backers were trying to overlook or forget.

In short, because he pointed out the obvious and refused to be stampeded by the crowd, he had survived and prospered where others had enthused and withered away. After nearly eight decades of avoiding gapingly unmistakable pitfalls, Larrimore was regarded by several generations of young executives with a respect that bordered on awe. This did not make him a happy man, however.

He was the first one to arrive in the conference room for the meeting with this new inventor that young Ransom had discovered. Larrimore walked stiffly to his accustomed chair, halfway down the polished mahogany table, his eyes fixed on the Byzantine complexity of electronic units stacked neatly against the back end of the conference room from wall to wall and floor to ceiling.

A uniformed security guard stood before the inert hardware. Larrimore snorted to himself and sat, slowly and painfully, in his padded chair. *Arthritis*, he groused inwardly. *They can cure pneumonia and give me a new heart, but the stupid sonsofbitches still can't do anything more for arthritis than give me some goddamned aspirins.*

William Ransom pushed the corridor door open and held it for a stocky, dark-complected young man who wore a denim leisure suit embroidered with flowers and sun symbols. *My God*, Larrimore thought, *that young twit Ransom has brought a goddamned Indian in here. An Apache, I bet.*

Ransom made a prim contrast to the solemn-faced redskin, being slim, tall, Aryan-blond and good-looking in an empty way. He always reminded Larrimore of a chorus boy from a musical about the Roaring Twenties.

"Oh, Mr. Larrimore, you're already here," Ransom said as he let the door softly shut itself.

"You get an A for visual acuity," Larrimore said.

Ransom grinned weakly. "Er . . . allow me to introduce Mr. Ja . . ."

"James Brightcloud. Who else would he be, Billy?" Larrimore chuckled inwardly. *What's the good of being a tyrant unless you can exert a little tryanny now and then?*

In a much-subdued voice, Ransom said to the inventor, "This is Mr. Larrimore, our president."

"How do you do?" Brightcloud said evenly.

"I do damned well," Larrimore answered. He did not extend his hand to the inventor. *A boy. He's a mere boy. He can't have anything worthwhile to show us.*

"The others will be here in a minute," Ransom chattered. "Would you like to have Mr. Brightcloud give you a briefing about his invention before they . . ."

"No," Larrimore snapped. "He can tell me the same

time he tells the others."

Ransom looked back to the inventor, uncertainty twitching in his left eye. "Er . . . do you need to, um, warm up the equipment or anything like that?"

Brightcloud shook his head. "You probably want to let the security guard go."

"Oh! Oh, yes, surely."

Larrimore sank back in his chair and watched the two young men take their places down at the end of the table. Ransom whispered a few words to the guard, who then quietly left the conference room. The door didn't get a chance to close behind him before the other board members started coming in.

Horace Mann was the first. The financial vice president always arrived on the stroke for every meeting, even though he could barely walk anymore. White-haired and bent with age, Mann had refused retirement every year for the past ten years. And since he knew financial details that were best kept locked within his head, he stayed in power. *We'll have to carry him out someday*, Larrimore thought.

Arnold Hawthorn and Toshio Takahashi arrived together. Hawthorn, the company's sales director, was sleek, silver-haired and devilishly handsome. He claimed to be bisexual, but no one had ever seen him so much as smile at a woman. Takahashi wore his saffron monk's robe even to board meetings. The foreign sales people worshipped him, almost literally, and his kindness and Oriental patience were legendary. *Good for morale*, Larrimore mused. *And he keeps those young squirts from trying to claw their way up the executive ladder.*

Borden C. Blude, the production manager, came in next and immediately began chatting amiably with Takahashi. Blude was in his eighties, almost as old as Larrimore himself, and clearly senile. He hadn't had a new idea since Eisenhower had resigned from Columbia, Blude's alma mater. They didn't let him do anything around the office, but Casanova—the man who actually owned Larrimore, Swain & Tucker—kept him around as a sort of mascot.

Cassanova was his usual punctual self, exactly ten minutes late. He was wheeled in by his nurse-secretary-assistant, Ms. Kim Conroy, who was known as Lollipop around the office, but never within Casanova's hearing. A tall, ravishing redhead who claimed she could type two hundred words a minute, her only obvious talent was a set of well-developed pectoral muscles—undoubtedly an asset in pushing Casanova's wheelchair.

The absolute master of Larrimore, Swain & Tucker, Casanova had lost the use of his lower extremities through a childish ambition to emulate Evel Knievel. By *almost* clearing twenty schoolbusses, Casanova went from a motorcycle to a wheelchair in his fortieth year, and turned his restless energy from race courses to board rooms. He owned LS&T, all of it. He was the sole stockholder. He had purchased the stock from this very board of directors when, after two of Larrimore's negative decisions, they had failed to get in on both the pocket calculator and CB radio booms and the company was about to go broke. Casanova had never told them where he'd gotten his money, and they had never asked. He merely bought them all out, kept them

all in their jobs, and showed up ten minutes late for
board meetings, glowering at them all.

*The titans of industry*, Larrimore thought as his gaze
swept along the conference table. *Old men who should
have been sent off to a farm years ago, a silver-haired
fag, a Jap saint, a cripple and his pet, and*, turning his
gaze inward, *an impotent old arthritic*.

"Very well, we're all here," Larrimore said, with a
nod in Casanova's direction. "What do you have to tell
us, Mr. Brightcloud?"

Brightcloud launched into his description of the
therapeutic machine. Larrimore knew the story;
Ransom had outlined it for him a week earlier, after
Brightcloud's first demonstration of the device.

"Do you mean," Hawthorn interrupted, "that
this . . . this *machine* can make people feel good?"

Brightcloud nodded, his face serious. "It can alleviate
nervous and muscular symptoms. It can even trigger
beneficial changes in some internal organs."

"Now that's pretty hard to believe, fella," old Blude
said. "I've been in this business for a lotta years
and . . ."

Casanova overrode him. "If this machine really
works, how useful would it be to us? We're in business
to market new products, not set up toys in our
infirmary."

"It would be a low-volume, high-dollar product. You
would market it the same way IBM does computers."

Ransom, who usually kept quiet at board meetings,
said, "I'd hardly call that low volume."

"I mean you would probably want to lease the
devices, instead of selling them outright."

Larrimore grumbled, "What about the FDA? If this machine has biological effects . . ."

"We would be bound in honor to submit the device for their evaulation," Takahashi said.

"Not legally," Brightcloud said. "There has never been a clear legal ruling about devices, the way there is about foods and drugs. Even artificial hearts are passed on by an *ad hoc* committee of the National Institutes of Health, not the FDA."

"That's something," Casanova murmured.

"You're gonna make people feel better by shining some ray on them?" Blude demanded. "I just don't believe it."

Brightcloud allowed himself a tight smile. "The device does work, sir."

"What about side effects?" Casanova asked.

"Practically none," Brightcloud said. "We've searched very carefully for side effects, believe me. There are a couple of very minor ones that are not physiologically damaging at all."

"What are they?" Larrimore asked, seeing out of the corner of his eye that he had beaten Casanova to the question.

"Very minor things. Less than you would get from standing in the sun for ten minutes."

"Do you mean that you could get a tan from this thing?" Hawthorn asked.

"If you want to," Brightcloud said. "It will stimulate the melanin cells in the skin if you adjust the output frequency properly, but tanning is only a minor effect. It would be an extremely expensive sunlamp."

"It's a shame," Horace Mann wheezed, "that it can't

change black skins into white. Now that would be an invention!" He cackled to himself.

Ms. Conroy took a deep breath and asked, "Is the device selective in any way? Will it work better on one type of person than another?"

Brightcloud stood impassively for a moment, then answered, "We have tested it on five hundred subjects in the laboratory, and several hundred more in the field. There are no significant differences among the subjects that we have been able to find."

"Were these subjects volunteers?" Takahashi asked.

"Almost all of them."

"And you found no harmful after effects?"

"None whatsoever. Everyone we interviewed afterward reported feeling much better than they had previously. Including Mr. Ransom."

Larrimore stirred in his chair. "Ransom? You didn't tell me that you had exposed yourself to this machine's radiation!"

The most-junior executive looked apologetic. "I tried to, but you were too busy to listen."

Casanova glared at both of them. "All right," he said, to Brightcloud, "I want proof that the damned thing really works."

"Right!" Blude slapped the table with the palm of his hand.

"I can show you all my data," Brightcloud offered.

"No," Casanova snapped. "You have to demonstrate the thing. I don't think it can possibly work the way you claim it does."

"It does work," Brightcloud said tightly.

"Then let it work on me. Take away the pain I've got.

Do that, and you've got a sale."

With a single nod of his head, Brightcloud went back to the racks of electronics lining the rear wall of the conference room and touched one button. He turned back toward the table.

"I expected that you'd want a demonstration, so I preset the beam focus for the head of the table, Mr. Casanova. There's no need for any of you gentlemen to move. Or you either, Ms. Conroy."

Larrimore watched the stacks of gadgetry. Nothing was happening. No noise, no electrical hum, no blinking lights. Nothing. He turned to look at Casanova, who was also staring at the machine with a quizzical smirk on his face.

"There may be some residual radiation leaking off to the sidelobes of the main beam," Brightcloud told them. "But there's no need for you to worry. The only possible effects you'll feel will be rather pleasant."

Larrimore swiveled his head back and forth between the inventor and Casanova in his wheelchair. Suddenly he realized that he was moving his neck without the usual arthritic twinges.

"The side effects, which are very minor," Brightcloud was saying, "come from a low-level stimulation of the glandular systems. . ."

A warmth was spreading over his body. Larrimore felt a pleasurable glow and . . . Startled, he looked sharply at Casanova. The man was smiling!

"There is one noticeable effect that hits men more than women," Brightcloud was still explaining. "It might have some embarrassing results in certain social situations, but on the whole our male test subjects have found it very favorable."

Larrimore couldn't believe it! But it was there all right. For the first time in decades.

He looked toward the others along the table. Ransom seemed red-faced and was trying hard not to stare at Ms. Conroy. Takahashi, the self-professed saintly ascetic, was actively leering at her. Casanova was smiling up at her with tears in his eyes. Mann seemed about to faint, Blude was slack-jawed and sweating. Hawthorn was fingering Takahashi's saffron robe.

"All right!" Larrimore croaked. It took all his strength to say it. "We're convinced. We're convinced. But don't turn it off!"

Ms. Conroy began to edge back toward the door.

James Brightcloud flew from New York to Santa Fe that afternoon. His equipment stayed in the LS&T building, after being moved from the conference room to Casanova's private suite. Larrimore wrote a seven-figure check on the spot, which Brightcloud deposited at the Citibank branch in LaGuardia.

He changed planes in Chicago and Albuquerque, and rented a car in Santa Fe. He spent more than a day driving to Phoenix, and when he boarded a Western Airlines jet there, he had washed off the dark makeup he'd used in New York and donned a sandy-blond curly wig.

In Los Angeles, the name he used for his next plane ticket was Julio Hernandez, and both his hair and his luxurious mustache were jet black. When he registered at the Sheraton Waikiki, the name he gave was John Johnston, and the moustache had disappeared. For two days he surfed and drank and sailboated, getting tan again naturally.

On the third day, as he lay belly-down on the sand at the public beach a few blocks away from the hotel, Ms. Conroy spread her beach towel next to his and stretched out beside him. She was no longer wearing her red wig, nor her tinted contact lenses. Her short-cropped thick blonde hair and light eyes marked her as a native of a far-off cold and northern land.

She lay on her stomach and put on a pair of sunglasses. He leaned over and undid the strap of her bikini top.

"Thank you," she said in accentless English.

"Thank *you*," he replied. "The machine worked like a charm."

"Of course. They paid the full amount?"

"Yep. It's deposited."

"Good."

"How's Casanova?" he asked.

She laughed, a deep-throated sound that had menace as well as mirth in it. "He is reliving all his childhood fantasies. I told him I was exhausted and had to get away for a few days. He easily agreed and began phoning every available woman in New York. He should be hospitalized by now."

"Or dead."

She shrugged.

"I still don't see why we sold the machine to them. I mean, wouldn't it have made more sense to get one into the White House . . . or the Congress?"

"No," she said, with a shake of her head that sent a golden curl tumbling over her eyes. She brushed it aside impatiently. "In Russia, the Kremlin, yes. In China, even though the leaders in Peking are ascetic, we are having successes among the provincial leaders. China will break up eventually. Time is on our side."

"And in America?"

"The business leaders, of course. And as subtly as possible. Not by . . . how do you call it, 'the hard sell?' "

"Yeah."

"Well, not that way. Subtly. Quietly. Let the word leak out from one office to another. The business leaders control the American government. As the businessmen use the machine to find their lost potency, the politicians will learn of it and demand that they get machines just like it."

"I hope you're right," he said.

"Of course I am right. They will destroy themselves. It is inevitable. The result of capitalist decadence."

'italist decadence? What about the Kremlin? The machines have been in use there longer than anyplace, haven't they?"

"Yes. Of course. I'm sorry. I shouldn't have lapsed into obsolete Cold War ideology. It's my childhood training. Forgive me, please."

"Okay. But let's keep this straight. It's *us* against *them*."

"Yes. We are agreed. The young against the old."

kids off to war anymore."

She nodded and brushed at the curl again. "It seems so simple and obvious. Do you think it really will work?"until your people developed the machinery to take advantage of it there was nothing we could do. But we're on our way now, baby. All around the world.

We'll get those impotent old bastards so dependent on these machines that they'll be too busy to do anything else."

"While those of us who don't need the machines take over the world."

"Why not, baby?" He broke into a broad grin. "After all, those who can, do."

# Build Me a Mountain

*Here's Kinsman again, about twenty years downstream from The Lieutenant and the Folksinger, and a few years before his appearance at the beginning of my novel about him, MILLENNIUM.*

A s soon as he stepped through the accoustical screen at the apartment doorway, the noise hit him like a physical force. Chet Kinsman stood there a moment and watched them. *My battlefield*, he thought.

The room was jammed with guests making cocktail-party chatter. It was an old room, big, with a high, ornately paneled ceiling.

He recognized maybe one-tenth of the people. Over at the far end of the room, tall drink in his hand, head slightly bent to catch what some wrinkled matron was saying, stood the target for tonight: Congressman Neal McGrath, swing vote on the House Appropriations Committee.

"Chet, you did come after all!"

He turned to see Mary-Ellen McGrath approaching him, her hand extended in greeting.

"I hardly recognized you without your uniform," she said.

He smiled back at her. "I thought Air Force blue

would be a little conspicuous around here."

"Nonsense. And I wanted to see your new oak leaves. A major now."

*A captain on the Moon and a major in the Pentagon. Hazardous duty pay.*

"Come on, Chet. I'll show you where the bar is." She took his arm and towed him through the jabbering crowd.

Mary-Ellen was almost as tall as Kinsman. She had the strong, honest fact of a woman who can stand beside her husband in the face of anything from Washington cocktail parties to the tight infighting of rural Maine politics.

The bar dispenser hummed absent-mindedly to itself as it produced a heavy scotch and water. Kinsman took a stinging sip of it.

"I was worried you wouldn't come," Mary-Ellen said over the noise of the crowd. "You've been something of a hermit lately."

"Uh-huh."

"And I never expected you to show up by yourself. Chet Kinsman without a girl on his arm is . . . well, something new."

"I'm preparing for the priesthood."

"I'd almost believe it," she said, straight-faced. "There's something different about you since you've been on the Moon. You're quieter. . . ."

*I've been grounded.* Aloud, he said, "Creeping maturity. I'm a late achiever."

But she was serious, and as stubborn as her husband. "Don't try to kid around it. You've changed. You're not playing the dashing young astronaut any more."

"Who the hell is?"

A burly, balding man jarred into Kinsman from behind, sloshing half his drink out of its glass.

"Whoops, didn't get it on ya, did . . . oh, hell, Mrs. McGrath. Looks like I'm waterin' your rug."

"It's disposable," Mary-Ellen said. "Do you two know each other?" Tug Wynne. . . ."

"I've seen Major Kinsman on the Hill."

Chet said, "You're with Allnews Syndicate, aren't you?"

Nodding, Wynne replied, "Surprised to see you here, Major, after this morning's committee session."

Kinsman forced a grin. "I'm an old family friend. Mrs. McGrath and I went to college together."

"You think the congressman's gonna vote against the Moonbase appropriation?"

"Looks that way," Kinsman said.

Mary-Ellen kept silent.

"He sure gave your Colonel Murdock a hard time this morning. Mrs. McGrath, you shoulda seen your husband in action." Wynne chuckled wheezily.

Kinsman changed the subject. "Say, do you know Cy Calder . . . old guy, works for Allied News in California?"

"Only by legend," Wynne answered. "He died a couple months ago, y'know."

"No . . . I didn't know." Kinsman felt a brief pang deep inside the part of him that he kept frozen. He made himself ignore it.

"Yep. He musta been past eighty. Friend of yours?"

"Sort of. I knew him . . . well, a few years back."

Mary-Ellen said, "I'd better get to some of the other guests. There are several old friends of yours here tonight, Chet. Mix around, you'll find them."

With another rasping cackle, Wynne said, "Guess we *could* let somebody else get next to the bar."

Kinsman started to drift away, but Wynne followed beside him.

"Murdock send you over here to try to soften up McGrath?"

Pushing past a pair of arguing cigar smokers, Kinsman frowned. "I was invited to this party weeks ago. I told you. Mrs. McGrath and I are old friends."

"How do you get along with the congressman?"

"What's that supposed to mean?"

Wynne let his teeth show. "Well, from what I hear, you were quite a hell-raiser a few years back. How'd you and Mrs. McGrath get along in college together?"

*You cruddy old bastard.* "If you're so interested in Mrs. McGrath's college days, why don't you ask her? Or her husband? Get off my back."

Wynne shrugged and raised his glass in mock salute. "Yes sir, Major, sir."

Kinsman turned and started working his way toward the other end of the room. A grandfather clock chimed off in a corner, barely audible over the human noises and clacking of ice in glassware. *Eighteen hundred. Cold and Smitty ought to be halfway to Copernicus by now.*

And then he heard her. He didn't have to see her; he knew it was Diane. The same pure, haunting soprano; a voice straight out of a legend.

Once I had a sweetheart, and now I have none.
One I had a sweetheart, and now I have none.

He's gone and leave me, he's gone and leave me.
He's gone and leave me to sorrow and mourn.

Her voice stroked his memory and he felt all the old joys, all the old pain, as he pushed his way through the crowd.

Finally he saw her, sitting cross-legged on a sofa, guitar hiding her slim figure. The same ancient guitar: no amplifiers, no boosters. Her hair was still long and straight and black as space; her eyes even darker and deeper. The people were ringed around her, standing, sitting on the floor. They gave her the entire sofa to herself, like an altar that only the annointed could use. They watched her and listened, entranced by her voice. But she was somewhere else, living the song, seeing what it told of, until she strummed the final chord.

Then she looked straight at Kinsman. Not surprised, not even smiling, just a look that linked them as if the past five years had never been. Before either of them could say or do anything, the others broke into applause. Diane smiled and mouthed "Thank you."

"More, more!"

"Come on ,another one."

" 'Greensleeves.' "

Diane put the guitar down carefully beside her, uncoiled her long legs, and stood up. "Would later be okay?"

Kinsman grinned. He knew it would be later or nothing.

They muttered reluctant agreement and broke up the circle around her. Kinsman took the final few paces and stood before Diane.

"Good to see you again."

"Hello, Chet." She wasn't quite smiling.

"Here Diane, I brought you some punch." Kinsman turned to see a fleshy-faced young man with a droopy mustache and tousled brown hair, dressed in a violet suit, carrying two plastic cups of punch.

"Thank you, Larry. This is Chet Kinsman. Chet, meet Larry Rose."

"Kinsman?"

"I knew Chet in L.A. a few years back, when I was just getting started. You're still in the Air Force, aren't you, Chet?"

"Affirmative." *Play the role.*

Diane turned back to Larry. "Chet's an astronaut. He's been on the Moon."

"Oh. That must be where I heard the name. Weren't you involved in some sort of rescue? One of your people got stranded or something and you——"

"Yes." Kinsman cut him short. "It was blown up out of proportion by the news people."

They stood there for a moment, awkwardly silent while the party pulsated around them.

Diane said, "Mary-Ellen told me you might be here tonight. You and Neal are both working on something about the space program?"

"Something like that. Organized any more peace marches?"

She laughed. "Larry, did I ever tell you about the time we tried to get Chet to come out and join one of our demonstrations? In his uniform?"

Larry shook his head.

"Do you remember what you told me, Chet?"

"No. . . . I remember it was during the Brazilian crisis. You were planning to invade the U.C.L.A. library or something. I had flying duty that day."

*It was a perfect day for flying, breaking out of the coastal haze and standing, the jet on her tailpipe and ripping through the clouds until even the distant Sierras looked like nothing more than wrinkles. Then flat out over the Pacific at mach 5, the only sounds in your earphones from your own breathing and the faint, distant crackle of earthbound men giving orders to other men.*

"You told me," Diane said, "that you'd rather be flying patrol and making sure that nobody bombs us while we demosntrated for peace."

She was grinning at him. It was funny now; it hadn't been then.

"Yeah, I guess I did say that."

"How amusing," Larry said. "And what are you doing now? Protecting us from the Lithuanians? Or going to Mars?"

*You overstuffed fruit, you wouldn't even fit into a flight crewman's seat.* "I'm serving on a Pentagon assignment. My job is congressional liaison."

"Twisting congressmen's arms is what he means," came Neal McGrath's husky voice from behind him.

Kinsman turned.

"Hello, Chet, Diane . . . eh, Larry Rose, isn't it?"

"You have a good memory for names."

"Goes with the job." Neal McGrath topped Kinsman's six feet by an inch. He was red-haired and rugged-looking. His voice was soft, throaty. Somehow the natural expression of his face, in repose, was an introspective scowl. But he was smiling now. *His cocktail party smile,* thought Kinsman.

"Tug Wynne tells me I was pretty rough on your boss this morning." McGrath said to Kinsman. The smile turned a shade self-satisfied.

"Colonel Murdock lost a few pounds, and it wasn't all from the T.V. lights," Kinsman said.

"I was only trying to get him to give me a good reason for funneling money into a permanent Moonbase."

Kinsman answered, "He gave you about fifty reasons, Neal."

"None that hold up," McGrath said. "Not when we've got to find money to reclaim every major city in this country, plus fighting these damned interminable wars."

"And to check the population growth," Diane added.

*Here we go again.* Shrugging. Kinsman said, "Look, Neal, I'm not going to argue with you. We've been making one-shot missions to the Moon off and on for fifty years now. There's enough there to warrant a permanent base."

McGrath made a sour face. "A big, expensive base on the Moon."

"Makes sense," Kinsman slid in. "It makes sense on a straight cost-effectiveness basis. You've seen the numbers. Moonbase will save you billions of dollars in the long run."

"That's just like Mary-Ellen saves me money at department store sales. I can't afford to save that money. Not this year. The capital outlay is too high. To say nothing of the overruns."

"Now wait. . . ."

"Come on, Chet. There's never been a big program that's lived within its budget. No . . . Moonbase is going to have to wait, I'm afraid."

"We've already waited fifty years."

A crowd was gathering around them now, and McGrath automatically raised his voice a notch. "Our first priority has got to be for the cities. They've become jungles, unfit for sane human life. We've got to reclaim them, and save the people who're trapped in them before they all turn into savages."

*Damn, he's got a thick hide.* "Okay, but it doesn't have to be either/or. We can do both."

"Not while the war's on."

*Hold your temper; don't fire at the flag.* "The war's an awfully convenient excuse for postponing commitments. We've been in hot and cold wars since before you and I were born."

With the confident grin of a hunter who had cornered his quarry, McGrath asked, "Are you suggesting that we pull our troops out of South America? Or do you want to let our cities collapse completely?"

*Do you still beat your wife?* "All I'm suggesting," Kinsman said with deliberate calm, "is that we shouldn't postpone building Moonbase any longer. We've got the technology—we know how to do it. It's either build a permanent base on the Moon, or stop the lunar exploration program altogether. If we fail to build Moonbase, your budget-cutting friends will throttle down the whole manned space program to zero within a few years."

Still smiling, McGrath said, "I've heard all that from your Colonel Murdock."

There was a curious look in Diane's dark eyes.

"Chet . . . why do you want to have a Moonbase built?"

"Why? Because . . . I was just telling you——"

She shook her head. "No, I don't mean the official reasons, I mean why do *you* dig the idea?"

"We need it. The space program needs it."

"No," she said patiently. "*You.* Why are you for it? What's in it for you?"

"What do you mean?" Kinsman asked.

"What makes you tick, man? What turns you on? Is it a Moonbase? What moves you, Chet?"

*They were all watching him, the whole crowd, their faces blank or smirking or inquisitive. Floating weightless, standing on nothing and looking at the overpowering beauty of Earth—rich, brilliant, full, shining against the black emptiness. Knowing that people down there are killing each other, teaching their children to kill, your eyes filling with tears at the beauty and sadness of it. How could they see it? How could they understand?*

"What moves you, Chet?" Diane asked again.

He made himself grin. "Well, for one thing, the Pentagon cafeteria coffee."

Everybody laughed. But she wouldn't let him off the hook. "No—get serious. This is important. What turns you on?"

*Wouldn't understand anyway.* "You mean aside from the obvious things, like girls?"

She nodded gravely.

"Hmmm. I don't know. It's kind of hard to answer. Flying. I guess. Getting out on your own responsibility, away from committees and chains of command."

"There's got to be more to it than that," Diane insisted.

"Well . . . have you ever been out on the desert at an Israeli outpost, dancing all night by firelight because at dawn there's going to be an attack and you don't want to waste a minute of life?"

There was a heartbeat's span of silence. Then one of the women asked in a near-whisper, 'When . . . were you. . . .''

Kinsman said, "Oh, I've never been there. But isn't it a romantic picture?"

They all broke into laughter. *That burst the bubble.* The crowd began to dissolve, breaking up into smaller groups, dozens of private conversations filling the silence that had briefly held them.

"You cheated," Diane said.

"Maybe I did."

"Don't you have anything except icewater in your veins?"

He shrugged. "If you prick us, do we not bleed?"

"Don't take dirty."

He took her by the arm and headed for the big glass doors at the far end of the room. "Come on, we've got a lot of catching up to do. I've bought all your tapes."

"And I've been watching your name on the news."

"Don't believe most of it."

He pushed the door open and they stepped out onto the balcony. Shatterproof plastic enclosed the balcony and shielded them from the humid, hazy Washington air—and anything that might be thrown or shot from the street far below. The air conditioning kept the balcony pleasantly cool.

"Sunset," Diane said, looking out toward the slice of sky that was visible between the two apartment buildings across the avenue. "Loveliest time of the day."

"Loneliest time, too."

She turned to him, her eyes, showing genuine surprise.

"Lonely? You? I didn't know you had any weaknesses like that."

"I've got a few, hidden away here and there."

"Why do you hide them?"

"Because nobody gives a damn about them, one way or the other." Before Diane could reply, he said, "I sound sorry for myself, don't I?"

"Well. . . ."

"Who's this Larry character?"

"He's a very nice guy," she said firmly. "And a good musician. And he doesn't go whizzing off into the wild blue yonder . . . or space is black, isn't it?"

He nodded. "I don't go whizzing any more, either. I've been grounded."

She blinked at him. "What does that mean?"

"Grounded," Kinsman repeated. "Deballed. No longer qualified for flight duty. No orbital missions. No lunar missions. They won't even let me fly a plane any more. Got some shavetail to jockey me around. I work at a desk."

"But . . . why?"

"It's a long dirty story. Officially, I'm too valuable to risk or something like that."

"Chet, I'm so sorry . . . flying meant so much to you, I know." She stepped into his arms and he kissed her.

"Let's get out of here, Diane. Let's go someplace safe

and watch the Moon come up and I'll tell you all the legends about your namesake."

"Same old smooth talker."

"No, not any more. I haven't even touched a girl since . . . well, not for a long time."

"I can't leave the party, Chet. They're expecting me to sing."

"Screw them."

"All of them?"

"Don't talk dirty."

She laughed, but shook her head. "Really, Chet. Not now."

"Then let me take you home afterward."

"I'm staying here tonight."

There were several things he wanted to say, but he checked himself.

"Chet, please don't rush me. It's been a long time."

*It sure as hell has.*

They went back into the party and separated. Kinsman drifted through the crowd, making meaningless chatter with strangers and old friends alike, drink in one hand, occasionally nibbling on a canape about the size and consistency of spacecraft food. But his mind was replaying, over and over again, the last time he had seen Diane.

*Five years ago.*

*Soaring across the California countryside, riding the updrafts along the hillsides and playing hide-and-seek with the friendly chaste-white cumuli, the only sound the rush of air across the glass bubble an inch over your head, your guts held tight as you sweep and bank and then soar up, up past the clouds and then you bank way* over so you're hanging by the shoulder harness and looking straight down into the green citrus groves below. Diane sitting in the front seat, so all you can see of her is the back of her plastic safety helmet. But you can hear her gasp.

"Like it?"

"It's wild . . . gorgeous!"

And then back on the ground. Back in reality.

"Chet, I've got to go to this meeting. Can't you come along with me?"

"No. Got to report for duty."

Just like that. An hour of sharing his world, and then gone. The last he had seen of her. Until tonight.

The crowd had thinned out considerably. People were leaving. McGrath was at the hallway door, making the customary noises of farewell. Kinsman spotted Diane sitting alone on the sofa, tucked against a corner of it, as if for protection.

He went over and sat down beside her. "I've got news for you."

"Oh? What?"

"An answer to your question. About what turns me on. I've been thinking about it all through the party and I've formed a definite opinion."

She turned to face him, leaning an arm on the sofa's back. "So what is it?"

"You do. You turn me on."

She didn't look surprised. "Do I?"

Nodding. "Yep. After five years, you still do."

Diane said, "Chet, haven't you learned anything? We're in two entirely different worlds. You want to go adventuring."

"And you want to join demonstrations and sing to the kids about how lousy the world is."

"I'm trying to make the world better!" Her face looked so damned intent.

"And I'm trying to start a new world."

She shook her head. "We never did see eye to eye on anything."

"Except in bed."

That stopped her, but only for a moment. "That's not enough. Not for me. It wasn't then and it isn't now."

He didn't answer.

"Chet . . . why'd they ground you? What's it all about?"

A hot spark of electricity flashed through his gut. *Careful!* "I told you, it's a long story. I'm a valuable public relations tool for Colonel Murdock. You know, a veteran of lunar exploration. Heroic rescuer of an injured teammate. All that crap. So my address is the Pentagon. Level three, ring D, corridor F, room——"

"Whether you like it or not."

"Yes."

"Why don't you quit?"

"And do what? To dig I am not able, to beg I am too proud."

Diane looked at him quizzically. They had both run out of stock answers.

"So there it is," Kinsman said, getting up from the sofa. "Right where we left it five years ago."

Mary-Ellen came over to them. "Don't leave, Chet. We're getting rid of the last of the guests, then we're going to have a little supper. Stay around. Neal wants to talk with you."

"Okay. Fine." *That's what I'm here for.*

"Can I fix you another drink?" Mary-Ellen asked.

"Let me fix you one."

"No, no more for me, thanks."

He looked down at Diane. "Still hooked on *tigers*?"

She smiled. "I haven't had one in years. . . . Yes, I'd like a *tiger.*"

By the time he came back from the bar with the two smoke-yellow drinks in his hands, the big living room was empty of guests. Diane and Mary-Ellen were sitting on the sofa together. Only when they were this close could you see that they really were sisters. Kinsman heard McGrath out in the hallway, laughingly bidding someone good night.

"Like a family reunion," Kinsman said as he sat on a plush chair facing the sofa.

"You're still here, Chet," McGrath called from the hall archway. "Good. I've got a bone to pick with you, old buddy."

As the congressman crossed to the bar, Mary-Ellen said, "Maybe Diane and I ought to hide out in the kitchen. We can see to supper."

"Not me," Diane said, "I want to be in on this."

Kinsman grinned at her.

McGrath came up and sat beside his wife. The three of them—husband, wife, sister—faced Kinsman. *Like the beginning of a shotgun wedding.*

"Listen, Chet," McGrath began, his voice huskier than usual from too much drinking and smoking. "I don't like the idea of Murdock sending you over here to try to soften me up. Just because you're an old friend doesn't give you——"

"Hold on," Kinsman said. "I was invited here two weeks ago. And I came because I wanted to."

"Murdock knew these hearings were coming up this week and next. Don't deny it."

"I'm not denying a damned thing. Murdock can do what he wants. I came here because I wanted to. If it fits Murdock's grand scheme, so what?"

McGrath reached into his jacket pocket for a cigaret. "I just don't like having space cadets from the Pentagon spouting Air Force propaganda at my parties. Especially when they're old friends. I don't like it."

"What if the old friend happens to believe that the propaganda is right and you're wrong?"

"Oh, come on now, Chet. . . ."

"Look, Neal, on this Moonbase business, you're wrong. Moonbase is essential, no matter what you think of it."

"It's another boondoggle——"

"The hell it is! We either build Moonbase or we stop exploring the Moon altogether. It's one or the other."

McGrath took a deep, calming drag on his cigaret. Patiently, he said, "There's too much to do here on Earth for me to vote for a nickel on Moonbase. Let alone the billions of dollars. . . ."

"The money is chickenfeed. We spend ten times that amount on new cars each year. A penny tax on cigarets will pay for Moonbase."

McGrath involuntarily glanced at the joint in his hand. Scowling, he answered, "We need all the money we can raise to rebuild the cities. We're going under, the cities are sinking into jungles——"

"Who's spouting the party line now?" Kinsman shot

back. "Everybody knows about the poor and the cities. And the population overload. And the whole damned social structure. That's a damned safe hobbyhorse to ride in Congress. What we need is somebody with guts enough to stand up for spending two percent of all that money on the future."

"Are you accusing me——"

"I'm saying you're hiding in the crowd, Neal. I don't disagree with the crowd; they're right about the cities and the poor. But there's a helluva lot more to life than that."

Diane cut in. "Chet, what about Moonbase? What good is it? Who will it help? Will it make jobs for the city kids? Will it build schools?"

He stared at her for a long moment. "No," he said at last. "It won't do any of those things. But it won't prevent them from being done, either."

"Then why should we do it?" Diane asked. "For your entertainment? To earn your Colonel Murdock a promotion or something? Why? What's in it for us?"

*Standing on the rim of a giant crater, looking down at the tired terraces of rock worn smooth by five eons of meteoric erosion. The flat pitted plain at the base of the slope. The horizon, sharp and clear, close enough to make you think. And the stars beyond. The silence and the emptiness. The freedom. The peace.*

"There's probably nothing in it for you. Maybe for your kids. Maybe for those kids in the cities. I don't know. But there's something in it for me. The only way I'll ever get to the Moon again is to push Moonbase through Congress. Otherwise I'm permanently grounded."

"What?"

Diane said, "Your man Murdock won't let you. . . ."

Kinsman waved them quiet. "Officially, I'm grounded. Officially, there are medical and emotional reasons. That's on the record and there's no way to take it off. Unless there's a permanent base on the Moon, a place where a nonpilot passenger can go, then the only people on the Moon will be flight-rated astronauts. So I need Moonbase; I need it. Myself. For purely personal, selfish reasons."

"Being on the Moon means that much to you?" Diane asked.

Kinsman nodded.

"I don't get it," McGrath said. "What's so damned attractive about the Moon?"

"What was attractive about the great American desert?" Kinsman shot back. "Or the poles? Or the Marianas Deep? How the hell should I know? But a while ago you were all asking what turns me on. This does. Being out there, on your own, away from all the sickness and bullshit of this world—that's what I want. That's what I need."

Mary-Ellen shook her head. "But it's so desolate out there . . . foresaken. . . ."

"Have you been there? Have you watched the Earth rise? Or planted footprints where no man has ever been before? Have you ever been anywhere in your life where you really challenged nature? Where you were really on your own?"

"And you still want to go back?" McGrath had a slight grin on his face.

"Damned right. Sitting around here is like being in

jail. . . . Know what they call us at the Pentagon?
Luniks. Most of the brass think we're nuts. But they use
us, just like Murdock is using me. Maybe we *are* crazy.
But I'm going to get back there if I have to build a
mountian, starting at my desk, and climb up hand over
hand."

"But why, Chet?" Diane asked, suddenly intent.
"*Why* is it so important to you? Is it the adventure of
it?"

"I told you—it's the freedom. There are no rule books
up there; you're on your own. You work with people on
the basis of their abilities, not their rank. It's—it's just so
completely different up there that I can't really describe
it. I know we live in a canned environment, physically.
If an air hose splits or a pump malfunctions, you could
die in seconds. But in spite of that—maybe *because* of
that—you're free emotionally. It's you against the
universe, you and your friends, your brothers. There's
nothing like it here on Earth."

"Freedom," Diane echoed.

"On the Moon," McGrath said flatly.

Kinsman nodded.

Staring straight at him, Diane said slowly. "What
you're saying, Chet, is that a new society can be built on
the Moon . . . a society completely different from
anything here on Earth."

Kinsman blinked. "Did I say that?"

"Yes, you did."

He shrugged. "Well, if we establish a permanent
settlement, I guess we'll have to work out some sort of
social structure."

"Would you take the responsibility for setting up that

social structure?" Diane asked. "Would you shoulder
the job of making certain that all the nonsense of Earth
is left behind? Would you do the job *right*?"

For a moment, Kinsman didn't know what to answer.
Then he said, "I would try."

"You'd take that responsibility?" Diane asked again.

Nodding. "Damned right."

Mary-Ellen looked totally unconvinced. "But who
would be willing to live on the Moon? Who would want
to?"

"I would," Diane said.

They all turned to look at her. Mary-Ellen shocked,
McGrath curious.

"Would you?" Kinsman asked. "Really?"

Very seriously, she replied, "If you're going to build a
new world, how could I stay away?"

Kinsman felt himself relax for the first time all
evening. "Well, I'll be damned. . . . If you can see
it. . . ." He started to laugh.

"What's funny?" McGrath asked.

"I've won a convert, Neal. If Diane can see what it's
all about, then we've got it made. The idea of a
Moonbase, of a permanent settlement on the Moon—if it
gets across to Diane, then the kids will see it, too."

"There are no kids in Congress."

Kinsman shrugged. "That's okay. Congress'll come
around sooner or later. Maybe not this year, maybe not
until after Murdock retires. But we'll get it. There's
going to be a permanent settlement on the Moon. In
time for me to get there."

"Chet," Diane said, "it won't be fun. It's going to be a
lot of work."

"I know. But it'll be worth the work."

They sat there, eye to eye, grinning at each other.

McGrath slouched back in the sofa. "I guess I'm simply too old to appreciate all this. I don't see how——"

"Neal," Kinsman said, "someday the history books will devote a chapter to the creation of man's first extraterrestrial society. Your name will be in there as one of the men who opposed it—or one of the leaders who helped create it. Which do you want to be put down beside your name?"

"You're a cunning bastard," McGrath mumbled.

"And don't you forget it." Kinsman stood up, stretched, then reached a hand out for Diane. "Come on, lunik, let's take a walk. There's a full Moon out tonight. In a couple years I'll show you what a full Earth looks like."

# The System

*This story was written while I was connected with a program to develop an artificial heart. Even at that time, there were committees sitting to decide who would get to use the rare and expensive kidney dialysis machines and who would die of renal failure.*

*Our artificial heart research eventually produced a temporary implantable pump that's saved hundreds of lives. But the device had to be developed, tested, and put into clinical use outside the existing Government R&D System.*

"Not just research," Gorman said, rocking smugly in his swivel chair, "*Organized* research."

Hopler, the cost-time analyst, nodded agreement.

"Organized," Gorman continued, "and carefully controlled—from above. The System—that's what gets results. Give the scientists their way and they'll spend you deaf, dumb, and blind on butterfly sex-ways or sub-subatomic particles. Damned nonsense."

Sitting on the front inch of the visitor's chair, Hopler asked meekly, "I'm afraid I don't see what this has to do . . ."

"With the analysis you turned in?" Gorman glanced at the ponderous file that was resting on a corner of his desk. "No, I suppose you don't know. You just chew through the numbers, don't you? Names, people, ideas . . . they don't enter into your work."

With an uncomfortable shrug, Hopler replied, "My job is economic analysis. The System shouldn't be biased by personalities . . ."

"Of course not."

"But now that it's over, I would like to know . . . I mean, there've been rumors going through the Bureau."

"About the cure? They're true. The cure works. I don't know the details of it," Gorman said, waving a chubby hand. "Something to do with repressor molecules. Cancerous cells lack 'em. So the biochemists we've been supporting have found out how to attach repressors to the cancer cells. Stops 'em from growing. Controls the cancer. Cures the patient. Simple . . . now that we can do it."

"It . . . it's almost miraculous."

Gorman frowned. "What's miraculous about it? Why do people always connect good things with miracles? Why don't you think of cancer as a miracle, a black miracle?"

Hopler fluttered his hands as he fumbled for a reply.

"Never mind," Gorman snapped. "This analysis of yours. Shows the cure can be implemented on a nationwide basis. Not too expensive. Not too demanding of trained personnel that we don't have."

"I believe the cure could even be put into worldwide effect," Hopler said.

"The hell it can be!"

"What? I don't understand. My analysis . . ."

"Your analysis was one of many. The System has to

look at all sides of the picture. That's how we beat heart disease, and stroke, and even highway deaths."

"And now cancer."

"No. Not cancer. Cancer stays. Demographic analysis knocked out all thoughts of using the cure. There aren't any other major killers around anymore. Stop cancer and we swamp ourselves with people. So the cure gets shelved."

For a stunned instant, Hopler was silent. Then, "But . . . I *need* the cure!"

Gorman nodded grimly. "So will I. The System predicts it."

# Orion

*This story was the result of being invited to turn out a tale with the "sense of wonder" tradition of the Thirties, as well as the technical accuracies of the Seventies. There will be sequels.*

**I** am not a superman.

I do have abilities that are far beyond those of any normal man's, but I am just as human and mortal as anyone on Earth.

The core of my abilities is apparently due to the structure of my nervous system. I am in complete conscious control of my entire body. I can direct my will along the chain of synapses instantly to make any part of my body do exactly what I wish it to.

Last year I learned to play the piano in two hours. My teacher, a mild, gray little man, absolutely refused to believe that I had never touched a keyboard before that day. Earlier this year I stunned an akido master by learning everything he had absorbed in a lifetime of work in less than a week. He tried to be humble and polite, but it was clear to me that he was furious with me and ashamed of himself for it. I left his class.

My powers are growing. I have always been able to control my heart rate and breathing. I thought everyone could, until I began reading about yogas and their "mystical" abilities. For me, their tricks have been literally child's play.

Four months ago I found myself sitting in a midtown Manhattan restaurant. I tend to be a solitary man, and usually take my lunch hour late enough to avoid the nosiy crowds. It was nearly 4:00 P.M. and the rsetaurant was almsot empty. A few couples sitting at scattered tables, speaking in hushed tones. Waiters standing back near the kitchen. One customer sitting at the bar—a strikingly handsome, gold-maned man. Even though he was wearing a conservatively dark business suit, he looked more like a movie idol or an ancient Greek god than a Manhattan executive who was getting an early start on the cocktail hour. There was an aura about him; the air almost seemed to glow where he was sitting.

Another man entered the restaurant and sat at the opposite end of the bar. If the first one was a golden angel, this second one had the presence of a dark netherworld figure. His face was heavy and thick; his muscular body bulged his clothing, his hair, his eyes, even his voice seemed dark and heavy with anger.

I was sitting not far from the bar, finishing my coffee and starting to look for my waiter to ask for the check. That's what saved me.

At the rear of the restaurant, a bald little man in a black coat popped out of the kitchen's swinging door momentarily and threw a gray egg-shaped object up toward the bar. A hand grenade.

I saw it all as if it were happening in slow motion. I realize now that my reflexes were suddenly operating at an incredibly fast rate. Maybe it was adrenaline. Every nerve in my body went into overdrive.

I could see the man ducking back inside the kitchen.
The waiters stiffening with surprise. The couples at the
other tables still talking, not realizing that death was a
second or two away. The bartender stared at the
grenade as it sailed the length of the restaurant and
thunked on the floor about five feet from my table.

The two men at the bar were as fast as I was. The
golden one dived over the bar like a trained acrobat.
The dark one merely ducked down behind it. I was
trying to shout a warning as I slid off my chair to the
floor, pulling the table over to make a shield for myself.

The clatter of the dishes hitting the floor was lost in
the roar of the explosion. The room flashed and
thundered. It shook. Then . . . smoke, screams, the heat
of flames.

I got to my feet, unharmed. The table was splintered
and the wall behind me was shredded by flying
shrapnel. Smoke was filling the room. Through it I
could see people mangled and bleeding, laying on the
floor, slumped against the walls.

I had carried two of them out to the sidewalk and was
going in for a third by the time the police, firemen, and
ambulances arrived. Eight people were already dead.

"Goddam IRA," a plainclothesman grumbled.

"Cheez—they tossin' bombs around here now?"

"Maybe it was the PR's," another cop suggested.

They questioned me for a few minutes, then turned
me over to the medics for a quick checkup.

"You're lucky, mister," said the white-jacketed
doctor. "Didn't even get your hair mussed."

I hardly paid him any attention. The important thing

to me was that there was no sign of either the golden man or the dark one. They had disappeared. The bartender had been decapitated by the blast. His two customers had vanished.

Once the police let me leave, I pushed through the crowd that had been drawn by the excitement and walked back to my office. By the time I reached the corner of the street there were only the usual throngs of a late Manhattan afternoon.

As evening fell, I was still sitting in my office, wondering why the grenade was thrown and how I had escaped being killed by it. Which led me to wondering why I have such abilities, and whether those two strangers at the bar have the same powers. Which, in turn, led me to wonder who I really am and where I came from.

The externals are easy. My name is Gilbert P. O'Ryan. I realized that my name had always made me feel uneasy, as though it wasn't the proper name for me, not my real name at all. Gil O'Ryan. It didn't feel right, somehow. I am an assistant to the director of marketing for Continental Electronics Corporation, an international company that manufactures lasers and other high-technology equipment. My personnel folder says that I'm thirty-six, but I've always felt more like thirty . . .

Always?

I tried again to remember back to my thirtieth birthday, and found that I still couldn't picture it. My thirty-third birthday was clear in my mind: that was the night I spent with Adrienna, the boss's private secretary. But beyond that my memory was a blank. I

frowned in concentration so hard that my jaw muscles
started to ache, but still I couldn't remember anything
more than three years back! No knowledge of who my
parents were. No memories of childhood. I didn't even
have any friends outside the small circle of
acquaintances here at the office. Cold sweat broke out
all over my body.

Who am I? *Why* am I?

I sat in my office for hours, as evening deepened into
darkness, alone in my quiet, climate controlled, chrome-
and-leather office, behind my sleek Brazilian mahogany
desk, and stared at my own personnel file. There wasn't
much in it. Names. Dates. Schools. None of them made
any sense to me.

I looked up at the polished chrome mirror across the
office. Dark hair, undistinguished face with a slight
Mediterranean cast to it (but why O'Ryan, then?),
medium build, light-colored jacket and slacks. The
personnel file said I had been a good athlete at school. I
still looked solid and trim. But totally "average." I
could fade into a crowd and become invisible quite
easily.

*Who am I?* I couldn't escape the feeling that I had
been put here, placed in this life, by some power or
agency that was beyond my knowledge and experience.

I had to find out who, or what, had put me here. And
I realized, with the total certainty of truly inbuilt
instinct, that to try to discover my origins would mean
mortal danger for me. Death. That grenade was meant
for me and no one else.

But I couldn't turn back. I had to find those two other
men—the angel and the dark spirit. One of them, or

perhaps both of them, knew the what and why of O'Ryan.

How do you find two individual men in a city of eight million? And what if all my certainties were wrong, and I was merely an amnesia victim, a paranoid, a madman building fantasies in his mind?

The answers to both questions were the same. It took me a sleepless night of thinking to find the single answer I needed, but I have never been much of a sleeper. An hour or two has always been sufficient for me; often I have gone several nights in a row with nothing but an occasional catnap. My fellow workers often complained, jokingly, about the amount of work I take home with me. Sometimes the jokes were bitter.

The morning after the restaurant bombing, I strode into my office exactly at nine, just as usual. I had to brush aside questions from my secretary and several of my co-workers, who had either seen the bombing on the evening TV news or were brandishing morning newspapers with my photo on the front page.

I sat at my desk and immediately called the company physician. I asked him to recommend a good psychiatrist. On the phone's small, flickering videoscreen, the doctor looked slightly alarmed, slightly puzzled.

"Is this about the blast you almost got caught in yesterday?" he asked. He had read the papers, too.

"Yes," I said. "I'm . . . feeling a little shaky about it." Which was no lie.

He peered at me through his bifocals. "Shaky? You? The imperturbable Mr. O'Ryan?"

I said nothing.

"Hmmm. Well, I suppose having a hand grenade go off in your soup would shake up anybody."

He gave me the name of a psychiatrist. I called the man and made an appointment for that afternoon. He tried to put me off, but I used the company's name and our doctor's, and told him that I only wanted a brief, preliminary talk with him.

The talk was quite brief. I outlined my lack of memory, and he quickly referred me to another psychiatrist, a woman who specialized in such problems.

It took many weeks, going from one recommended psychiatrist to another, but I finally reached the one I wanted.

He was the only specialist who agreed to see me at once, without argument, the day I phoned. His phone had no videoscreen, but I didn't need one. I knew what he looked like.

"My schedule is very full," his rich tenor voice said, "but if you could drop by around five-thirty or six o'clock, my office ought to be empty by then."

"Thank you, Doctor, I will."

His office was indeed empty. I opened the door to the anteroom of his suite, and no one was there. It was already getting dark outside, but there were no lights on in the anteroom. Gloomy and dark. Old-fashioned wood furniture. Bookshelves lining the walls. No nurse, no receptionist. No one.

A short hallway led back from the anteroom, and a glow of light came from its end. I followed the light to a partially closed heavy wooden door.

"Doctor . . . ?" I didn't bother saying the name that was on the door. I knew it wasn't the true name of the man inside the office.

"Mr. O'Ryan," that same warm tenor voice called. "Come right in."

It was the golden man from the restaurant. The office was small and oppressively overfurnished with two couches, a massive desk, heavy window drapes, thick carpet. He sat behind the desk, smiling expectantly at me. The only light was from a small floor lamp in one corner of the room. But the man himself seemed to glow, to radiate golden light energy.

He was wearing a simple open-neck shirt. No jacket. He was broad-shouldered, handsome; he looked utterly capable of dealing with anything. His hands were clasped firmly together on the desktop. Instead of casting a shadow, they seemed to make the desktop slightly brighter.

"Sit down, Mr. O'Ryan," he said calmly.

I sat in the leather armchair that was in front of the desk.

"You said you have a problem with your memory."

"You know what my problem is," I told him. "Let's not waste time."

He arched an eyebrow and smiled more broadly.

"This isn't your office. It's nothing like you. So since you know my name, and yours isn't the one stencilled on the door, who are you?"

"Very businesslike, O'Ryan." He leaned back in the swivel chair. "You may call me Ormazd. Names don't really mean that much, you understand, but you may use that one for me."

"Ormazd."

"Yes. And now I will tell you something about your own name. You have been misuing it. Your name is Orion . . . as in the constellation of stars. Orion."

"The Hunter."

"Very good! You *do* understand. Orion the Hunter. That is your name and your mission."

"Tell me more," I said.

"There is no need to," he countered. "You already know. But much of the information stored in your brain remains blocked from your active memory."

"Why is that?"

His face grew serious, as if he were pondering, trying to make a decision. "There is much that I cannot tell you. Not yet. You were sent here on a hunting mission. Your task is to find the Dark One . . . Ahriman.

"The one who was in the restaurant with you?"

"Exactly. Ahriman."

"Why? Who sent me here? From where?"

He sat up straighter in his chair, and something of his self-assured smile returned to his lips. "Why? To save the human race from destruction. Who sent you here? Your own people. From where? From about fifty thousand years in the future."

I should have been shocked, or surprised, or at least skeptical. Instead, I heard myself saying, "My own people. And they live fifty thousand years in the future."

Ormazd nodded gravely. "That is your time. You have been sent backward in time to this so- called twentieth century."

"To save the human race from destruction."

"Yes. By finding Ahriman, the Dark One."

"And once I find him?"

For the first time, he looked surprised. "Why, you must kill him, of course."

I shook my head. "No."

"You don't believe what I have told you?"

I wished I could truthfully say that I didn't. But somehow I knew that he was speaking the truth.

"I believe it. But I don't understand it. Why can't I remember any of this? Why . . ."

"Temporal shock, perhaps," he interrupted. "Or maybe Ahriman has already reached your mind and blocked its capacities. Do you have any idea of what you can *do*?"

"Some," I said.

"Do you know the capacities of your mind? The training that you've had? Your ability to use each hemisphere of your brain independently?"

"What?"

"Are you right-handed or left-handed?"

That took me off-guard. "I've always been . . . both."

"You can write with either hand? Throw a ball with either hand, play a guitar either way?"

I nodded.

"You can also use both sides of your brain independently of each other," he said. "For example, you could run a computer with one hand and paint a landscape with the other. Simultaneously."

That sounded ridiculous. "So I could get a job in a freak circus, is that it?"

He smiled again. "Far more than that, Orion. Far more."

"What about this Ahriman?" I demanded. "What danger does he pose to the human race?"

"He seeks to destroy the entire race. He would scour the Earth clean of human life, if we allowed him to."

Strangely, my mind was accepting all this and working at it very logically. "But . . . if I actually came here from fifty thousand years in the future, that means that the human race still exists at that time. Which means that the human race was not destroyed here in the twentieth century."

"Precisely," Ormazd said. "It was not destroyed because you saved it."

"But if I fail to?"

He stared at me for a long moment, and his aura seemed to glow brighter. He radiated light, like a miniature star. "You cannot fail to. *It has already happened.* There remains nothing for you to do but to play out your part."

"I can refuse. I can turn my back on all of this nonsense."

"You won't!" he snapped.

"How do you know?"

The light around him seemed to pulse, as if in anger. "As I told you . . . it has already happened. You have found Ahriman. You have saved the human race. It is inescapable! All that you need to do in this time era is to play out your part."

"But if I refuse?"

"That is unthinkable."

"If I refuse?" I insisted.

He glittered like a billion fireflies. His face became grim. "If you do not play out your predestined role . . . if you do not stop Ahriman . . . the very fabric of time itself will be shattered. The human race will die.

All of time will be shifted to a different track, a different continuum. Perhaps the entire planet Earth will be dissolved. This whole universe of space/time could disappear—vanish—as though it had never existed."

It had the ring of truth in it.

"And if I do cooperate?"

"You will find Ahriman. You will save the human race from destruction. The time continuum will remain on its present track. The universe will continue."

"I will kill Ahriman, then?"

He hesitated a long, long time before answering. "No," he said slowly. "You will stop him. But . . . he will kill you."

"That has also already happened?"

"Yes."

Suddenly I stood bolt upright, leaned across the desk, and reached for Ormazd's arm. My hand went right through his shimmering, gleaming image.

"Fool!" he snapped. And he faded into nothingness.

I was alone in the psychiatrist's office. I had seen holographic projections before, but never one that looked so convincingly solid and real. It was the scintillations that gave it away. But even though I searched that office until dawn, I could find no lasers or other projection equipment of any kind. Nothing that could produce a hologram.

It was a wisp of memory that put me on Ahriman's trail.

By the time I returned to my own dark and quiet apartment that dawning morning, I had remembered (remembered!) the origin of the names the golden man had used: Ormazd, the god of light and truth; Ahriman, the god of darkness and death. They were from the ancient religion of Persia, Zoroastrianism, founded by the man the ancient Greeks called Zarathustra.

So the Golden One considered himself a god of light and goodness. Was he a time traveler? Obviously so. Was he indeed Ormazd? Did he appear to Zarathustra long eons ago in Persia? Was he struggling against Ahriman even then? Of course. Then and now, future and past, all are the same in time.

The memory that started my hunt for Ahriman was a different one, however. I sat in my apartment and watched the dawn slowly brighten the city, thinking back over every scrap of memory I could coax from my mind.

And at last it came. I knew why I had been placed in this time era, why I had come to this particular company and this exact job.

I closed my eyes and recalled Tom Dempsey's long, serious, hound-dog face. It had been at the office Christmas party last year that he had told me, a bit drunkenly, "Th' lasers, man. Those goddam big-ass ol' lasers. Most important thing th' company's doing. Most important thing goin' on in the' whole wide world!"

The lasers for the thermonuclear fusion reactor. The lasers that would power a man-made sun, which in turn would provide the permanent answer to all of the human race's energy needs. The god of light made real in a world of science and technology. Where else would the Dark One strike?

It took me nearly a week to convince my superiors that I should be assigned to the last project. Continental

Electronics was producing the lasers for the world's first
CTR—Controlled Thermonuclear Reactor. By the end
of the week I was on a company plane bound for Ann
Arbor, Michigan, where the fusion reactor and its
associated power plan thad been built. Tom Dempsey
was sitting beside me as we watched the early winter
clouds forming along the shore of Lake Erie, some thirty
thousand feet below our speeding jet.

Tom was grinning happily at me.

"First time I've seen you really take an interest in this
fusion project. I always thought you couldn't care less
about this work."

"You convinced me of its importance," I said, not
untruthfully.

"It *is* damn important," he said, unconsciously
playing with his seat belt as he spoke. Tom was the kind
of engineer who kept everything neat, polished, in its
place. His hands were never still.

"The fusion reactor is ready for its first test?" I led
him on.

"Yep." He nodded emphatically. "You put in
deuterium, which you get from ordinary water, zap it
with our lasers, and out comes mucho *power*.
Megawatts of power, man. More power in a bucket of
water than all the oil fields in Iran."

It was a slight exaggeration, but not much of one. I
had to smile at his mention of Iran—modern-day
Persia.

The flight was smooth, and the company had a car
waiting for us at the airport. I was surprised at the small
size of the fusion lab building, but Dempsey kept telling
me that CTRs could be made small enough to fit into the

basements of private homes.

"No need for electric utility companies or any other kinds of utilities, then, except for water. Turn on the tap and filter out enough deuterium in five minutes to run your house for a year."

He was a happy engineer. His machines were working. The world was all right.

Except that as we came up to the front gate of the lab, we saw there were pickets marching along the wire fence. Many of them were young, students most likely. But there were plenty of older men and women who looked like teachers, housewives, and even blue-collar workers. The placards they were carrying were neatly printed:

WE DON'T WANT H-BOMBS
IN OUR BACKYARD!

PEOPLE YES! TECHNOLOGY NO!
FUSION POWER HAS TO GO!

RADIATION CAUSES CANCER

The car slowed down as we approached the gate. Our driver, a company chauffeur, said over his shoulder to Tom and me, "The lab security guards don't wanna open the gate. They're afraid the pickets will rush inside."

There were only a couple of dozen of them, but as we got closer to the gate they seemed like a larger mob. They crowded around the car so that we couldn't move and shouted at us:

"Go back where you came from!"

"Stop poisoning us!"

In a flash they were all chanting their "People yes!
Technology no!" slogan and pounding the car with their
fists and placards.

"Where are the police?" I asked the driver.

He merely shrugged.

"Shit on this," Dempsey snapped. "I'm not gonna let
a bunch of punk kids keep me out of the lab."

Before I thought to stop him, he pushed open the car
door on his side and got out, shouting, "Get the hell out
of our way! Go on, get lost! There's nothing for you to be
afraid of. Get out of here!"

The demonstrators wouldn't move. Dempsey shoved
one of them, a frail-looking boy who seemed no older
than high school age. An older one, football-player size,
pushed Dempsey against the side of the car.

I began to get out as Dempsey grappled with the
football player. The driver opened his door suddenly
and hit somebody hard enough to make him or her
scream with pain. Someone else swung a fist at me. I
blocked it automatically, while out of the corner of my
eye I saw a girl crack Dempsey on the head with the
corner of the placard she was holding. He went face
down on the grimy pavement. The chauffeur grabbed at
the girl's placard. She yelled and tried to squirm out of
his reach. Another guy socked the chauffeur and
suddenly a half-dozen angry young men were yelling at
me.

"Let's teach 'em a lesson!"

They tried to pin me against the side of the car. I
moved sideways to straddle Dempsey's body. I could see
a thin trickle of blood coming from his scalp.

I took a punch on the side of the face. Before the youngster could pull his arm back I had him by the wrist and elbow. I flung him against the others, lifting him off his feet and knocking them down like tenpins. With two short steps I was on the goons beating the chauffeur. Everything happened very quickly. Suddenly they were gone, except for the five on the ground with various concussions and fractures. The rest of them were running down the street.

In the lab's infirmary I spoke with the security chief, a waspish little man named Mangino, whose skin was the color of cigarette tobacco.

"I don't understand it," he muttered, as Dempsey's head was being bandaged. "We never had a speck of trouble until today. This bunch of nuts just pops outta nowhere and starts parading up and down in front of the main gate."

They were meant for me. I knew. But I said nothing.

"Our public relations people have been telling everybody that this reactor isn't like the old fission power plants. There's no radioactive waste. No radiation at all gets outside of the reactor shell. And it can't explode."

Dempsey, tight-lipped, said, "You can't talk sense to those people. They get themselves all worked up and they don't want to listen to facts."

"No," I corrected him. "They don't get themselves all worked up. Somebody works them up."

They stared at me.

"And I think it might be a good idea if we found out who—and what—that someone is."

Mangino said, "I guess so. It could be Arabs, or oil

companies, or any of a dozen nut groups."

Or, I added silently, *Ahriman*.

It wasn't difficult to find the local headquarters of th
demonstrators. It was an organization that called itsel
STOPP, an acronym for Stop Technology from Ove
Powering People.

STOPP's headquarters was an old four-story fram
house across the main avenue from the universit
campus. I parked my rented car in front of the hous
and sat watching for a while. Plenty of students walkin
by; more congregating around the pizza and fast-foo
shop on the corner of the street. This side of the avenu
was strictly urban: houses and shops packed side b
side, right down the street for block after block. Acros
the avenue was the campus: tall green hedges, tree
reaching bare branches toward the gray, early winte
sky, brooding stone buildings set off by spacious lawn
and walkways.

And all the noise of city traffic honking, growling
clattering along the main thoroughfare itself. Trucks
cars, buses, motorcycles, even a few electrically
powered bikes.

I got out of the car and decided the best approach wa
the direct one. I walked up the wooden steps and acros
the porch that fronted the house, pushed the antique
rusting bell button, opened the front door, and steppe
in.

The outside of the house looked Victorian, turn- of
the-century, Middle American tasteless. Inside, it wa
decorated in late Student Activist style. Yellowin
posters covered most of the walls in the front hallway. A

library table was heaped high with pamphlets. I glanced at them; none of them mentioned the fusion laboratory.

Doors were open on the right and left of the hallway. I looked left first, but the big, high-ceilinged room was devoid of people. A couple of old sofas, three tattered army cots, a big square table with a typewriter on it. But no people.

I tried to room on the right. A bright-looking young woman was sitting behind an ultramodern portable phone switchboard, which rested incongruously on a heavy-legged Victorian mahogany table. The girl had an earphone-and-pin-mike arrangement clamped over her short-clipped blonde hair. Without breaking the conversation into the microphone, she waved me into the room and pointed to one of the frail plastic chairs that lined the wall.

I sat and waited while she finished her conversation and switched off. Their phones had no videoscreens.

"Welcome to STOPP," she said cheerfully. "What can we do for you, Mr. . . . er?"

"Orion," I said. "I want to see the chief of this organization."

Her pert young smile clouded over. "You from the City? Fire Marshal?"

"No. I'm from the CTR facility. The fusion lab."

"Oh!" That took her by surprise. The enemy in her boudoir.

"I want to see the head person around here."

"Don Maddox? He's in class right now."

"Not him. The one he works for."

She looked puzzled. "But Don's the chairperson. He

organized STOPP. He's the . . ."

"Is he the one who decided to demonstrate against the fusion lab?"

"Yes . . ." It was an uncertain answer.

"I want to know who put him up to it."

"Now wait a minute, mister . . ." Her hands began fidgeting along the switchboard buttons. A barely discernible sheen of perspiration had broken out along her upper lip. Her breathing was slightly faster than it had been a moment earlier. A very highly trained interrogator might have noticed these reactions of fear. I recognized them immediately.

"All right then," I said easily. "Who first suggested demonstrating at the fusion lab? It wasn't one of the students, I know that."

"Oh, you mean Mr. Davis." She sat up straighter, her voice took on a ring of conviction. "He's the one who woke us up about your fusion experiments and all that propaganda you people have been handing us!"

There was no point in arguing with her. Davis. I smiled inwardly. With just a slight change in pronunciation I came up with *Daevas*, the gods of evil in the old Zoroastrian religion.

"Mr. Davis," I agreed. "He's the one I want to see."

She was instantly suspicious. "Why? You trying to arrest him or something?"

I had to grin at her naivete. "If I were, would I tell you? No one got arrested at the lab this morning, did they?"

Shaking her head, she said, "From what I heard, they had a platoon of Sonny Chibas out there breaking heads."

"Whatever. I'd still like to see Davis. Is he here?"

"No." I could easily see that it was a lie. "He won't be around for a while . . . maybe tonight. I don't know."

With a shrug I said. "All right. Try to get in touch with him. Tell him Orion wants to see him. Right away."

"Mr. O'Ryan?"

"Orion. Just plain Orion. I'll be waiting in my car outside. It's parked right in front of the house."

She frowned. "He might not be back for a long while. Maybe not even tonight."

"You just try to contact him and give him my name. I'll wait."

"Okay," she said in that tone that implied *"but I think you're crazy."*

I waited in the car less than an hour. It was a cold, gray afternoon, but I adjusted easily enough to it. Clamp down on the peripheral blood vessels, so the body heat isn't radiated away so fast. Step up the metabolic rate a bit, so that some of the fat stored in the body's tissues gets burned off. This keeps the body temperature up despite the growing cold. I could have done the same thing by going to the corner and getting something to eat, but this was easier and I didn't want to leave the car. I did begin to get hungry after half an hour. As I said, I'm no superman.

The blonde girl came out on the porch, shivering in the cold. She had thrown a light sweater over her shoulders. She stared at my car. I got out and she nodded to me, then ducked back inside.

I followed her into the house. She was waiting in the

hallway, her arms clamped tight across her body.

"It's really cold out there," she said, rubbing her arms. "And you don't even have an overcoat!"

"Did you reach Mr. Davis?" I asked.

Nodding, she replied, "Yes. He . . . came in through the back way. Down at the end of the hall. He's waiting for you."

I thanked her and walked to the door at the end of the hall. It opened onto a flight of steps leading down to the cellar of the house. *Logical place for him*, I thought, wondering how many legends of darkness and evil he had inspired over the span of eons.

It was dark in the cellar. The only light came from the hallway, at the top of the stairs. I could make out a bulky, squat, old-fashioned heater, spreading its pipes up and outward like a metal Medusa. Boxes, packing crates, odd-shaped things hugged the shadows.

I took a few tentative steps into the dimness at the bottom of the stairs and stopped.

"Over here." The voice was a harsh whisper.

Turning slightly, I saw him, a darker presence among the shadows. He was big: not much taller than I, but very broad. Heavy, sloping shoulders, thick, solid body, arms bulging with muscle.

I walked toward him. I couldn't see his face, the shadows were too deep for that. He turned and led me back toward the heater. I ducked under one of the pipes . . .

And was suddenly in a brightly lit room! I squinted and staggered back half a step, only to bump against a solid wall behind me. The room was warmly carpeted, paneled in rich woods, furnished with comfortable chairs and couches. There were no windows. No decorations on the walls. *And no doors.*

"Make yourself comfortable, Orion," he said, gesturing to one of the couches. His hand was thick-fingered, blunt and heavy.

I sat down and studied him as he slowly eased his bulk into a soft leather reclining chair.

His face was not quite human. Close enough so that you wouldn't look twice at him on the street, but when you examined him carefully you saw that the cheek-bones were too widely spaced, the nose was too flat, the eyes a reddish color. His hair was gray and cropped so close to his broad, flat skull that he almost looked bald. His chin sloped and quickly vanished into a bull-like neck.

But it was the color of his skin that startled me most. It was gray. Not black or any mixture of Negroid. Gray. Almost like the color of an elephant's skin. The color of ashes.

"You are Ahriman," I said at last.

He almost smiled. "You don't remember me, of course. We have met before." His voice was a whisper, like a ghost's, or an asthmatic's tortured gasping.

"We have?"

With a slow nod, "Yes. But we are moving in different directions through time. You are moving back toward the War; I am moving forward toward the End."

*The War? The End?* But I said nothing.

"Back and forward are relative terms in time travel, you understand. But the truth is, we have met before. You will come to those places in time and remember that I told you of it."

"You're trying to destroy the fusion reactor," I said.

This time he did not smile. It was not a pleasant thing to see. "I am trying to destroy your entire race."

"I'm here to stop you."

"You may succeed."

"Ormazd says that I will ... that I *already have* succeeded." I didn't mention the part about being killed. Somehow, I couldn't.

"Ormazd knows many things," Ahriman said, "and he tells you only a few of them. He knows, for example, that if I prevent you from stopping me this time ..."

*This time? Then there have been other times!*

"... Then not only will I destroy your entire race of people. I will smash the time continuum and annihilate Ormazd himself."

"And demolish this whole planet," I added.

"Phfft! This one planet? I will bring down the pillars of the universe. *Everything* will die. The whole space/time continuum will come crumbling down. Stars, planets, galaxies ... everything." He clenched his massive fists.

He believed it. He was making *me* believe it.

"But why? Why do you want to ..."

He silenced me with a gesture. "You will find out. You will learn. But not now. Not here. Not this time."

I tried to see past his words, but my mind struck an utterly blank wall.

"I will tell you this much," Ahriman whispered. "This fusion reactor of yours is the third nexus in your race's development. If you make the fusion process work, you will be expanding out to the stars within a generation. *I will not allow you to accomplish that.*"

"I don't understand."

"How could you?" He leaned closer to me, and seemed almost glad of the chance to explain it to someone, as if he'd been alone for eons and needed a companion, a listener, even if it was an enemy.

"This fusion machine—this CTR, as you call it—is the key to your race's future. If it is successful, within ten years fusion power plants will be supplying energy everywhere on earth. The fuel comes from the sea. The energy is limitless. Your people could stop playing with their puny chemical rockets and start building real starships. They could expand throughout the galaxy."

"They *have* done so," I realized.

"Yes they have. But if I can change the nexus here, at this point in time . . . if I can destroy that fusion reactor . . . He smiled again.

I shook my head. "I don't see how one machine's failure can kill the whole human race."

"It is simple, thanks to the inherent manic nature of your race's mentality. The fusion reactor explodes . . ."

"It can't explode!" I snapped.

"Of course not. Under ordinary circumstances. But I do have access to extraordinary means, you must realize. I can create a sudden surge of power from the lasers strong enough to detonate the lithium shielding that surrounds the reactor's ignition chamber. Instead of a microgram of deuterium being fused and giving off its energy, a quarter-ton of lithium and heavier metals will explode."

"That can't . . ."

"Instead of a tiny, controlled, man-made star radiating energy in a manageable flow, I will create an artificial supernova, a lithium bomb. The explosion will destroy Ann Arbor totally. The fallout will kill millions of people from Detroit to New York."

I sagged back, stunned.

"Your people will immediately react against the very idea of fusion power. Their reaction against the uranium and plutonium fission power plants will be as child's play compared to this. Their reaction will be swift, violent and total. There will be an end to all nuclear research everywhere. You will never get fusion power. Never."

"But even so, that won't kill off everyone."

"Not at once. But I have all the time in the world to work with. As the next few years go by, your increasing energy needs will go unmet. Your mighty nations will continue to struggle against each other for the possession of petroleum, of coal, of food resources. There will be war, inevitably. And for war, you have fusion devices that *do* work—H-bombs."

"Armageddon," I said.

He nodded triumphantly. "At the time when you should be expanding outward toward the stars, you will destroy yourselves with nuclear war. Your planet will be scoured clean of life. The fabric of time itself will be so twisted that the entire universe will collapse and die. Armageddon indeed."

I wanted to stab him, to silence him. I grabbed for his arm. It was real enough: strong and alive. But he easily pulled away and got to his feet.

"Despite what Ormazd has told you, I will succeed in this. You will fail. You are trapped here, and will remain here while I destroy your precious CTR."

"But why?" I asked, my voice pleading—not so much in fear as in desperate curiosity. "Why do you want to wipe out the human race?"

He stood a moment, staring at me. "You really don't know, do you? They never told you . . . or they erased your memory of it."

"I don't know," I said. "Why do you hate the human race?"

"Because you wiped out *my* race," Ahriman replied. "Your people killed mine. You annihilated my entire species. I am the only one of my kind left alive. And I will avenge my race by destroying yours—and your masters, as well."

The strength left me. I sat weakly on the couch, unable to challenge him, unable to move.

"And now good-bye," Ahriman said. "I have much to do before the first test run of your fusion reactor. You will remain here . . ." He gestured around the tiny room. It had no windows or doors. No exits or entrances of any kind. *How did we get in here?* I wondered.

"You will be comfortable enough in here," he went on. "If I succeed, it will all be over in a few hours. Time itself will stop and the universe will fall in on itself like a collapsing balloon. If I fail, well . . ." that ghastly smile again, . . . you will spend the rest of your life in this room. It will not be long, I promise you. The air will give out long before you starve."

"The air will give out? We're in space, in a satellite?"

"Hardly," he answered. "We are thirty miles underground, in a temporary bubble of safety and comfort created by warping the energies of the atoms around us. Think about it as you suffocate— you are only a step away from the house in Ann Arbor. One small step for a man . . . if he truly understands the way the universe is constructed.''

He turned abruptly and walked *through* the wall and disappeared.

For long minutes I sat on the couch, unmoving, my body numb with shock, my brain spinning in turmoil.

*You wiped out my race . . . your people killed mine . . . and I will avenge my race by destroying yours—and your masters, as well.*

It couldn't be true. And what did he mean by all that talk about him and me moving on different time tracks, of having met each other before. *Our masters?* What did he mean by that? Ormazd? Because he said *masters*, plural. Is Ormazd a representative of a different race, an alien race from another world that controls all of humankind? Just as Ahriman is the last survivor of an alien race that we humans battled so long ago?

How many times had we met before? Ahriman said that this point in time, this first test of the fusion reactor, marked a nexus for the human race. If it succeeded, we would use fusion energy to reach out to the stars. If it failed, we would kill ourselves within a generation. There must have been other nexuses back through time, the discovery of electricity, perhaps, Columbus's voyages, the invention of steel tools, the discovery of language, agriculture, the taming of fire.

Somewhere back along those eons there was a war, The War, between the human race and Ahriman's kind. When? Why? How could we fight invaders from another world back thousands of years ago?

All these thoughts were bubbling through my brain

until finally my body asserted itself on my con-
sciousness.

"It's getting hot in here," I said aloud.

My attention snapped to the present. To this tiny
room. The air was hot and dry. The room was now hot
enough to make me sweat.

I got up and felt the nearest wall. It was almost too
hot to touch. And although it looked like wood
paneling, it felt like stone. It was an illusion, all of it.

*One small step for a man . . . if he truly understands
the way the universe is constructed.*

I understood nothing. I could remember nothing. All I
could think of was that Ahriman was back on the
Earth's surface, in Ann Arbor, working to turn the CTR
test run into a mammoth lithium bomb that would
eventually destroy the entire human race. And I was
trapped here, thirty miles underground.

*You are only a step away from the house in Ann
Arbor,* he had said.

"One small step for a man," I muttered. How *is* the
universe constructed? It's made of atoms, I answered
myself. And atoms are made of smaller particles. These
particles are made of energy, tiny bits of frozen energy
that can be made to thaw and flow and surge . . .

This room was created by warping the energies of the
atoms in the Earth's crust. Those energies were now
reverting back to their original form; slowly the room
was turning back into hot, solid rock. I could feel the air
congealing, getting hotter and thicker by the second. I
would be embedded in rock, thirty miles below the
surface, rock hot enough to be almost molten.

Yet I was only a step from safety, according to

Ahriman. Was he lying? No, he couldn't have been. *He* walked directly through the rock wall of this room. He must have returned to the cellar of the house in Ann Arbor. If he could do it, so could I. But how?

*I already had!*

I had stepped from the cellar into this underground dungeon. Why couldn't I step back again?

I tried doing it and got nothing but bumps against hot solid rock for my efforts. There was more to it than simply trying it.

But wait. If I had truly traveled thirty miles through solid rock in a single step, it must mean that there is a connection between that house and this room. Not only are the atoms of the Earth's crust being warped to create this room, but the geometry of space itself is being warped, to bridge a thirty-mile distance by a human step.

I sat down on the couch again, my mind racing. I had read stories about space warps, where futuristic starships could cover thousands of light-years of distance almost instantaneously. And astrophysics had discovered "black holes" that warped space with their titanic gravitational fields. It was all a matter of geometry, a pattern, like taking a flat sheet of paper and folding it into the form of a bird or a star.

And I had seen that pattern, I had gone through it, on my way into this troom. But it all happened so quickly that I couldn't remember it in detail.

Or could I?

Data compression. Satellites in orbit can accumulate data on magnetic tapes for days on end, and then spurt it all down to a receiving station in a few seconds, on command from the ground. The compressed data is played out at a lower speed by the technicians, and all the many days' worth of information is intact and usable.

Could I slow down my memories to the point where I could recall, microsecond by microsecond, what happened to me during that one brief stride from the house to this underground burial chamber? I leaned back in the couch and closed my eyes.

A thirty-mile stride. A step through solid rock. I pictured myself in the cellar of that house. I had ducked under a heating pipe and stepped into darkness . . .

And cold. The first instants of my step I had felt a wave of intense cold, as if I had passed through a curtain of liquefied air. Cryogenic cold. The kind that physicists use to make superconducting magnets of enormous field strength.

In those few microseconds of unbearable cold I saw that the crystal structure of the atoms around me had been frozen, almost utterly stopped. Nearly all the energy of those atoms had been frozen down into stillness, close to absolute zero temperature.

All around me the atoms glowed dully like pinpoints of jeweled lights, but sullen and almost dark because nearly all their energies had been leached away from them. The crystal latticework of the atoms formed a path for me, a tunnel, as my body moved in slow motion in that one thirty-mile-long step through the darkness of a place where space and time had been frozen, suspended, warped out of their natural flow and shape.

I opened my eyes. The tiny room was glowing now, the walls themselves were radiating heat. It was difficult to breathe. But I understood how I had gotten there.

There was a crystal lattice of energy connecting this room with the house in Ann Arbor. A tunnel that connected *here* with *there*, using the energies stolen from the atoms in between to create a safe and almost instantaneous path between the two places. But the tunnel was dissolving just as this room was dissolving; the energies of those tortured atoms were returning to normal. In minutes, all would be solid rock once again.

I understood now the connection, the tunnel. But how to find the opening? I concentrated again, but no sense of it came through to me. I was sweating, both from the heat and from the effort of forcing myself to understand. But it did no good at all. My brain could not comprehend it.

My brain could not . . . *Wrong!* I realized that so far I had been using only half my brain to attack the problem.

Every human brain is divided into two hemispheres, left and right. I remembered Ormazd telling me that I could use both halves simultaneously, something that most humans cannot do. So far, I had been using one half of my brain to see the geometrical patterns of the energy warp that connected my underground chamber with the Earth's surface.

But this half of my brain could *only* perceive geometrical problems, relationships involving space and form.

With a conscious effort, I forced the other half of my brain to consider the problem. I could almost hear myself laugh, inside my head, as the unused portion of my mind said something like, "Well, it's about time."

And it *was* about time. The solution to the problem of how to find the gateway to the crystal latticework of atoms was a matter of timing. All those dully glowing atoms were still vibrating: slowly, unnaturally slowly, because most of their energies had been drawn from them. But still they vibrated, and only when they were all in precisely the exact positions was their alignment such that the tunnel's entrance could open. Most of the time they were shifted out of phase, as unaligned and mixed-up as a crowd milling through a shopping mall. But once every minute or so they reached precisely the right arrangement necessary to form the tunnel that led back to safety. Like a swarm of meandering ants that suddenly arrange themselves into an exact battle formation, the atoms would "get together" for a bare microsecond or two to from the tunnel I needed.

Only during those incredibly tiny moments of time was the tunnel open. I had to step into the crystal latticed work, through the searing hot wall of the room, at the exact momenty—or not at all.

I stood and forced myself close to the wall. The heat was enough to curl the hair of my eyebrows and the backs of my hands. I kept my eyes closed, simultaneously picturing, with one side of my brain, the crystal pathway itself, while calculating with the other side of my brain the precise moment when the lattice would be open for me to step through.

With my eyes still closed I took a step forward. I felt an instant of roasting heat, then cold beyond the most frigid ice fields of Antarctica. Then nothing.

I opened my eyes. I stood in the cellar of the STOPP

house. For the first time in what seemed like years. I let out my breath.

I found a back door to the cellar and stepped out into the cold night air. It felt beautiful. There was an alleyway between the house and its next-door neighbor leading to the street. My car was still parked out there, adorned with a yellow parking ticket affixed to the windshield wiper. I stuffed the ticket into my pocket and got behind the wheel. I was glad that no one had towed the car away or stolen it.

It took me twenty minutes to get back to the fusion lab. I didn't even think about speed limits or highway police. Once in the deserted lobby of the building, I phoned for Tom Dempsey, Mangino the security chief and the lab's director of research. It was close to midnight, but the tone of my voice must have convinced them that something important was happening. I got no arguments from any of them, although the phone's computer system had to try three different numbers before it located Dr. Wilson, the research director.

They all arrived in the lab within a half-hour; thirty minutes during which I checked with every security guard on duty. No one had reported any problems at all. They were on constant patrol around the entire laboratory, inside and out, and everything seemed quiet and normal.

Dr. Wilson was a lanky, long-faced Englishman who spoke quietly and seemed completely unflappable. He arrived first, but as I was explaining that someone might try to detonate the fusion reactor—and he was smiling patiently and saying it was totally impossible—Dempsey and the security chief came into the lobby together.

Dempsey looked more puzzled than angry, his dark hair an uncombed tangled mess. He must have been asleep when I called and had merely pulled on his clothes helter-skelter. Mangino was definitely angry; his deep-set brown eyes snapped at me.

"This is a lot of hysterical nonsense," he said as I repeated my fears. I didn't tell them about Ormazd and Ahriman, of course; nor about the underground chamber I'd just escaped from. It was enough to convince them that a real danger existed. I didn't want them to bundle me off to a psychiatric ward.

Dr. Wilson tried to explain to me that the reactor simply could not be turned into a bomb. I let him talk; the longer he explained, the longer we stayed on the scene, available to counter Ahriman's move.

"There simply isn't enough deuterium in the reactor at any given moment to allow an explosion," Dr. Wilson said in his soft, friendly voice. He was slouched on one of the plastic couches that decorated the lab's lobby. I was leaning against the receptionist's desk. Dempsey had stretched out on another couch and apparently gone back to sleep. Mangino was behind the desk, checking out his security patrols on the videophone.

"But suppose," I stalled for more time, "there was a way to boost the power of the lasers . . ."

"They'd burn out in a minute or two." Dr. Wilson said. "We're running them at almost top capacity now."

". . . And an extra amount of deuterium was shot into the reaction chamber." I went on.

Dr. Wilson shook his head. "That can't happen. There are fail-safe circuits to prevent it. Besides, even so, all that would happen is that you'd get a mild little *poof* of a detonation—not a hydrogen bomb."

"What about a lithium bomb?" I asked.

For the first time, his brows knit worriedly. "What do you mean?"

"If things worked out the right way, couldn't that *poof* of a detonation trigger the lithium in the shielding around the reactor chamber? And wouldn't the lithium go off . . . ?"

"No, no. That would be imposs . . . that would be very unlikely. *Very* unlikely. I'd have to work out the calculations, of course, but the chances against it are . . ."

"Forty-four, *report*." Mangino's voice broke into our conversation.

I turned and looked at the security chief. He was frowning angrily, "Dammit, forty-four, answer me!"

He looked up at me, eyes blazing. As if I were responsible. "One of those outside guards doesn't answer. Patrolling the area around the loading dock."

"Good grief!" Wilson was on his feet. I could sense his body trembling. "The loading dock . . ."

Mangino held up a hand. "Don't get excited, Doc. I've got the area on one of the outside TV cameras. Everything looks normal. Just no sign of the guard. He might be sneaking a smoke somewhere . . ."

I went around the desk and peered at the TV screen. The loading-dock area was brightly lit. There were no cars or trucks anywhere in sight. All looked quiet and calm.

Just the same, "Let's take a walk down there," I said.

We roused Dempsey and told him to stand guard over

the phones and TV screens. He rubbed his eyes sleepily and nodded okay. Then Dr. Wilson, Mangino, and I hurried down the building's central corridor toward the loading dock. Mangino reached inside his coat and pulled out a slim, flat, dead-black pistol. He hefted it once as we quick-stepped down the corridor, then slipped it into a hip pocket.

Lights turned on automatically ahead of us as we hurried along the corridor, and switched off behind us. The loading area looked like a miniature warehouse, stacked cardboard cartons, steel drums, all sorts of exotic-looking equipment wrapped in clear plastic.

"You could hide a platoon of men in here," Mangino grumbled.

"But everything seems to be in order," said Dr. Wilson, looking around.

I started to agree, but felt the slightest trace of a breeze on my face. It was coming from the direction of the loading-dock doors, big metal roll-up doors that were shut and locked. Or were they?

I walked slowly toward the doors and saw a man-size doorway that had been cut into one of them. A single person could slip in or out without raising and lowering the big doors. This smaller door was windowless and tightly shut. I reached for it.

"It's locked," Mangino said. "Electronic lock . . . if anybody tried tampering with it . . ."

I pulled the door handle and it swung open effortlessly. Mangino gaped.

Kneeling, I saw that the area around the edge of the lock had been bent slightly, as if massive hands had pried it open, bending the metal until it yielded and opened. The slight breeze I had felt came through the bent area after the door had been carefully closed again.

"Why didn't the electronic alarm go off?" Mangino wondered out loud.

"Never mind that," I said. "He's inside the lab! Quick, we don't have any time to lose!"

We ran to the fusion reactor area, Wilson protesting breathlessly all the way that no one could tamper with the lasers on the reactor in any way that could cause an explosion.

We skidded to a clattering halt in front of the doors to the laser control room. They should have been shut. They were open. A quick look inside showed us that no one was there. The control boards seemed untouched.

Mangino was yelling into his palm-size radio, "All security guards, converge on the fusion reactor area. Apprehend anyone you see. Shoot if he resists. Call the police and the FBI, at once!"

We entered the big double doors that led into the long, cement-walled room where the lasers were housed. Again, the overhead lights snapped on automatically as soon as we crossed the doorway.

"Those doors should have been closed too," Dr. Wilson said. "And locked."

The lasers were long, thin glass rods, dozens of them, mounted on heavy metal benches, one behind the other, like a series of railway cars. In between each pair of lasers were lenses. Faraday rotators, all sorts of sensors. The double line of lasers marched down the room for nearly fifty feet and focused on a narrow slit cut into a five-foot-thick cement and steel wall at the far end of the chamber. Beyond that slit was the reactor itself, where the deutèrium pellets received the energy from the lasers.

The three of us stood there uncertainly for a moment. Then the lasers began to glow greenish, and an electrical hum vibrated through the air.

"They're turning on!" Dr. Wilson shouted.

Mangino and I swung our attention to the far end of the room, where the control section was. In the shadows up there, behind the thick protective-glass window, bulked the heavy dark form of Ahriman.

Mangino pulled out his gun and fired. The glass starred. He fired again and again. The glass shattered, but by then Ahriman was gone.

The lights went out. All we could see was the green glow of the lasers, twin paths of intense green light aiming at the slit. And beyond that was the reactor.

We stumbled out into the hallway. It was dark everywhere. From somewhere far off I could hear running footsteps. Then shots.

"They've got him!" Mangino yelled. But to me it sounded as if the running and shooting was going in the direction away from us. The shots grew fainter. As long as they continued, they didn't have Ahriman, I knew.

"I'm going after him," said Mangino, and he moved off into the darkness.

"We've got to stop the lasers," I said to Dr. Wilson, "before they build up enough power to detonate the lithium."

"I told you that can't happen!" he insisted.

"Let's stop them anyway." With that he didn't argue.

But the laser control room was now in a shambles. In the eerie green light of the lasers themselves, we could see that the control panels had been smashed, dials shattered, metal paneling bent out of shape. Wires sagged limply from broken consoles. It was as if an elephant had gone berserk in the tiny room.

Wilson's jaw hung slackly. "How could anyone . . ."

The electrical whine of the lasers suddenly went up in pitch several notches. The lasers glowed more fiercely. I heard a glass lens pop somewhere down on the the floor of laser room.

I pulled Wilson out of the control room, and we stumbled down the darkened hallway toward the reactor chamber.

"How do we turn the darned thing off?" I shouted into his ear.

He seemed dazed, bewildered. "The deuterium feed . . ."

"That's been jury-rigged and smashed too, I'll bet. We won't be able to turn it off any more than we can turn off the lasers."

I could sense him shaking his head in the shadows as we stumbled to a step in front of the reactor room.

"Main power supplies," he mumbled. "I could get to the main power switches and shut down everything . . ."

"Okay! Do it!"

"But . . . it'll take time . . . five, ten minutes at least."

"Too long! By then it'll be too late. She'll blow up in another minute or so."

"I know."

"What else can we do?"

"Nothing."

"I don't belive it! There must be *something* . . ."

"Damper," he muttered. "If we could place a damper between the deuterium and the lithium shielding . . ."

I knew enough about the fusion reactor to understand what he meant.

The deuterium fuel for the fusion reaction was in tiny lexan pellets that dropped out of a tube like water droplets leak from a faucet. Ordinarily the pellets dropped one at a time, one a second. And the laser pulses were timed to flash exactly when the pellets were at the focal point of the laser beams. The laser energy smashed the pellets flat; the deuterium was squeezed and instantly heated to the hundred-million-degree temperature where fusion processes take place. Energy came out—some of the energy was heat: most of it was fast, deadly neutrons, subatomic particles that could kill a man very quickly if they ever got outside the five-foot-thick shielding around the reactor.

Under ordinary circumstances, the neutrons impacted against the inner wall of the reactor chamber, which consisted of hundreds of pipes carrying liquefied lithium. The neutrons transmuted the lithium into more deuterium, providing fresh fuel for the reactor. The lithium absorbed the neutrons and made the outside of the reactor completely safe. Under ordinary circumstances.

What was happening now, though, was that the deuterium pellets were being forced into the reactor at an insanely fast rate, and the lasers had been jury-rigged to zap them just as fast as they entered the reactor. Thousands of times more neutrons were boiling off the deuterium pellets and hitting the lithium; within a minute or less, the lithium would be energized to the point where it would explode.

How many megatons of energy would be released in the explosion? Enough, I knew, to destroy much of the human race.

We needed a damper, some sort of material that could be inserted between the deuterium pellets and the lithium pipes. Or better yet, something that could block off the incoming laser energy.

"A damper," I snapped at Wilson. "Okay . . . you find the main power switches. I'll find a damper."

"But there's nothing . . ."

"Get moving!" I commanded.

"You can't get anything in there without going inside the reactor itself! That'll kill you!"

"Go!"

I pushed him away from me. He staggered off, then hesitated as I yanked open the door to the reactor room.

"For God's sake . . . don't . . . !" Wilson screamed.

I ignored him and stepped inside.

The high-ceilinged room was bathed in the greenish light from the lasers. In its center was the round metal reactor already beginning to glow a deep red. It looked like a bathysphere, but it had no portholes in it. There was no way to interrupt the laser beams from the outside; they were linked to the reactor chamber by a thick quartz light pipe. I couldn't break it, even if I had the time to try.

There was only one hatch in the metal sphere. I yanked it open and was literally pushed back by the overwhelming intensity of light and heat blazing inside. A man-made star was running amok in there, getting ready to explode.

My burning eyes squeezed shut, I grabbed the hot edges of the metal hatch and forced myself inside the chamber. I flung my body in front of the laser beams.

I knew then what hell is like.

Pain. Searing agony that blasts into your skull even though your eyes have been burned away. Agony along every nerve, every synapse, every pathway of your entire body and brain.

All the memories of my mind stirred into frantic life. Past and present and future. I saw them all in that instant, that never-ending infinitesimal flash of time.

I stood flayed and naked and burning as my mind saw tomorrows and yesterdays.

Newspaper headlines blaring ATTEMPT TO SABOTAGE FUSION LAB FAILS.

Puzzled FBI agents searching for some trace of my body as Dr. Wilson is wheeled into an ambulance, catatonic with shock.

Ahriman's presence looming over my horizon of time, brooding, planning vengeance.

Ormazd shining against the darkness of space itself.

And me. Orion the Hunter. I see all my pasts and futures. At last I know who I am, and what, and why.

I am Orion. I am Zeus. I am Krishna. I am Zarathustra. I am the Phoenix who dies and is consumed and rises again from his own ashes, only to die once more. The never-ending agony of life and death and renewal.

From fifty thousand years in Earth's future I have hunted Ahriman. This time he escaped me, even though I thwarted his vengeance. Humankind will have fusion power. We will attain the stars. That nexus has been passed successfully, just as Ormazd told me. It required my death, but the fabric of time and the continuum has not been broken.

I have died. And I live. I exist, and my purpose is to hunt down Ahriman, wherever and whenever he is.

I will live again.

# The Future of Science

*I've been in love with gray-eyed Athena ever since I first met the lady, back in grammar school. To me, she represents most of what's good in the human race—our striving to outgrow our brutish beginnings and use our intellect to raise ourselves to the stars. When I was asked to write a piece about where science is heading, for the ninth Nebula Awards anthology, this was the result.*

Where is science heading? Is it taking us on a one-way ride to oblivion, or leading the human spirit upward to the stars? Science fiction writers have been predicting both, for centuries.

"I have but one lamp by which my feet are guided," Patrick Henry said, "and that is the lamp of experience. I know of no way of judging of the future but by the past."

Look at the past, at the way science and technology have affected the human race. Look far back. Picture all of humanity from the earliest *Homo erectus* of a half-million years ago as a single human being. Now picture science as a genie that will grant that person the traditional three wishes of every good fable.

We have already used up one of those wishes. We are working on the second one of them now. And the future of humankind, the difference between oblivion and infinity, lies in our choice of the third wish.

Our three wishes can be given classical names: Prometheus, Apollo, and Athena.

### Prometheus

Long before there was science, perhaps even before there was speech, our primitive ancestors discovered technology. Modern man thinks of technology as the stepson of scientific research, but that is only a very recent reversal of a half-million-year-long situation. Technology—*toolmaking*—came first. Science—*understanding*—came a long time later.

Look at the Prometheus legend. It speaks the truth as clearly as any modern science fiction story. It speaks of the first of our three wishes.

Prometheus brought the gift of fire. He saw from his Olympian height that man was a weak, cold, hungry, miserable creature, little better than the animals of the fields. At enormous cost to himself, Prometheus stole fire from the heavens and gave it to man. With fire, man became almost godlike in his domination of all the rest of the world.

Like most myths, the legend of the fire-bringer is fantastic in detail and absolutely correct in spirit. Anthropologists who have sifted through the fossil remains of early man have drawn a picture that is much less romantic, yet startlingly close to the essence of the Prometheus legend.

The first evidence of man's use of fire dates back some half-million years. The hero of the story is hardly godlike in appearance. He is *Homo erectus*, an ancestor of ours who lived in Africa, Asia, and possibly Europe during the warm millennia between the second and third glaciations of the Ice Age. *Homo erectus* was scarcely five feet tall. His skull was rather halfway between the shape of an ape's and our own. His brain case was only two-thirds of our size. But his body was fully human: he walked erect and had human, grasping hands.

And he was dying. The titanic climate shifts of the Ice Age caused drought even in tropical Africa, his most likely home territory. Forests dwindled. Anthropologists have found many *H. erectus* skulls scratched by leopard's teeth. Our ancestors were not well-equipped to protect themselves. Picture Moon Watcher and his tribe from Arthur C. Clarke's *2001*.

It was a gift from the skies that saved *Homo erectus* from oblivion. Not an extraterrestrial visitor, but a blast of lightning that set a bush afire. An especially curious and courageous member of the *erectus* clan overcame his very natural fear to reach out for the bright warm promise of the flames. No telling how many times our ancestors got nothing for their curiosity and courage except a set of burnt fingers and a yowl of pain. But eventually they learned to handle fire safely, and to use it.

With fire, humankind's technology was born.

Fire, the gift of Prometheus, satisfied our first wish, which was: feed me, warm me, protect me.

Fire not only frightened away the night-stalking beasts and gave our ancestors a source of warmth, it helped to change the very shape of their faces and their society.

*Homo erectus* was the world's first cook. He used fire to cook the food that had always been eaten raw previously. Cooked food is softer and juicier than raw food. Cooking cuts down greatly on the amount of chewing that must be done. Our ancestors found that they could spend less time actually eating and have more time available for hunting or traveling or making better spear points.

More important, the apelike muzzle of *Homo erectus*, with its powerful jaw muscles, was no longer needed. Faces became more human. The brain case grew as the jaw shortened. No one can definitely say that these two face changes are related. But they happened at the same time. The apelike face of the early hominids changed into the present small-jawed, big-domed head of *Homo sapiens sapiens*.

Beyond that, fire was the first source of energy for any animal outside its own muscles. Fire liberated us from physical labor and unleashed forces that have made us masters of the world. Fire is the basis of all technology. Without fire we would have no metals, no steam, no electricity, no books, no cities, no agriculture, nothing that we would recognize as civilization.

The gift of Prometheus satisfied our first wish. It has fed us, kept us warm, protected us from our enemies. Too well. It has led to the development of a technology that is now itself a threat to our survival on this planet.

The price Prometheus paid for giving fire to us was to be chained eternally to a rock and suffer daily torture. Again, the myth is truer than it sounds. The technology that we have developed over the past half-million years is gutting the earth. Forests have been stripped away, mountains leveled, our air and water fouled with the wastes of modern industry.

For our first wish, the wish that Prometheus answered, was actually: feed me, warm me, protect me, *regardless of the consequences.* Our leopard-stalked ancestors gave no thought to the air pollution arising from their primitive fires. And our waist-coated entre-preneurs of the Industrial Revolution did not care if their factories turned the millstream into an open sewer.

But today, when the air we breathe can kill us and the water is often unfit to drink, we care deeply about the consequences of technology.

The gift of Prometheus was a first-generation tech-nology. It bought the survival of the human race at the price of eventual ecological danger. Now we seek a second-generation technology, one that can give us all the benefits of Prometheus's gift without the harmful by-products.

This is our second wish. We have already asked it, and if it is truly answered, it will be answered by Apollo. The sun god. The symbol of brilliance and clarity and music and poetry. The beautiful one.

## Apollo

Although our first-generation technology predated actual science by some half-million years, the second-generation technology of Apollo can not come about without the deep understandings that only science can bring us. To go beyond the ills of first-generation technology, we must turn to science, to the quality of mind that sees beyond the immediate and makes the desire to know, to understand, the central theme of human activity.

Science is something very new in human history. As new, actually, as the founding of America. In the year 1620, when the Puritans were stepping on Plymouth Rock, Francis Bacon published the book that signaled the opening of the scientific age: *Novum Organum.*

Men had pursued a quest for knowledge for ages before that date. Ancients had mapped the heavens, tribal shamans had started the study of medicine,. mystics had developed some rudimentary understandings of the human mind, philosophers had argued about causes and origins. But it was not until the first few decades of the seventeenth century that the deliberate, organized method of thinking that we now call science was created.

It was in those decades, some 350 years ago, that Galileo began settling arguments about physical phenomena by setting up experiments and measuring the results. Kepler was deducing the laws that govern planetary motion. Bacon was writing about a new method of thinking and investigating the secrets of nature: the technique of inductive reasoning, a technique that requires a careful interplay of observation, measurement, and logic.

Bacon's landmark book, *Novum Organum,* was written and titled in reaction to Aristotle's *De Organum,* written some fifteen hundred years earlier as a summarization of all that was known about the physical universe. For fifteen hundred years, Aristotle's word was the last one on any subject dealing with "natural philosophy," or what we today call the physical sciences. For fifteen hundred years it was lindly accepted that a heavy body falls faster than a ight one, that the Earth is the center of the universe, hat the heart is the seat of human emotion. (And when 1ave you seen a Valentine card bearing a picture of the orain or an adrenal gland?)

For fifteen hundred years, human knowledge and understanding advanced so little that the peasant of Aristotle's day and that of Bacon's would scarcely seem different to each other. This was not due to a Dark Age that blotted out ancient knowledge and prevented progress. For this fifteen-hundred-year stasis affected not only Europe, but the Middle East, Asia, Africa, and the Americas as well.

The lack of advancement during this long millennium and a half was due, more than anything else, to the limits of the ancient method of thought. Only incremental gains in technology could be made by people who accepted ancient authority as the answer to every question, who believed that the Earth was flat and placed at the exact center of the universe, who "knew" that empirical evidence was not to be trusted because it could be a trick played upon the senses by the forces of evil.

In the three-hundred fifty years since the scientific method of thought has become established, human life has changed so enormously that a peasant of Bacon's time (or a nobleman, for that matter!) would be lost and bewildered in today's society. Today the poorest American controls more energy, at the touch of a button or the turn of an ignition key, than most of the high-born nobles of all time ever commmanded. We can see and hear the world's history, current news, the finest artists, whenever we choose it. We live longer, grow taller and stronger, and can blithely disregard diseases that scourged civilizations, generation after generation.

This is what science-based technology has done for us. Yet this is almost trivial, compared to what the scientific method of thinking has accomplished.

For the basic theme of scientific thought is that the universe is knowable. Man is not a helpless pawn of forces beyond his own ken. Order can be brought out of chaos. Albert Einstein said it best: "The eternal mystery of the world is its comprehensibility."

Faced, then, with a first-generation technology that threatens to strangle us in its effluvia, we have already turned to science for the basis of a second-generation technology. We have turned to Apollo.

We recognize that it is Apollo's symbol—the dazzling sun—that will be the key to our second-generation technolgy. The touchstone of all our history has been our ability to command constantly richer sources of energy. *Homo erectus*' burning bush gave way to fires fueled by coal, oil, natural gas—the fossils of antediluvian craetures. Today we take energy from the fission of uranium atoms.

Tomorrow our energy will come from the sun. Either we will tap the sunlight steaming down on us and convert  it into the forms of energy that we need, such as electricity or heat, or we will create miniature suns here on Earth and draw energy directly from them. This is thermonuclear fusion, the energy of the H-bomb. In thermonuclear fusion, the nuclei of light atoms such as hydrogen isotopes are forced together to create heavier nuclei and give off energy. This is the energy source of

he sun itself, and the stars. It promises clean, inexpensive, inexhaustible energy for all the rest of human
history.

The fuel fusion is deuterium, the isotope of hydrogen
that is in "heavy water." For every six thousand atoms
of ordinary hydrogen in the world's oceans, there is one
atom of deuterium. The fusion process is energetic
enough so that the deuterium in one cubic meter of
water (about two-hundred twenty-five gallons) can
yield 450,000 kilowatt-hours of energy. That means
that a single cubic kilometer of sea water has the energy
equivalent of all the known oil reserves on Earth. And
that is using only one-six-thousandth of the hydrogen in
the water.

Fusion power will be cheap and abundant enough to
be the driving force of our second-generation technology. The gift of Apollo can provide all our energy
needs for millions of years into the future.

There will eventually be no further need for fossil
fuels or even fissionables. Which in turn means there
will be no need to gut our world for coal, oil, gas,
uranium. No oil wells. No black lung disease. No
problems of disposing of highly radioactive wastes.

The waste products of the fusion process are clean,
inert helium and highly energetic neutrons. The neutrons could be a radiation danger if they escape the
fusion reactor, but they are far too valuable to let loose,
for energetic neutrons are the philosopher's stone of the
modern alchemists. They can transform the atoms of
one element into atoms of another.

Instead of changing lead into gold, however, the neutrons will be used to transmute light metals such as lith-

ium into the hydrogen isotopes that fuel the fusion
reactors. They can also transmute the radioactiv
wastes of fission power plants into safely inert sub
stances.

The energy from fusion can also be used to make th
ultimate recycling system. Fusion "torches" will be abl
to vaporize anything. An automobile, for example
could be flashed into a cloud of its component atoms–
iron, carbon, chromium, oxygen, etc. Using apparatu
that already exists today, it is possible to separate thes
elements and collect them, in ultra pure form, for reuse
With effective and efficient recycling, the need for fresh
raw materials will go down drastically. The mining an
lumbering industries will dwindle; the scars on the fac
of the Earth will begin to heal.

Fusion energy will produce abundant electricit
without significant pollution and with thousands o
times less radiation hazard than modern power plants
With cheap and abundant energy there need be no suc
thing as a "have-not" nation. Sea water can be desalte
and piped a thousand kilometers inland, if necessar
The energy to do it will be cheap enough. All forms o
transportation—from automobiles to spacecraft—wil
either use fusion power directly or the electricit
derived from fusion.

The gift of Apollo, then, can mark as great a turnin
point in human history as the gift of Prometheus. Lik
the taming of fire, the taming of fusion will so chang
our way of life that our descendants a scarce centur
from now will be hard put to imagine how we coul
have lived without this ultimate energy source.

Apollo is a significant name for humankind's secon

wish for another reason, too. Apollo was the title given to humanity's most ambitious exploration program. In the name of the sun god we reached the moon. Not very consistent nomenclature or mythology, perhaps, but extremely significant for the future of science and the human race.

For to truly fulfill our second wish, we must and will expand the habitat of the human race into space.

We live on a finite planet. We are already beginning to see the consequences of overpopulation and over-consumption of this planet's natural resources. Sooner or later, we must begin to draw our resources from other worlds.

We have already "imported" some minerals from the moon. The cost for a few hundred pounds of rocks was astronomically high: more than $20 billion. Clearly, more efficient modes of transportation must be found, and scientists and engineers are at work on them now.

It is interesting to realize that the actual cost of the energy it takes to send an average-size man to the moon and back—if you bought the energy from your local electric utility—is less than $200. There is much room for improvement in our space transportation systems.

Improvements are coming. Engineers are now building the Space Shuttle, which will be a reusable "bus" for shuttling cargo and people into orbit. Fusion energy itself will someday propel spacecraft. Scientists are working on very high-powered lasers that could boost spacecraft into orbit. And the eventual payoff of the esoteric investigations into subatomic physics might well be an insight into the basic forces of nature, an insight that may someday give us some control over gravity.

There is an entire solar system of natural resources waiting for us, once we have achieved economical means of operating in deep space. Many science fiction stories have speculated on the possibilities of "mining" the asteroids, that belt of stone and metal fragments in orbit between Mars and Jupiter.

There are thousands upon thousands of asteroids out there. A single ten-kilometer chunk of the nickel-iron variety (which is common) would contain approximately 20 million million tons of high-grade iron. That's $2 \times 10^{13}$ tons. Considering that world steel production in 1973 was a bit less than a thousand million tons ($10^9$), this one asteroid could satisfy our need for steel for about ten thousand years!

The resources are there. And eventually much of our industrial operations will themselves move into space: into orbit around Earth initially, and then farther out, to the areas where the resources are.

There are excellent reasons for doing so. Industrial operations have traditionally been sited as close as possible to the source of raw material. This is why Pittsburgh is near the Pennsylvania coal fields and not far from the iron-ore deposits farther west. It is cheaper to transport finished manufactured products than haul bulky raw materials.

The very nature of space offers advantages for many industrial processes. The high vacuum, low gravity, and virtually free solar energy of the space environment will be irresistible attractions to designers of future industrial operations. Also, the problems of handling waste products and pollution emissions will be easier in space than on Earth.

The pressures of social history will push industry off-planet. We cannot afford to cover the Earth with factories. Yet the alternative is a cessation of economic growth—as long as industrial operations are limited to our finite planet.

Although studies such as the MIT/Club of Rome's "Limits to Growth" have urged a stabilized society, human nature usually wants to have its cake and eat it, too. It should be possible to maintain economic growth by expanding off-planet, and thereby avoid the catastrophic effects of polluting our world to death.

What about the ultimate pollution: overpopulation? Will our expansion into space simply allow the human race to continue its population explosion until civilization collapses under the sheer groaning weight of human flesh?

Many science fiction stories have depicted a rigidly stabilized future society, where vocation, recreation, and even procreation are strictly controlled by the state. Given modern techniques of behavior modification and genetic manipulation, this might someday be possible. Indeed, this is the world that the "Limits to Growth" inevitably leads to.

There is an alternative. In all of human history, the only sure technique for leveling off an expanding population has been to increase the people's standard of living. War, famine, pestilence inevitably lead to a higher birth rate. Modern science has reduced the death rate to the point where even a moderately rising birthrate is a threat to society.

If economic growth can be maintained or even accelerated by expanding the economy into space—and this growth is shared by all people everywhere on Earth—we may have the means for leveling off the population explosion without the repressions that most science fiction writers are haunted by.

Eventually, people will go into space to live. There will be no large-scale migrations—not for a century, at least. But within a few decades, we may see self-sufficient communities in orbit around the Earth, on the moon, and eventually farther out in space.

For the first time since the settling of the Americas, humankind will have an opportunity to develop new social codes. In the strange and harsh environments we will encounter in space, we will perforce evolve new ways of life. Old manners and customs will wither; new ones will arise.

Scientists such as astronomer Carl Sagan look forward to these "experimental communities." They point out that social evolution on Earth is stultified by the success of Western technological civilization. Nearly every human society on this planet lives in a Westernized culture. Variety among human cultures is being homogenized away. The new environment of space offers an opportunity to produce new types of societies, new ways of life that might teach those who remain on Earth how to live better, more fully, more humanly.

Which brings us to the last of humankind's three wishes, the most important one of all, the wish for the gift of Athena.

### Athena

The gray-haired goddess of civilization and wisdom. The warrior-goddess who was born with shield and spear in her hands, but who evolved from Homer's time to Pericles' into a goddess of counsel, of arts and industries, the protectress of cities, the patron deity of Athens.

It is to Athena that we must turn if we are to succeed in our long struggle against the darkness. For human history can be viewed as an attempt to countervene the inevitable chaos of entropy. We succeed as individuals, as a society, as a species, when we are able to bring order out of confusion, understanding out of mystery. Athena, whose symbol is the owl, represents the wisdom and self-knowledge that we so desperately need.

Knowledge we have. And we are acquiring more, so rapidly that people suffer "future shock" from their inability to digest the swift changes flowing across our lives. Wisdom is what we need; the gift of Athena. Self-understanding.

Human beings are understanding-seeking creatures. But when we seek understanding from authorities—in ivied towers of learning, or marbled halls of government, or dark caves of mysticism—we fall short of our goal. Proclamations from authorities are not understanding. When we as individuals give up our quest for understanding and allow others to think and decide for us, we allow the inevitable darkness to gather closer. The brilliant Aegean sunlight is what we seek, and we must turn to Athena's gift of wisdom to find it.

Science will be the crucial factor in finding Athena's gift. As a mode of thinking, a technique for learning and understanding, it is central to our search for self-knowledge.

Our first two wishes were largely focused outside

ourselves. They were aimed at manipulating the world outside our skins. Our third and final wish concerns the universe within us: our bodies, our brains, our minds. Until now, scientific research has been mainly concerned with the physical world around us. Physics, chemistry, astronomy, engineering—all deal with the universe that we lay hands on. Even biology and sociology have dealt mainly with matters external to the individual human being. Medical research has been confined to chemistry, mysticism, and sharper surgical tools, until very recently.

But starting with psychology, the major thrust of scientific research has been slowly turning over the past century or so toward the universe inside our flesh.

Molecular biology is delving into the basic mechanics of what makes us what we are: the chemistry of genetic inheritance. Ethnology and psychology are probing the fundamentals of why we behave the way we do: the essence of learning and behavior. Neurophysiology is examining the basic structure and workings of the brain itself: the electrochemistry of memory and thought.

Many view this research with horror. From Mary Wollstonecraft Shelley's vision of Frankenstein, generations of writers and readers have feared scientists' attempts to tamper with the human mind and body. "There are some things that man was not meant to know," has become not only a cliche, but a rallying cry for the fearful and the ignorant.

Genetic manipulation could someday create an elite of geniuses who rule a race of zombies. Behavior modification techniques can turn every jailbird into a model prisoner, and make prisoners of us all. Psychosurgery is performed on the poor, the uninformed, the helpless.

Yet molecular biology may erase the scourge of cancer and genetic disease, bringing the human race to a pinnacle of physical perfection. Behavior modification techniques will someday unravel the tangled engrams of hopeless psychotics and restore them to the light of healthy adulthood. Brain research could bring quantum leaps in our abilities to understand and learn.

Human societies have developed in such a way that new ideas and new capabilities are acquired by the rulers long before the ruled ever hear of them. All societies are ruled by elites. But the eventual effect our new knowledge is to destroy the elite, to spread the new capabilities among all the people. Far from fearing new knowledge, or shunning it, we must seek it out and embrace it wholeheartedly. For only out of the new knowledge that scientists are acquiring will we derive the understanding that we need to survive as individuals and as a species.

The gift of Athena is what we must have. And it must be shared by all of us, not merely an elite at the top of society. The gift of Prometheus gave us mastery of this world. The gift of Apollo is bringing us powers so vast that we can turn this planet into a paradise or a barren lifeless wasteland.

Only the wisdom of Athena can control the powers of modern science and technology. Only when all the people know what is possible will it be possible to know what to do. As long as an elite controls the power of science and technology, the masses will be manipulated. And such manipulation will inevitably lead to collapse and destruction.

We stand poised on the brink of godhood. The knowledge and wisdom that modern scientific research offers can help us to take the next evolutionary step, and transform ourselves into a race of intelligent beings who truly understand themselves and the universe around them. It is possible, by our own efforts, to climb as far above our present condition as we today are above primitive little *Homo erectus.*

The anthropologist Carleton Coon painted the prospect twenty years ago, in his book, *The Story of Man:*

> A half-million years of experience in outwitting beasts on mountains and plains, in heat and cold, in light and darkness, gave our ancestors the equipment that we still desperately need if we are to slay the dragon that roams the earth today, marry the princess of outer space, and live happily ever after in the deer-filled glades of a world in which everyone is young and beautiful forever.

We have the means within our grasp. The gift of Athena, like our first two gifts, actually comes from no one but ourselves.